The Star Child

Stephanie Keyes

THE STAR CHILD

The characters and events in this book are fictitious. Any similarity to real persons, living or dead, places, or events is coincidental and not intended by the author.

The Star Child

Paperback ISBN: 978-0-9856562-4-9
ePub ISBN: 978-0-9856562-3-2

Inkspell Publishing
18, Scott Court, C-4
Ridgefield Park
07660 NJ

Edited By Melissa Keir.
Cover art By Najla Qamber

You can visit us at www.inkspellpublishing.com

The Star Child is dedicated to the memory of my father, Russ Jones.

CHAPTER ONE
GRADUATION DAY

My eyes snapped open. For a moment, I looked around the room, trying to recall where I was, the time of day, and what I'd been doing before falling asleep. I couldn't remember what I'd been dreaming about specifically, though I had a good idea.

Rubbing my eyes wearily, the rushing in my ears subsided as I sat up and began the return journey to my current reality. It was my college graduation day and I'd be the youngest student in three generations to graduate with a degree from the prestigious Yale University. *Great.* More attention.

My ears popped. Able to hear again, I realized that Gabe, my roommate, was talking to me as he ran around the room packing up the last of his belongings. It was a task that he'd put off for quite some time, as did I, but now I was packed and ready to go.

Normally, our apartment was small and cluttered, but homey. Gabe's mother had decorated it during the first year that we roomed together. The resulting product was a combination of Senior Citizen and IKEA, almost disturbing but too contemporary to be tacky. Gabe had managed to trash the place within the time that I was sleeping and it looked like a bomb went off.

Looking back at the clock, I stood up. "We really need to leave now."

Sparing a glance in the mirror, I attempted to tidy up my chin-length black hair before making a lame effort to de-wrinkle my clothes. My suit was well made, tailored in the height of fashion. However, no amount of custom design could save it from my impromptu nap on the sofa. I met my own green eyes in the mirror. This was as good as it was going to get.

Gabe, who'd been rummaging boxes, stopped and threw up his hands. "Yeah, you're right. There's plenty of time to get this stuff, right?"

"Sure." If Gabe wasn't packed by the end of the day, his entire family would probably come in and pack up his belongings en mass. That was how they did everything, as one large, loud group. I loved them all.

Without another word, we both donned our blue caps and gowns. Grabbing some essentials—keys, cell phone, iPod music player, and a Snickers candy bar, I followed Gabe out the door, taking in a final glance at the room on the way out. I would miss this place; it had been more of a home to me than most of my former dorm accommodations. Still, it was time to say goodbye.

Old Campus and the designated congregation area for graduates was a short walk from our dorm. Despite the lateness of the hour, we took our time cutting across the vast lawns to enjoy the beautiful Connecticut day. When we reached the large group of volunteers that sat behind an endless row of tables, we searched for the table with a large S suspended above it, then got in the short line to register.

"Name?" barked a commencement volunteer.

"Stewart. Gabriel Stewart." Gabe was adjusting his clothes, most likely uncomfortable about the gown's cut on his tall frame. He straightened the cap perched atop his head and checked his shoelaces before unfolding himself to his full six-foot-three height.

The volunteer dismissed Gabe with a check of a box and looked at me. "Okay, your name?"

My feet carried me toward to the table. "St. James, Kellen."

The volunteer didn't look me in the eyes. *I get that a lot.* After we'd checked in, we went to stand in the large line of graduates with whom we'd walk onto the field.

Gabe, who was two places in front of me, walked back and stood next to me. "So, do you think…do you think your father will come today?" He scratched his head—a behavior he often demonstrated when he was nervous.

The reason for his anxiety was obvious to me: he wanted to know the answer, but he didn't want to upset me. He wasn't sure if he should've brought it up, and I wished that he hadn't. My shoes caught my eye. They were polished black loafers with the customary tassel on the front. I stared at them for a moment.

For weeks, I'd been wondering if my father would show at my graduation. I'd certainly held up my end of the bargain, graduating five years early *and* from his alma mater. Would this mean that he'd finally be pleased with me? Call me crazy, but I found myself hoping, though the realist in me cautioned against it. "I really don't know. He knows the date, but since I only speak to him when absolutely necessary, I'm not holding my breath."

"But maybe if you talked to him..." Gabe frowned and scratched his head again and knocked his cap off-center.

It was clear that he was unhappy about this turn of events. It was easy to understand his perspective if you thought about it. Gabe had a very close, tight-knit family, and he couldn't fathom anyone else not having the same.

Sighing, I glared at him. This discussion was old. "Sounds great in theory, but the execution is flawed. He doesn't have it in him. Besides, I really don't care if he shows up."

My father, or Stephen as I often referred to him, had never been there for me, either before or after he'd shipped me off to an expensive boarding school in England, where I'd spent the majority of my school years before coming to Yale. Incidentally, that's a long way away for a little boy to travel from New York after losing his mother. Not that my feelings had ever mattered to him. We had no relationship, and I refused to bestow upon him the term "father" or even "Dad". Those titles belonged to a special kind of person. They were honors that he did not deserve.

"If he does come," said Gabe, "he's going to be really angry when he finds out that you didn't take the medical school track or even take the MCATs."

Snorting, I shared a smile with Gabe. He was right; Stephen would be furious. That would be a fun conversation when he found out that he'd paid the bills for me to study literature and not biology.

It wasn't in my nature to try to pull one over on Stephen, but he never listened to anything I had to say. When I first enrolled at Yale, I found that he'd pre-registered me for a biology major. I spent the first week vomiting into a garbage can during most of the lessons. Biology clearly wasn't the right path for me, so I changed my major. My teachers were relieved; so was my lab partner.

Besides, the humanities were clearly my strength. I'd even been called a prodigy when I was five, though I preferred not to think of myself that way. Writing was my first love and I wrote constantly: novels, short stories, anything that came to mind. I've always believed that you should play to your strengths. Stephen, on the other hand, wanted a "Doogie Howser, MD" in the family. If you've never heard of him, Google it.

I changed my major and convinced Sarah, the cook, who also thought that Stephen was a jerk, to switch the quarterly grade reports that arrived at the house for the fabricated ones that I'd created on my Mac. Thank God for Photoshop.

The procession started and we began our walk onto the field. The graduating class ranged from the pranksters, who were snorting and laughing, to the serious rich boys, with their straightened ties and aristocratic heads held high. We were somewhere in the middle. After taking our seats, the keynote speaker began his commencement address. He was an alumnus and a successful executive who'd founded a charity that donated electronic equipment to underprivileged kids.

The speaker was only about five minutes into his speech when it happened. As I looked past the speaker into the space behind him, there was a spot of green hovering in the air to his right. At first, I assumed that it was a trick of the light or a retinal burn from the sun's rays. Leaning my head forward, I confirmed that the space was semi-transparent and shimmered before me.

Glancing around, I wondered if anyone else had taken notice. People stared at their shoes, their phones, their programs, everywhere but at me. That told me all that I needed to know: whatever this was, it was meant for me alone. As the green space increased in size, it was suddenly on the move and heading straight for me. It continued until it came to a stop right in front of me, almost at eye level. Looking around, I noticed a change. Everyone seemed frozen, unmoving. Even the light spring breeze that had touched my face only a second ago had stopped.

Exercising caution, I leaned toward the opening. There was music filtering through. The faint sound of pipe and drum got my attention. Inching forward, I brought my face close to the opening and looked inside.

On the other side sat my grandmother's house in the late-day sun.

My stomach dropped. Placing both hands on the base of the opening, I pulled. It gave like Saran Wrap. Tugging on it, I continued this motion until the opening was large enough to step into. Looking back to verify that nothing had changed, I stepped through the hole and onto the grass by Gran's house in Ireland.

***

Two things I noticed immediately were my change of clothes (I was now sporting a pair of jeans and a hunter green sweater) and my close proximity to the ground. I was no longer seventeen, but instead six years old. Whether this was the dream that I'd memorized so well or something else entirely didn't matter. Whenever I came to this place in my dreams, I was always six because that's how old I was when I first met her.

It was the autumn after my mother Addison's death and I'd come with Stephen and my brother to visit Gran in Ireland. This wasn't our first trip abroad; Stephen made these pilgrimages annually, insisting that we stay in the home where he was born. Nothing, not even my mother's death, would dissuade him.

Some people would have regarded him as a caring son for visiting his mother regularly, despite the distance. However, they'd have been vastly mistaken. He visited out of duty, not out of love or concern for Gran. There was always something tainted about him.

The ghostly pangs of loss and loneliness tugged at me now, pulling at my clothes and at the unexplored fringes of my mind. Tearing my gaze from the empty house, I looked to the steps that led down to the cove and started walking toward them.

On that day, the day I met her, I'd gone down to the rocks deliberately to avoid my older brother, Roger. His favorite game involved taunting me verbally, being much too ineffective as a bully to do any damage to me physically. He'd follow me around, telling me how hated and worthless I was.

The cove was my preferred place to visit, though Gran hadn't exactly deemed me old enough to walk to the cove on my own. Roger, who was generally a wimp, was too afraid to make the journey. He believed the cove was haunted, which meant that this place was safe territory for me. I wasn't afraid of ghosts. My mother was a ghost *now*.

The wind was picking up and blew harshly against my skin, ruffling my hair. The style was rather long for a young boy, and I got picked on a lot in school for the look. I'd refused to have it cut; my mother was the only one who cut my hair. No one was allowed to touch it until I was ten. It was around that time when I'd given up hope that she'd return.

I only needed to close my eyes to bring her to the front of my mind. My photographic memory made it extremely easy for me to remember my mother in vivid detail.

Although I'd demonstrated perfect recall in my lessons early on, Stephen was so wholly unobservant that he didn't know until I picked up our cook's Bible on my fifth birthday and recited the Book of Luke in its entirety after a single reading. Stephen didn't even know I could read.

Naturally, after that incident, he took every opportunity he could to brag, taking full credit for this anomaly. The types of remarks that he made on these occasions included: "Obviously my advanced parenting skills should be credited in this instance" or "He doesn't get this ability from his mother's side of the family".

Once at the bottom of the cove's staircase, I walked tentatively out onto the gray pebbles that dotted the shore. It was low tide, but the water was on its way back in. My shoes started to soak through as I walked further out onto the rocks.

At that moment, it occurred to me that I wasn't really six, but seventeen, and I'd climbed straight into this other world from my own graduation. I still hadn't seen anyone and instantly began to get annoyed. What was the point of bringing me here if she wasn't going to show? I wasn't going to wait. It was my graduation, which had been interrupted. I'd better things to do than to stand along the coast freezing. Pivoting on the spot, I headed in the direction of the lawn, then came to a halt.

The girl was standing ahead of me but off slightly to my left. I stared at her and my lungs filled with air as if I'd been holding my breath. I knew, without knowing how, that she was exactly my age, yet she seemed wiser than her years. Dark brown hair flowed down her back, so thick in appearance that it reminded me of a horse's mane. It hung straight, framing her face and complimenting her shockingly blue eyes. Even when I saw her that first time at the age of six, I had no problem identifying beauty when it crossed my path. This young girl was excruciatingly beautiful.

Initially, she gave every appearance of a normal girl in a gingham dress, tights, and shoes. But she was a contradiction. Despite the common wardrobe, she held herself with an almost regal air that implied there was nothing ordinary about her.

Our eyes met. There was an intense jolt of recognition that rocked my senses. It was as if we'd planned to meet here on the shore, on this day, and she was exactly on time. It was the same that first time and again today. A blush overcame me and I became tongue-tied, despite a desire to appear cool and collected.

"Hello." She smiled a dazzling smile and all of my feelings of inferiority went away. Still, I simply didn't have it in me to speak.

When she took my hand in hers, all of the loneliness, the sadness that I'd been fighting vanished instantly. Her skin was extremely warm against my chilled palm. Suddenly, I was freezing, almost shaking with cold.

"Calienta, we must be going," a man's voice called out in the distance.

She turned at the sound of the voice, but reluctantly, it seemed. She didn't let go of my hand.

When she gazed at me again, her smile began to fade. I had only moments with her.

There was a crunch of rock on the beach, and we both turned to look up as the fading sun was blocked by perhaps the tallest man in the world. He practically loomed over both of us, so great was his height.

He smiled kindly, possibly wanting to reinforce that he truly meant no harm. He was a good man, that much was clear, and I found that I respected him. That I knew nothing about him mattered very little.

"It's time to go," he repeated, touching the girl's arm. His expression conveyed a sense of urgency.

"I know, Father." Despite her words, she didn't release my hand but, instead, squeezed it tighter.

I tried to speak, tried to ask what this visit was about and to get more information, but I found that I couldn't. When I opened my mouth, nothing came out. Perhaps it was a reminder that I had to stick to the script from that first encounter so many years ago.

Turning back in my direction, she kissed me lightly on the cheek, and my entire body flooded with warmth. The cold had left me.

"I don't want to leave you." There was an overtone of grave sadness in her voice. She meant what she said. I truly believed that. After another brief smile, however, she pulled her hand from mine and placed her hand in her father's as they both started to walk away.

Instantly, I was seized with panic. She was leaving. "Wait." Before I could think, I was running after her.

At the sound of my voice, both Calienta and her father turned around. I couldn't bear for her to leave. Letting her go would be akin to losing my mother all over again. I couldn't explain it, but I needed her to stay with me like I needed air to breathe. "Can't I come with you?"

Some part of me wanted to go with them; where they were going didn't matter. I was simply starved for attention from the one person whom I needed it from the most: Stephen. I didn't want this feeling of warmth to end.

The man looked down at his daughter with such doting adoration, such obvious love. Jealously flooded my veins, took the driver's seat for a moment. I'd wanted this from my own father for so long that to watch this type of caring was torment. It was surely akin to showing a cool glass of water to a man who'd been lost in the desert but not letting him drink it.

Today, my reasons were different for wanting to go with her than they'd been when I was six. Mainly it was my curiosity; my need to understand was getting the better of me. Why had this moment replayed in my dreams every night for the last eleven years? Why was I here yet again on my graduation day? Yet, I'd be disappointed this time as well.

Calienta's father, whose name hadn't been spoken, smiled and knelt down before me. In deep rich tones he said, "You cannot come with me today, Kellen. Not yet. You have much growing to do and a gran that will miss you."

"You're wrong. My gran's dead now. There's nobody who'll miss me." Calienta and her father gave me twin looks of such compassion that I knew they understood my pain. In the next moment, they were gone.

My toes were starting to get wet. I stood alone on the beach, unwilling to climb the stairs and see the lonely house that was a dim shadow of its former self without Gran.

"I'm ready to go back." And whatever force of nature had brought me to that place listened.

***

SLAM! I was suddenly thrust back into my chair in the middle of the commencement speech, winded and dazed. The green spot in the air was gone and, as I looked around, everyone still wore the same bored expressions on their faces.

"…to move on and let a new generation lead us into further successes…" The speaker droned on.

What did this mean? What happened? It wasn't as though I hadn't dreamed about that day at the cove before, only about a million times, but *never* in the middle of the day. This clearly wasn't a dream. It was something else.

I looked down at my shoes and found them covered in sand, my dress socks soaked through. This caused my heart to pound even more. Looking around, I searched for some other sign, some other indication that *she* was here, but there was nothing else out of the ordinary. After a few moments, I forced myself to relax, but the urge to leave was strong.

Gabe and I were among the last called to receive our diplomas, and it didn't seem to take very long to get up front and return to our seats. Before I could further contemplate my experience, we were throwing our caps in the air and laughing with our fellow classmates.

From across the lawn, Gabe's family ran to greet him and he was engulfed in a sea of aunts, uncles, cousins, and other relatives. That left me standing awkwardly, the only one without an excited family member, in the middle of a green field filled with happy people. The nearest exit beckoned to me.

Gabe must have noticed because he ran back to my side, yelling to his family that he'd meet them at the reception. As always, he was unswervingly loyal. He was constantly checking to make sure I was included.

"Hey, man, I almost forgot. Happy seventeenth birthday." Gabe handed me a Snickers candy bar with a ribbon tied around it.

Birthday presents weren't a common occurrence in my life, so this small gift was unexpected. My right hand closed around the candy immediately.

"Thanks." Snickers candy bars were my staple food item, along with caffeine-free Pepsi. This combination was a good balance, given the amount of caffeine in the chocolate. Slowing down, we patted each other on the back in the awkward way guys have of trying to make it look like they aren't hugging. I smiled at him.

I considered telling Gabe, not for the first time, about that day at the cove. However, again I kept it to myself. Today my hesitation had more to do with Gabe's own excitement and his obvious desire to get back to his family. This wasn't the day.

"I guess I'll be seeing you," I said.

"What? What do you mean? I thought you weren't leaving until Wednesday. Plus the Commencement Ball is tonight. You can't miss that. I bet there'll be a lot of hot graduates there." He winked. Gabe was always talking about hot girls, but he never got a date. In his freshman year, one girlfriend dumped him after a month, and Gabe spent the next three months crying like a baby.

"No. I don't dance. Besides, they all still think of me as jail bait, you know?" This was true. When you're under eighteen and in college, people either beat you up or avoid you like the plague; you are always overlooked. A pair of eyes would rest on mine, only to flitter away. "It's better not to make them feel uncomfortable," I added, continuing to head in the direction of my car, through the crowd of celebrating graduates.

"You're gonna go, just like that?"

I cleared my throat, wishing I could leave, run away. I'd known this goodbye would be difficult, which is why I never told him about it beforehand.

"You don't need to go right now, Kellen. Stay the next few days with me. Let's hang out."

I sighed. “I can’t. I’ve got a plane to catch tonight and a few things to do before I take off. You’ve got my cell number.”

“Yeah, I have your cell number, but where are you gonna go?” The tone in Gabe’s voice made me stop.

I often pictured myself as the older of the two of us, guiding Gabe through his important decisions, helping him cope with some of the more challenging areas of his life. Now I suddenly realized that he’d see this as abandonment.

“Kellen! K?” His brows rose up above his blue eyes to meet the start of his sandy brown hairline.

We’d entered the parking area. He waited, one eyebrow still raised, while I walked over to a nearby garbage can and tossed in the commencement program and my gown and cap. These things mattered very little to me. They represented Stephen’s dreams, not mine. I returned, passing Gabe to unlock my car, which was parked slightly to his right.

As I slid the key in the lock, Gabe’s sharp intake of breath made me smile. “Dude. Since when do you drive an Audi TT?”

I smiled slightly, knowing he'd react this way. Gabe was beside himself and brushed past me to touch the hood of the little sports car, its black exterior gleaming in the sun. It was a gorgeous car, but there was no way I was going to keep it.

“It was a graduation present from my father.”

“This little beauty is…” He mouthed the word “amazing” as though afraid to say it out loud. When I didn't reply, he turned to look at me. "You don't seem too excited for someone who got such an incredible car for graduation."

I shook my head. "This is typical of my father. He can't be bothered to show up for anything, so he buys everyone off. I don't want his money and I don't want his car." I sounded self-indulgent, even to myself, but didn't care.

"If you aren't looking for a free handout man, I am. Why don't you call up your dad, eat some crow sandwich, and say thanks?"

"No. But hey, give me a penny."

Gabe stared at me as if I had two heads.

"Give me a penny." I enunciated every syllable as I spoke, like I was speaking to a small child.

After some more hesitation, he reached into his pocket and pulled out a single penny, curiosity evident on his face. Holding it between his thumb and forefinger, he dropped into my open palm.

I smiled as I caught it and pocketed it. "There's your handout. You bought yourself an Audi. If you don't mind driving to Syracuse International Airport to pick it up, that is."

"Kellen, you don't want to—you'll want to—" he stammered.

"This gift means nothing to me, so I have to find something that does."

He nodded, not even close to understanding.

"I'll text you the lot and row, okay?" I tried not to get choked up as I leaned over, this time really hugging him. There was no one around to see anyway.

"Where are you off to? You never said you were going to leave like this." His words were an accusation, his eyes a reflection of his own disappointment.

"Look, Gabe, I need to get away from here. It's time to start living a life for myself. I need a fresh start."

"You didn't answer my question." He crossed his arms in front of him, an indication that I'd let him down.

"I'm going home. I'm going to Ireland." And with a nod in Gabe's direction, I hopped in the car, put the key in the ignition, and sped out of the parking lot, leaving him in my wake. I already wished he could come along.

CHAPTER TWO
NEW BEGINNINGS

The car purred beneath me as I drove to Stephen's house that afternoon. Shaking off the out-of-body experience—or whatever had happened at graduation—seemed an impossibility. My mind replayed the events of that first meeting yet again.

After Calienta disappeared that night, I remembered that I could hear my name being called as I got closer to the cottage. It was Gran, my favorite person after my mother. Though she was Stephen's mother, there was very little of Gran's personality in him. How he'd become so horrible after having such wonderful parents was beyond anything I could understand.

Gran had wrapped me in a plaid blanket and I let her *tut-tut* over my wet clothes as she led me inside the warm little house. "Where have you been? You're absolutely freezing."

Stephen glanced up from his book long enough to nod curtly and returned to his reading. He hadn't asked where I'd gone, nor did he appear the slightest bit curious.

Roger, pouting after having been denied the pleasure of harassing me all day, glared in my direction from across the table. "Where were you, dog breath?"

"None of your bees-wax." I glared right back.

"What were you doing, picking up turds because you are one?" He laughed, chuckling at his own subpar insults.

"No. I met a girl on the beach." I was proud to mention Calienta, because it was well known that Roger was taunted by all of the girls at our school because of a chronic case of bad breath.

"What, was she a sheep? Kellen was kissing a sheep," Roger said in a singsong voice.

I stuck out my tongue fiercely at him before turning away, checking once to make sure no adult was watching. However, I still got caught.

"Kellen, quit fighting with your brother." Stephen conveyed this message without looking up from his book. Rolling my eyes, I walked away.

Passing Gran, I went upstairs to the modest guest room that Roger and I were sharing and changed into a pair of gray sweatpants and a sweatshirt that had the name of my prep school from back home on it. Though the clothes were warm, I hated wearing them as I detested the prep school.

When I returned downstairs, dinner was laid on the table. The fare was basic, a simple stew and bread that Gran had made that day. It smelled like heaven. The cold slowly started to seep out of my bones as I sat in the seat closest to the fire.

Stephen raised an eyebrow. "This is interesting, Mother." He always looked down his nose at anything offered to him here. He was a snob; there was no other word for it.

"It should be. You had it often enough growing up, before you got too big for your britches." She winked at me.

The potatoes were velvety on my tongue as they practically melted in my mouth. Each carrot was a savory jewel that was complemented by thick, rich broth. Beside my plate, a slim pat of butter slowly melted on a slice of brown bread that was still hot from the oven.

We ate in silence, with Gran making several attempts to catch my gaze again throughout the meal. Under normal circumstances, I'd have met her stare, even shared a conspiratorial wink with her. After all, when you're one of two normal people at a table of weirdos, you tend to forge a bond. This evening, however, I only wanted to be alone so I could think about Calienta some more.

Once everyone had retired for the evening, I crept back downstairs and sat in front of the remnants of the fire. The fireplace was large and dominated the kitchen, with heavy gray stones covering the front of the hearth. In the darkened room, with the crackling of embers providing the backdrop, my mind replayed the scene at the cove, wondering if it had been a dream, hoping that it had been real.

Sitting down, Gran wrapped her arms around me, surprising me; she'd never made a sound. Her weathered hand against my back was calming, and I found myself leaning against her. This closeness was something I hadn't experienced much since my mother died. I closed my eyes against the memory of my mother's touch.

Gran had always seemed to prefer me to Roger, although she never demonstrated this either in her words or actions. Then again, Roger was such a loser, who could blame her?

"You mustn't worry over your father and Roger. They love you in their own way, you know."

I realized she'd made the assumption that my pensiveness was due to hurt feelings, which, given the nature of my family, was a logical conclusion. She smiled to add emphasis, though she was lying to make me feel better. Stephen and Roger hated me. Even at that young age, I suppose I felt little more than apathy for the pair of them, though I found myself constantly hoping for something more. At present, however, I had more pressing concerns.

"Have you—" My voice sounded rough, as though I hadn't spoken in a long time.

She shifted her position slowly on the bench, so that she was able to meet my eye. Gran was always careful to give me her utmost attention whenever I spoke.

"Have you ever had a dream that was so real…so real that you thought it might actually have happened?" Anxiety had overtaken me and I sat practically on the edge of my seat in anticipation of her answer. I truly hoped that my dream was real. I needed it to be real.

Gran considered my question for a moment before speaking. "Yes, Kellen, I've experienced that feeling many a time. Why, just last week I went to the market and Lily O'Shea was wearing a pair of red leather pants. I thought for sure it must have been a dream. After all, she's seventy-five, for goodness' sake."

She chuckled, finding humor in her own experience. I laughed with her but didn't say anything further.

After silence ensued, she must have realized that she hadn't reached the heart of the matter. "Did you have a dream like that?"

"Well…well, how do you know if the dream really happened?" I ignored her question, keeping my head down and my arms around her. I refused to meet her eyes.

"Mmm. I suppose that you have to go with whatever your heart tells you."

My heart leapt inside my chest. This was exactly the kind of information that I wanted to hear. I needed to believe in Calienta.

"Where were you today, Kellen? I was worried about you."

"I was at the cove again. I think that I fell asleep there."

"That's not the safest of places for a nap. Why on earth–"

"I didn't want Roger to find me. I know he's afraid of that place, so that's why I went." I mumbled this into her side as she held me.

"Well, I suppose that's a good reason. You ought to be more careful, though. Is that where you had your dream?"

I nodded in response.

"Do you want to tell me about it? I like to talk about my dreams. It always makes me feel better."

That was the encouragement that I needed and I launched into a full explanation of the girl, her father, and the happenings at the cove. The excitement was evident in my voice, and if I looked in the mirror, I knew that my eyes would seem a little too bright. "They were leaving and I tried to stop them, but they had to go. They were so nice to me." My voice sounded small.

When I looked into my grandmother's eyes, her expression was confused, her forehead creased. She gave the appearance of someone considering this carefully, which was precisely the level of attention that this case needed.

"A young girl. Maybe you dreamed about Bridget or Emily, one of the girls from the village. They're both very nice." She smiled as she drew the conclusion.

"No. That wasn't the girl's name. I met a girl named Calienta today."

Gran seemed startled by this and pulled back, looking closely at me. In her gaze was the same look of scrutiny that she gave whenever she was trying to discern if I was telling the truth or not. Why would she think I was lying? I didn't care for the intensity of her expression and looked at my socks, plain white with a single red stripe across the toe.

"That couldn't be." A look of bewilderment crossed Gran's face and she seemed to teeter once again on the edge of believing my tale. Her eyes flicked to the window closest to us; her anxiety seemed to mirror my own.

I didn't understand what she'd need to be concerned about. Wanting to put her inexplicable fears to rest, I added, "I don't think you know them. They were on vacation. They had to leave today. I was sad. She was my only friend."

And somehow this was the truth, even though I'd spent less than five minutes with her. Calienta would have been my very closest friend. She was the most kindred of spirits.

Gran's face suddenly appeared centuries old as she looked down into my eyes. In that solitary moment, I could read the sympathy that she had for me there, but also the pain. "Oh, I know who she is, but I don't know if you do."

A smile lit my face. Gran knew her. Maybe we could be friends after all. "You know her? Where does she live? Can we go and see her now? I thought she was only visiting."

Leaping up, I ran to the door as I spoke and started putting my shoes on. There was no doubt in my mind that I was prepared to run out into the wind-swept night in search of a girl that I had barely met.

Gran laid a hand on my arm and shook her head. "Come with me. You won't need your shoes," she added as I made to retrieve them.

It was unusual for Gran to take me out at night. Irish folklore was ingrained in her daily life. Faeries and other local legends were a reality that was acknowledged and respected. As such, we rarely went outside of the house at night, and there were a variety of charms around the perimeter of the house to keep the "wee folk" at bay. *This must be serious.*

Taking her hand, the two of us stepped out onto the back porch and Gran closed the door behind us. The air was crisp and the sky blacker than black, except for the points of light where several stars dotted the sky.

Gran put her arm around me. "Child, you won't be able to find her tonight or any other, for she doesn't live in the village here."

I stomped my foot impatiently on the stone, causing my toes to throb mildly with pain. Didn't she say she knew her? Why would Gran lie to me? Why would she get my hopes up?

"Where does Calienta live?"

"I'm not sure exactly, as I know her only from the old stories that I grew up with. We won't be able to find her on any map. I know that she lives somewhere there."

And I looked on as Gran slowly raised an aged finger to point to the star-covered sky. "You see, Kellen, Calienta is a Star Child."

My eyes flickered to the sky for a moment and then back to hers. Before I could question her further, movement behind her caught my eye. I could have sworn that Calienta's father was watching us in the distance.

***

Trying to shake off the feeling of unease, I slowly began to push the experience to the back of my mind. Instead, I chose to reflect on the changes, both past and future, that would have an impact on my life.

Of course, the biggest change had taken place today. Not only had I graduated, but also, thanks to Gran, I no longer needed to depend on Stephen, though I hadn't gone public with this information yet.

We went to Ireland for Gran's funeral about three months ago, after receiving word that she'd died suddenly in her sleep. It was a low-key event for Gran. She'd enjoyed a nice dinner with a close friend at the local pub before going home to bed. She never felt a thing, from what we were told, which was something that I was incredibly grateful for.

When we got the news that Gran had passed, there was never any question that we'd attend the funeral. Stephen always did what was expected of a son. He sent money every month, visited every year for two weeks, and went to his mother's funeral. Shedding a tear, however, was another matter.

In contrast, the entire experience had been among the most painful of my life. Gran was my best friend, the person that I was closest to in the world since my mother's death. She was the only one that I could be myself with. When she died, part of my heart went with her.

Even when I graduated early and went to college, we still stayed in touch. I'd call her every few days, making sure that Yale billed it to my room so Stephen could pick up the tab. In turn, she'd send a care package to me every two weeks, filled with sweets and other goodies.

Ironically, the care packages continued right up until my graduation, despite her death. Obviously she'd arranged for someone to manage them in case something happened to her. She was always worried about me, calling me such a "skinny thing".

She wasn't far off. I'd always been thin and lanky, though not unusually tall, about five-foot-nine. My body never seemed to gain any muscle no matter what I tried. My complexion was fair and pale, though my need to surround myself with books in the library was most likely a contributing factor to the latter.

When I received a care package the week before my graduation, I acknowledged that there'd be no more correspondence from Gran. The package was light, bendable, and I remembered carrying it back to my place and not really hearing much of what was going on around me as I walked.

The box contained the usual assortment of sweets and baked goods, but this time there was also a letter. It was in a plain white envelope and was addressed to me in Gran's hand. As I picked up the letter, my heart started to pound. Having spent only a few months in this world without Gran's infectious enthusiasm for life, the letter connected me to her.

I smiled as I read my name and could almost hear her reading aloud to me as I unfolded the letter and began to read.

Kellen,

If you're reading this, then I've gone on to be with your Grandda. As happy as that thought makes me, it also saddens me because I won't get to see you again in this lifetime. I'm sorry for the life that you've lived and for my son. Although you already know this, I have to say it: You deserved a better father. I'm disappointed in the man that my son has become and you, my darling boy, have had to suffer. But that's neither here nor there now.

There are two things that I need to tell you. The first is that you're old enough to know the truth about your mother and her life. In this envelope, there's a ticket to London. You must go to your grandfather Alistair. I've left a box with him that contains a letter from your mother that you need to read.

Second, I've taken the money that your father gave me and saved it for you. It's in a fund and will become yours upon my death. I've also willed you my house and my books. I know you'll take care of them. You may choose to do whatever you wish with the remainder of my belongings. Alistair will act as your attorney and help you negotiate the legalities.

I've tried to reach out to your brother, but he has made it more than clear that he finds no fault with your father and isn't in need of my help. I'll leave it to you how to deal with him.

Regardless, you're free of Stephen and you can get a proper start out on your own now. No matter what happens or what you find out, you should know that you're the greatest joy in my life and proof that I didn't fail in life.

My love to you,

Gran

I was reeling. It wasn't as if I hadn't thought of going it alone before; running away from Stephen, school, everything, was something that I considered on an almost daily basis. However, there'd always been a certain amount of fear associated with starting out on my own. Still just a kid, in my mind. Though emotionally I'd been on my own for a long time, I'd never been responsible for my own financial independence.

The level of risk seemed further intensified by the knowledge that Stephen controlled the purse strings, and I had no plan and no idea where to go. Over time, I found that I could easily convince myself that I didn't need to leave "right now".

It would be Gran who instinctively provided the funding, the plan, and the motivation that I needed to start out on my own. Her letter included information regarding a bank account that she'd set up for me and a debit card with my name on it. After that, it was a very small matter to arrange to use my ticket immediately after graduation.

It also didn't hurt that Gran had invested the money from Stephen over the years, which I came to find out resulted in a little over a million dollars. I had plans to invest a large portion of this money once I got to London. With any luck, I could ride out many years on those funds until my writing got published. Smiling, I envisioned writing for a living in a cottage by the sea. Those thoughts swirled around in my head now.

So that was where I stood. I had my degree, I had money, but what I craved now was closure. I certainly didn't have any belongings at Stephen's house; everything that was important to me was in the car. However, I needed to close the door on Stephen for good.

***

It was getting quite hot out. Spring was fading into summer and the temperature was already in the mid-eighties as I drove toward Syracuse. Shrugging out of my jacket, I switched to the next song in my music playlist: "Take On Me" by A-ha. Turning up the volume, I tried not to think about where I was going or what I was about to do.

In the years that I'd been at Yale, I'd managed to avoid going home. Every holiday, every birthday, every break was spent with Gabe's family. The Stewarts always made me feel at home; I even had my own room there. The last time that I was at Stephen's home was the summer before I started college. That was also the last time that I'd had an audience with him.

When I arrived at the estate four hours later, I half expected the circular drive in front of the house to be empty, but it wasn't. Up to that point, some part of me still hoped that there was a reason he'd blown off my college graduation. Guess not.

I parked and hopped out of the car, not bothering to lock up behind me. As I walked toward the front door, I glanced up at the Tudor-style manor house in disgust.

Though the home's stately façade and aged wood exterior would have impressed some, maybe even coerced them to visit each of the home's four floors and thirty rooms, it had the opposite effect on me.

Yet I reached for the ornate brass handle that dominated the front door and tugged it open, not bothering to close the door behind me. Stephen's study was on my right and he was sitting there, reading, with a look on his face that indicated the presence of an unpleasant smell under his nose.

"At least you missed my graduation ceremony for something important." I gestured to the book. "You certainly can't read 'Freeing Your Child from Anxiety' enough, given that that was such a priority with me." My words were daggers of ice in the otherwise warm room. At least that was how I intended them.

He glanced up about a fraction of an inch but otherwise didn't acknowledge that I was present. This was a typical response from him, so I can't say that I should have been hurt or surprised, yet I always was.

These days, Stephen St. James was an esteemed professor at Syracuse University who specialized in Child Psychology. In the last thirty years, he'd earned two PhDs, written twelve books, and been on television countless times.

One of his books was featured in the Oprah Book Club and he made a point of mentioning this whenever possible to anyone who'd listen. *"Oh, it's going well. Had a book in the Oprah club last month, you know. I was very lucky."*

Actually, he believed that this was not due to good fortune at all but instead to his own brilliance. Regardless of the book club, his psychology degrees, or his success in the academic arena, none of these experiences qualified him to raise his own children.

The bottom line was that his only claim to fame was having a compelling public persona and an even more compelling agent. Marketing himself was his life, and this was something he did exceptionally well. This meant that the speaking engagements continued to pile up, along with the line of women that wanted to date him.

"Since you aren't interested in speaking to me, I wanted to stop by and tell you that I'm moving out on my own. Goodbye, Father, have a nice…whatever." I couldn't think of anything more to say to him. The desire to turn and leave overwhelmed me; I turned away to do just that.

"There's certainly a note of finality in your tone. Given that you're penniless, I'd recommend at least finishing college first." He hid behind the pages of his book, refusing eye contact.

"Did you not hear me? I'm done. I graduated today. I'm moving out." I turned back again as a look of astonishment crossed his face. I wondered if it had only just occurred to him that I'd aged at all.

"Today?" His brow furrowing, he looked at the calendar as if he might find the answer there. "You might as well stay. I know that you've nowhere to go and no way to survive on your own. I'll cut off your allowance as soon as you walk out that door." He was so obviously proud to lord his money over my head.

I reflected that he'd never struck me in my life. He made sure we were fed, clothed, gave us the best education, and provided a more than generous roof over our heads. Giving his money was easy. He never gave of *himself.*

"I have a nice little stash set aside. I won't have to worry for a while."

"How could you possibly have any money set aside, you insolent child?" This was obviously enough to spark some emotion, and he threw his book onto the desk in time with the phrase "insolent child". He did have a flare for the dramatic. "You've absolutely no concept of how much medical school costs. Plus I'll have to buy your way into some school, as I'm sure you screwed up. I wasn't informed about a single interview."

"Insolent child, huh? Is that the best you can come up with?" *You'd think he'd make more of an effort to be original. What a disappointment.* Turning fully, I faced him again. "Let's think about it this way. How much money would I have if your mother took every cent that you ever gave her and instead of spending it, put it in a trust fund for me? I'd be willing to bet that would be quite a nice little sum, wouldn't you?"

He blanched at my words. His face flushed in anger before he regained control. If I didn't know his measured reactions so well, I'd have missed the moment entirely.

"I don't want you to feel particularly concerned over my financial well-being, Father."

"I suppose that I shouldn't be surprised. You always did have so much of your mother in you. This is exactly the type of thing that she'd do."

He spoke in such a way that he implied this type of behavior was reckless and undesirable. Despite his attitude, I still stopped breathing. This was unheard of; he never spoke of my mother.

Throughout my childhood, questions were forbidden and there were no pictures of her in the house. She was there one day, a vibrant, beautiful part of our world, and then suddenly she didn't exist.

In this tense moment, as I stood in the ornate den with a man whose approval I'd never receive, I was suddenly thrust back in time to the day that my mother passed away.

We had been taken aside by Stephen's estate manager and told that she'd died suddenly and that we should go to our rooms. No further explanation was given beyond that. Roger and I wept at the news, unable to reconcile a mother whom we'd seen the night before with one that wouldn't be coming back. However, this reaction wasn't one Stephen had the patience for.

Upon returning to the house, he'd locked us in our rooms for the remainder of the day. When we were released the following morning, we were asked to restrict our tears to a minimum and informed that it was Stephen's wife who'd died, and he was the only one who should be allowed to cry.

However, I missed my mother too much and I needed something, some memento of hers, something to hold in my hand. I snuck into her study the next day, using a paperclip technique that I had read about in a book to pick the lock. Even now, I could still recall the hush of the darkened room, the grateful rush of familiarity I recognized in being among those things that had only recently been hers, things she'd once touched.

Her scent still hung there—a woodsy smell that linked my mother to the nature that she loved and the forest she loved to walk in. That day, I progressed tentatively into the room, touching everything and seeing nothing through my tear-filled eyes. I stayed there for hours, feeling close to her, yet missing her with a longing so intense that it was unbearable.

Eventually I got up to leave, taking pains not to make any sound lest I be discovered. Then I noticed the crumpled piece of paper at the bottom of the empty wastebasket. My hand lunged forward into the basket as I opened it up greedily. In my hands was simply an old grocery list from the previous month in her handwriting. Yet it was more than that to me. I held it close, feeling as though I'd struck gold.

That piece of paper went everywhere with me for months. I slept with it under my pillow every night. I opened and closed it so many times that the writing was worn and faded, the paper starting to tear.

One evening after dinner, it fell from my pocket onto the floor. Stephen picked it up, and there was a rushing sound in my ears as I waited for his reaction. Looking at me in disgust, he tore it up into tiny pieces despite my cries of panic.

That wasn't enough for him, however. He further punished me by not speaking to me for the next two weeks. In many ways, this was much worse than being

beaten. At least a beating would eventually end, whereas being ignored seemed without end.

After that day, the study was emptied and all of her things removed, her scent replaced by the harsh burn of bleach. There were no reminders of my mother left in the cold house, no indicators of her presence, which had once filled every room. These memories haunted me now. Though I processed quite a bit, my silence lasted only a few seconds.

"I'll take that as a compliment, Father, as I'd rather have my mother in me than the alternative." I turned to leave again, but before I could make it to the doorway, I remembered something that I needed to say. "I almost forgot. Thanks for the graduation present. Since I only had it a week, though, I wanted to let you know that I sold it and thought that you should have the proceeds."

Before Stephen could speak, I tossed a single penny high in the air in his direction. I'd just about made it through the door before he voiced his outraged realization.

Without a backward glance, I reached the car and hopped over the door and into the driver's seat "Dukes of Hazzard"-style. Starting the little car's engine, I navigated my playlist to the Police's "Ghost in the Machine" album and cranked up the music. I was always a bit of an eighties aficionado, in case you hadn't noticed. They were simpler times, with sitcoms that featured families who were happy, brothers and sisters who got along, and music that was mostly rap and booty-free. *What's not to like?*

My phone rang persistently, but I didn't answer. It was Stephen, of course. I'd have to make arrangements for a new number once I got to Ireland. I wouldn't come back here again, I vowed to myself. I'd given up on Stephen for good now, and I had already given up on Roger years ago.

Thinking of him, I glanced up at the window on the topmost floor. Roger was staring down at me from the window of his bedroom. As I continued to look at him, he slowly raised his right hand and I thought for a moment that he was going to wave. Instead, he simply extended his middle finger. Shaking my head, I muttered under my breath, "He's all yours, dog breath."

Turning the key, I drove off with the top down, speeding toward the airport and the plane that would take me to my new life.

CHAPTER THREE
A LIFE BEGINS

When I got to the airport, I sent a text with the location and the pin number for the car to Gabe, and left the keys under the mat. Opening the trunk, I extracted two small duffle bags and a backpack, and shut the lid. I believed in packing light.

After negotiating the airport, I looked forward to a peaceful flight. For me that meant that I could eat unlimited Snickers candy bars and nap under a hobbit-sized blanket.

After navigating through security and waiting through the long boarding process, I finally made it to my seat. An attractive blonde who was sitting in an aisle seat across from me smiled invitingly. This was nothing new in my experience. I'd been told before that I looked five years older and was therefore used to having older women hit on me.

After my mother's death, Stephen was never without a beautiful woman on his arm. He rarely introduced any of them to Roger and me, so I couldn't say that I recalled even one name. Since I had no interest in turning out like Stephen, I generally ignored these types of situations when they came up.

Ironically, girls my own age refused to give me the time of day. It had never helped matters that I'd had the ideal girl in my mind for quite a long time, most of my life actually, and wasn't willing to relinquish the dream yet. I gave the woman across from me a small smile before deliberately closing my eyes and turning my head toward the window; the blonde's disappointment was almost tangible.

I slept deeply, falling into the familiar dream almost at once, as though it was merely waiting for me to close my eyes to start replaying it.

Alone, I stood on the rocky coast by Gran's small village, letting the water soak my shoes. It was almost sundown and I'd decided to turn back to the house when…there she was. The young girl with dark brown hair and eyes as blue as the sea.

Let me come with you. Thoughts that I was unable to voice clouded my mind. This was the part where she always shook her head sadly and slowly faded away.

This dream didn't disappoint. When I woke, I discovered that we were approaching the London airport and the seatbelt sign had been turned on. I'd slept through the flight in its entirety, without even waking for the sub-par meal and over-salted pretzels.

My eyes roamed the cabin. To my right, the blonde across the aisle held a cosmetic kit with a rather large mirror angled in my direction. What I saw when I looked in the mirror nearly brought me out of my seat. Instead of the blonde's reflection, looking back was a man with fierce eyes and white-blond hair staring at me.

I looked around behind me and down the aisle to see if this stranger was anywhere around me. However,

there was no one. When I looked back, the imposing visage was gone. *That was weird.*

Trying to calm down, I looked out the window into the early morning light. Now, with sweat beading on my forehead and running down the back of my neck, the dream seemed too real, too vivid.

The blonde closed the compact roughly, giving me an irritated look when she caught my eyes on her. Averting my gaze, I focused on the bag under my seat.

The face I'd seen did little to remove the sense of unease that dreams of Calienta always left me with. After that first encounter, whether it was real or imagined, I'd dreamed about Calienta every night without fail. The dreams didn't scare me, but they always left me feeling alone and with the impression that there were unmet expectations surrounding me. The endless stories that I wrote about her helped me document both my dreams and my schoolboy fantasies of another life. They were a diversion, and a welcome one at that, from the lonely life that I led.

Even into my college years, I couldn't wait to escape to my journal and write about what might have been or what my life could have been like if I went with her. Not that I ever admitted any of that to Gabe. Though I'd far less free time once my intense Yale schedule kicked in, I always thought of her.

As I eased into an upright position and worked out the kinks in my neck, the pilot announced that fog had moved into the area and landing would be a challenge. The backup of other airplanes resulted in ours being placed in an extensive holding pattern. We remained in flight an additional forty-five minutes longer than I'd anticipated.

By the time we landed and claimed our luggage, I found that I was practically running to the cab bay. There was no point to hurrying, but I hurried nonetheless. Spotting an empty taxi, I wrenched open the door, tossed in my bags first before climbing in, and shut it firmly behind me.

"Where to?" asked the cabbie.

"Three-o-nine Upper Pembroke," I instructed. It was a little early for social calls, but my grandfather would be expecting me.

***

When I was ten years old, Stephen had informed me that I was being sent to boarding school in North Yorkshire. He explained that I'd be leaving the next day and should keep my packed belongings to a minimum as there wouldn't be much room for luggage.

My voice tentative, I asked, "Where's North Your Shirt, Father?"

Roger snorted in the background. Stephen looked annoyed. He didn't respond well to questions. He expected everyone to have all of the answers, like he did. He barked at me impatiently, "It's in the UK. England."

The place couldn't be any worse than home. Maybe I could see Gran; England was right next door to

Ireland anyway, I thought, trying not to let my excitement show.

"Will Roger be going with me?" Roger looked smug and Stephen didn't answer, which told me all that I needed to know. Roger was staying; I was being sent away.

"Go and pack your bags." That was the extent of the conversation.

The school was good for me. I made friends among my classmates, and my roommate, Simon, became my best friend. Some of the teachers were nice too, which was more than I could have hoped for. The topics were too simple, though, and I found that I was often bored in my classes. I didn't mind, because I never received bad marks, which meant that I got to stay. I'd have been happy to stay there forever. Plus, if I hadn't gone, if I hadn't been shipped off, I might never have met my grandfather, Alistair.

***

Gran had shared quite a bit about him, but definitely not the entire story. It was with interest that I greeted Alistair when I first met him as he visited me at boarding school.

Alistair and Gran had met while he was visiting Dublin on a business trip and she was visiting a cousin. He was leaving a restaurant with a client at the end of his trip, and Gran was sitting alone at a table by the door. Alistair excused himself and went immediately to Gran's table, where he struck up a conversation. He'd ended up extending his trip a week to stay with her.

Although they cared for each other very deeply, once they returned to their own worlds it became apparent that they weren't suited. Gran never wanted a life with "fancy cars and chambermaids", as Alistair had put it, and Alistair was entirely too fond of his "silk pajamas lifestyle", as Gran had put it.

More out of heartbreak than love, he became engaged to a young woman, Imogen, that his parents had recommended. A classic tale, it would eventually become a marriage based on love, though it certainly had a rocky beginning. Within months of leaving Ireland, he was married and living in China with a new business to focus on.

When Gran found out that she was pregnant with Stephen, she couldn't find Alistair. Her letters were returned, not having been received at all. Forced to have a child alone, she'd had no way to inform Alistair that he had a son. She even traveled to Dublin to try to find him through his business contact there. Yet when the secretary couldn't provide Alistair's whereabouts, Gran left without speaking to anyone else.

In actuality, it would be several years later, when a colleague asked him if he'd ever connected with the very pretty, and very pregnant, Irish girl who'd come looking for him in Dublin, before he found her.

That brief conversation triggered a series of events that resulted in Alistair ending up on Gran's doorstep with a lot of apologies. He found a nine-year-

old Stephen that he'd never known about. Gran had married a local fisherman who'd had no problem accepting both Gran and her young child, not having the ability to father a child himself.

Alistair and Gran found so much contentment in their lives that their friendship was reformed, and plans were made to introduce Stephen to Alistair's family. Alistair had two sons, Percy and Heath, who were close to Stephen's age, and both Alistair and Gran believed that there was no reason that they shouldn't get on famously.

With my Grandda's blessing, it was agreed that Stephen would come for an extended visit to London. Yet despite their shared enthusiasm, Stephen was undeniably a bad seed. Whatever hope Alistair had had that they could have a relationship vanished within a month of Stephen's arrival.

Initially, Stephen had been an angel, winning over Alistair's wife, Imogen, and befriending both of the boys. Alistair had even gone through the process of formally adopting Stephen and giving him the St. James name. He even added him to his will.

After the initial introductions to the household were made, things started to go downhill and the accidents started happening. If you could call them "accidents".

First, the dog was poisoned. Percy had started screaming early one Sunday morning when he'd found Cleo, his best friend, dead on the kitchen floor. Percy had

clung to the animal sobbing, unable to leave him as Alistair had held him close.

Further investigation had uncovered that straight bleach had been poured into the dog's water dish. Alistair was forced to fire the horrified servant that fed the dog, though he wasn't entirely convinced at the time that the woman was to blame.

As terrible as that was, it was far worse when Percy almost drowned in the river the following week. Percy had blamed Stephen, stating that the older boy had pushed him in. However, the butler claimed that Stephen was in his room studying the entire time and didn't remember seeing him leave the house.

It all came to a head when Alistair caught Stephen in Heath's room with a pillow positioned above Heath's face, as though to suffocate him. When Stephen met Alistair's eyes, they held a decidedly evil glint to them.

Stephen was immediately removed to the drawing room, where Alistair confronted him. Alistair had been disgusted and demanded to know why he was doing these things. The conversation was a long one. Stephen was a practiced liar, yet Alistair, who'd become a successful barrister in years past, had no qualms about pressing the matter again and again. It was finally enough to make Stephen snap.

Stephen screamed at Alistair, disclosing that he hated him and his rich family. He claimed that Alistair's uptight sons hadn't the faintest idea what it was like being known as the son of a fisherman and the village whore.

Alistair hit him, though he immediately regretted it. He was shocked and amazed that this amount of anger was possible from a boy. He pleaded with Stephen, explaining that if he'd only known about his existence, he never would have left.

Stephen wasn't interested. He vowed that one-day things would be different and he'd be the one with the money and titles.

Alistair reprimanded him, tried to turn him around, but it did no good. After Stephen attempted to trip Imogen at the top of the stairs, it was clear that there was something wrong with him. Alistair had little choice but to send Stephen to St. Bernard's Care Home, a reformatory school in the Berkshire town of Reading.

It broke Gran's heart to hear Alistair's stories, knowing somehow that they were true. After all, she'd glimpsed of this type of behavior before; try as she might to pretend they weren't real. Alistair was adamant for Gran's own safety, as there was nothing to stop Stephen from harming her as well. So off Stephen went to school.

When he was sent home for good several years later, he was a stranger to Gran. He refused visits from both parents during his stay, and the young man that arrived at her doorstep was cold and controlled. He stayed with Gran long enough to get into college.

Once Stephen got accepted on a partial scholarship to Yale, he packed up everything and left in the middle of the night. No goodbye to Gran or phone calls to Alistair, although his tuition checks were cashed quickly enough.

Alistair continued to try and have a relationship with Stephen, but his son wanted nothing to do with him. Even when his grandchildren were born, he was not allowed to see them, though my mother sent photographs. When Alistair came to see me, though his name was familiar to me, we'd never met.

"Why are you coming to see me, Grandfather, if you know how horrible my father is?"

"Kellen, I have the opportunity to act as role model with you and your brother in a way that I couldn't be with Stephen, though goodness knows I tried. If you'll let me."

"Sure, but I don't know about Roger. Good luck with that one."

Roger, staying in character, showed no interest in Alistair when he reached out. I, on the other hand, had plenty of interest.

From that day on, I had another grandfather. Alistair called once a week to check on me. Imogen sent packages of sweets and baked goods. Trips to London were arranged during long weekends, and I met my uncles and their families as well. No one seemed to care that I was Stephen's son, though he was rarely mentioned.

Alistair and Gran provided me with the sense of family that I never received from Stephen. He hadn't spoken to me since he sent me to the school. No arrangements were made for me to come home for Christmas, so I'd spent it with Gran and Grandda.

After a full year away, Stephen finally called me. I'll never forget the chattering between the other students as I was removed from my Ancient History class to take the phone call.

"Kellen." I found this a very cold greeting after having no contact for over a year.

"Yes, sir." I tried to make my voice sound obedient, not wanting to draw much attention to myself, even on a phone call. In my experience, attention generally resulted in criticism.

"The Headmaster tells me that you're doing incredibly well." There was smugness to his tone and I wondered dimly what right he had to that emotion, since he'd done little to ensure my success in this place.

When I didn't respond, he continued. "The best news is that he says that you can graduate early and he'll write a personal recommendation to Yale. Imagine, Kellen, you could be in college at thirteen."

One couldn't mistake the note of triumph in his voice. Yale was Stephen's alma mater. He wanted nothing more than for both Roger and me to walk in his footsteps. Although I was quite certain that Roger would have reveled in this honor (had he not been a complete moron), it wasn't for me.

I started to panic as I realized that this would mean yet another move. This wasn't what I wanted; I didn't want to leave. Boarding school was the first time that I'd ever experienced any sort of stability and I didn't want to go. I made the mistake of objecting, one of many

unfortunate occasions when I decided to share my feelings.

"Father, I want to stay in this school. I like it and I have friends here." There was a pleading tone to my voice and I could tell he was sneering at me over the phone as I spoke. He didn't even have to respond for me to know that I'd lost the battle.

"Friends. Friends. You want to stay behind in school because of friends? That's absurd. No, you'll be going to Yale."

The conversation ended and there was no going back. The rest of the year was occupied by a series of advanced prep classes. Though, I tried to do poorly so that they'd keep me behind, there was nothing for it. When I turned thirteen, I was off to Yale, my request to stay behind viciously ignored. My friends and my life in England were left in the dust.

***

The cab jostled me from my reverie as it pulled up to the curb, rousing me from my musings.

"Here we are son," the cabbie announced, hopping out and setting my bags on the curb. "Fourteen quid," he continued, holding out a ruddy palm, not bothering to look my way.

Climbing out of the cab, I paid the fare and grabbed my bags, slinging a gray and orange backpack roughly over my shoulder. "Thanks for the ride."

I looked up at the townhouse directly in front of me before jogging up the steps. After a butler answered the door, I was immediately ushered into Alistair's study.

"Kellen, good to see you." Alistair St. James jumped to his feet and ran over to hug me.

I stepped into his embrace and patted him on the back. "Hey Grandfather."

With a glance around the room, I took in the familiar flowery chintz and wood paneling. Alistair called this room "The Floral Explosion". His reasoning was that any room with that many different kinds of flowers in it deserved a title that began with the word "The".

However much it was not to his liking, his beloved, now late wife, Imogen, had decorated it. There wouldn't be redecoration anytime soon, if at all. Alistair gestured to a seat on a beige-colored lowboy next to a short, squat, mahogany table.

Despite the wide array of pastels, the room was comfortable, as was the home itself, like putting on a favorite pair of socks. All who graced its doorstep were welcome, regardless of the fancy London address. Fortunately, breakfast had been laid out and my stomach, constantly in search of any chocolate or Pepsi products, growled insistently in the absence of both.

"Tuck in." Alistair reached for a fork and pulled a tray closer to him. He usually preferred that we eat in the dining room, but he chose the setup for me. He was trying to make me feel at home and I wasted no time taking him up on his offer of breakfast.

We ate while I updated Alistair on the graduation ceremony and Stephen's absence. Alistair had been sick and unable to attend, but he listened intently now, nodding in all the right places.

"I'm sorry that no one was there for you, Kellen. I really wanted to be." His eyes held disappointment for himself and I was sure for his son.

After I'd plowed through three platefuls of eggs and ham, two lukewarm Pepsis, and some biscuits, my outlook seemed much brighter. My stomach full, I moved to a more comfortable divan and lay back against the fluffy cushions, content.

"It's nothing. Come on, Alistair, I'm used to this by now." This was only partially true, but there was no point in upsetting him.

"That doesn't make it right."

"When has it ever been right, Alistair?"

***

I stayed with Alistair for about a week, only delaying the inevitable. There was a house along the Irish coast that was waiting for me. And, as my dreams kept telling me, it was time to go home.

On the last day of my visit, we ate a casual lunch before Alistair got up and went to his desk to retrieve Gran's will. Since I was her sole heir and Alistair the executor of her estate, there was no need to include Stephen or Roger. Reading Gran's will would make her

departure more real to me, so I wasn't looking forward to this.

Alistair sat back in his seat with a sigh and arranged the papers in front of him. He locked his gaze with mine. "Let's get this over with, shall we?" His smile seemed insincere and he appeared at that moment much older than his sixty-five years.

Clearing my throat, I sat up straighter, nodding as I did so, unable to give any further consent. My left hand gripped the pillows until my knuckles turned white. My fingers throbbed in response.

After some momentary shuffling of documents, Alistair went on to read the will in his brusque barrister-like manner. He discussed such things as property taxes and title transfer. These were terms that I vaguely understood, but I fought the urge to plug my fingers in my ears and shut my eyes the entire time. I'd never missed Gran more.

It was simple, I thought, as I listened to Alistair run through all of the details. Gran had had very few expenses, and her estate paid those that did exist. Alistair had already taken care of this, so everything was fairly cut and dried.

The land and the house had been given to me, although they were in trust until I reached twenty-four years of age. Until that time, Alistair would oversee everything and keep an eye on the funds for me. I didn't have any plans to sell Gran's home. It had been more of a home to me than my own had been; there would be nothing to gain by getting rid of it now. There was already more than enough money in my account to get by on.

Everything in the house was mine now as well. I'd have the rather daunting task of sorting through Gran's memories, something else that I was not looking forward to. It would only bring more painful reminders that I would never hear Gran's voice again, see her face. Touching those things would be like ripping my heart out.

Alistair handed everything over to me to review. Getting up from his chair, he went to find someone to witness my signature. After a few moments, they returned to the room and the young man went to wait in a corner until I was ready.

Both gentlemen waited patiently as I read through each line of the paperwork, though the silence in the room was overwhelming as they waited for me to finish. Alistair didn't move from his seat until I looked up and handed the signed stack back to him.

"What's next?" I expected some sort of red tape to deal with. Whether interference from Stephen or some government restrictions, I assumed that there would be more to do.

"Well, Kellen, that's about it. What's next is up to you." He handed me a large manila envelope and a set of keys.

"What about Stephen? I'm still a minor, after all. What if he tries to force me to come back?"

"I've started the paperwork that will make you an emancipated minor. It will tie Stephen up for a year, easily. In the meantime, let's just say you're studying abroad."

"Are you okay with me living alone in a foreign country?"

Alistair laughed. "Kellen, you've been on your own for a long time, grown up a lot faster than any child your age should have to. I think you can handle the cottage on your own. However, if you need me, I expect you to pick up the phone."

His voice was kind, sympathetic, as he continued. "I've included a few extra things for you to review." He nodded to the envelope in my hand. "There's a letter from Gran in that, but also one from your mother. I hope that you'll take the time to read both."

I didn't speak. My heart was pounding at the mere idea of anything from my mother being made so readily available. However, I set those emotions aside and allowed myself a small smile as I turned to put the manila envelope and set of keys into my bag. Zipping it back up, I realized that I didn't feel the sense of relief that I'd expected. Instead, I was overwhelmed by a sense of sadness at the finality.

CHAPTER FOUR
GRAN'S HOUSE

"Kid, we're here. Wake up." The driver pulled to a stop. Somewhere in the corner of my mind, I heard him get out of the front seat to take my bags out of the trunk, stomping on the gravel road as he walked.

A yawn escaped me and I rolled my head in slow circles, peering out from the window into the small garden that wrapped around the cottage. It was littered with flowers in every color of the rainbow. With no skills or knowledge of plants, I sighed, resigned to the knowledge that I'd probably kill them within the week.

The exterior of the house was whitewashed brick, the roof slate. Beyond the cottage, I could hear the crash of the sea against the rocks. The entire perimeter was surrounded by a stone wall, which identified the property's barriers and kept out most unwanted livestock. Most of it, anyway. There was a small cow grazing in the yard that I didn't think belonged there. I'd have to deal with him or her eventually, but one step at a time.

It was around dinnertime and my stomach grumbled. The smell of the salt air always made me feel hungry, for some reason.

The sun was slowly starting to set beyond the hills; it would be dark soon. I was immediately anxious to get inside and settled, afraid of getting stuck outside trying to figure out how to unlock the door in the dark.

There was a lonely feeling here; the nearest house was about a half mile away. The dramatic landscape haunted me; each mountain and ruin was a ghost peeking out at me. Gran had loved the solitude of it all and reveled in the aloneness. Although I'd probably love it for the same reasons, I couldn't help but wish, as I had many times before, that I wasn't quite so on my own.

After paying the cab driver, I pulled the very modern-looking keys that Alistair had given me from my bag. At first they didn't seem to belong at the cottage, but I remembered that Stephen had had a new door installed at the house for security reasons in the prior year. *Why did he bother?* I smirked as I looked at my surroundings in the fading light. Surely no one would ever think to rob this little place.

The key slid easily into the lock and I walked into the small entryway, taking off my coat in the process. My hand paused in mid-air as I went to hang my coat on the hook by the door. Gran's work coat was still hanging there, as if Gran had only just entered the house. Stephen was such a Type-A personality that I assumed he'd have handled cleaning out her things already. Then reality hit me. As the sole heir, that was my responsibility. There was a lot of work ahead of me.

Slowly, I walked through the house, turning on lights as I went. Out of sheer luck, the utilities weren't turned off. As I passed a warming radiator, I took a moment to stand in front of it as the faintest traces of heat warmed my skin. Gran had often chosen to build a peat fire for warmth, mostly for sentimental reasons. *Thank God I wouldn't have to figure that out.*

A persistent tapping sound turned my attention to the window at the front of the house. A light rain had begun to fall, pattering against the windows and striking the roof. Gran's cottage had always lost power at the drop of a hat and I prayed now that we wouldn't have a storm. Despite my book smarts, I was still a seventeen-year-old who'd never lived alone. The last thing I needed was a wrestling match with my own fears in the dark Irish countryside.

As I walked into the kitchen, I noted that it was a contradiction of itself. On one hand, there was aged brick flooring that had clearly seen better days, along with a wide open hearth for cooking. On the other, there were also several stainless steel appliances that functioned well, but looked out of place.

On the wooden kitchen table there was a flowered tablet with the heading "To Do" printed daintily across the top. Gran was a list-maker, like me. Grabbing the pen next to it, I made a note on the first page to find out how utilities worked in Ireland, along with whom I needed to call if the power went out. I didn't imagine that twenty-four-hour-service was an option.

My glance shifted to another note on the table, one that I hadn't seen earlier. It was from one of Gran's neighbors who wanted to let me know that she'd been in to clean out the refrigerator and "tidy up a bit".

I shuddered, trying not to imagine what she would have found. There'd probably been a bunch of rotting, smelly food in the fridge. However, as I glanced around again, I took in a pleasant lemony smell and noted the gleaming tables and countertops. It made me smile to think that someone cared about my well-being here.

Thankfully, the note also indicated that there were groceries in the fridge, which had been billed to Gran's account. There was only the one little shop in town. It was poorly stocked, but I assumed that she'd have given me some essentials.

Putting on a kettle for tea, I opened the fridge. Happily, I noted several covered dishes inside with instructions for reheating. The closest to the front would do nicely. The spoon dug into it easily and I placed some on a plate before putting it into the microwave and firing it up.

After eating two generous portions and enjoying a cup of tea, I cleaned up and set off to explore the rest of the house. The flowered tablet came with me, and I used it to indicate which things should be removed and which should stay. Most I'd sell or donate. This systematic approach might have seemed callous or cold, but the action of planning calmed me. It made me feel more adult, and more in control of my situation because I was taking action.

I continued my punch list upstairs, moving through each of the two handkerchief-sized bedrooms and the small bathroom. When I entered Gran's bedroom, I noticed a book by the bed and mistakenly assumed it was a Bible. Closer examination told me that it was her journal.

"I'm not going there." I spoke to the empty room, touching my hand to the front of the leather volume but resisting the temptation to open it. Although I was sure she'd want me to read it, I wasn't ready yet.

I headed out to the conservatory at last, smiling. Completely enclosed by glass, such a modern luxury seemed bizarre in such an antiquated place. Gran had spent a lot of her time out there, looking out over the horizon.

***

The sky was an inky black now and it was impossible to see anything, yet I opened the french doors leading out to the backyard anyway and listened to the sea for a few moments. It was unsettling, the darkness, as not even a single star lit the sky. My eyes took their time adjusting to my surroundings before I noticed the wooden steps to my left that led down the cliffs and to the shore below. They led directly to my childhood refuge: the cove.

I pushed back a wave of emotion as I realized that Gran would never again chide me for being down there in the cove by myself. We were cheated out of time like a gambler cheated at cards.

Leaving the house, I walked to the top of the steps and looked down. The way was burned into my brain. Grandda had built those steps years ago when he came home to find his new bride trying to scale down the cliffs with a rope. She'd wanted to swim in the sea and that was the most efficient way to get down to it.

Suddenly I knew where I wanted to go. Running easily back into the house, I set my list on the table and grabbed my jacket and a flashlight, shutting the doors after me. I pulled my hood over my head to keep the rain and the cool night air at bay and jogged to the end of the grassy lawn.

The steps weren't in the best condition and I exercised caution on the weathered, rickety wood that was slippery from the harsh, salty sea air. After a few near falls, I made it to the bottom, my feet crunching on the small rocks.

The cove was exactly as I'd remembered. Though nearly covered with water, I could clearly see the rocks on the pebble-covered beach as the tide receded. Using my flashlight, I navigated carefully on the wet stones, not wishing to stray far from the stairs that led back to the house. There was a large boulder on the pebbled beach, the same one I remembered from my youth. Carefully, I climbed atop it and wrapped my arms around my legs.

I was completely isolated, and had to admit that I was afraid of the aloneness. Yet I felt a need to prove to myself that I could live on my own, that I was man enough. That was exactly what drove me—the need to battle total solitude and win.

Only moments after sitting down, however, I became conscious of water running down my face. Initially I blamed the rain but realized, with some degree of mortification, that I was crying. The wind started to pick up as the tide rose, and I realized that I was fairly close to being stranded on this rock by the incoming sea. The rock's jagged exterior scraped against my arm as I climbed down. The rough water teased with pulling me under, but I ran straight to the stairs. I'd only reached the first step when something compelled me to turn around.

Following the instinct, I glanced back, and my heartbeat increased as I realized that I wasn't alone. There was someone standing on the perimeter, outside of my range of focus, but I was afraid to look.

Less hesitant during the return trip, I took the steps two at a time, falling twice in the process.

When I got to the top, I glanced back toward the foot of the staircase. Despite my sense of unease, it appeared as though I was alone. Turning, I ran across the lawn to the cottage, pleased to reach the safety of the house. Heat started to fill the space and it was homey, so normal. Then I remembered that I was the only one there, and any illusion of a *home* instantly disappeared.

Once the warmth began to permeate my skin, I realized that I was soaking wet; the rain had changed from a light drizzle to a heavy downpour without my noticing. Shaking my head, I removed my wet things in the conservatory, hanging them up on a small line in the corner.

The darkness outside intrigued me, and my gaze kept being drawn to the windows again and again. There was something out there, though I couldn't name it. Glancing into the darkness once again, I started as a form began to take the shape of a woman. Some part of me responded, urged me to leave the house, to see who—

"Yeah, I don't think so." Talking to oneself was never a good sign. Without waiting to see if I was right, I turned abruptly and entered the main part of the house, shutting the door behind me, and headed straight for the shower.

When I looked out the window again after my shower, there was no sign of the girl, but I did see a dog sitting at attention on the back lawn. It was in reach of the backyard light that I'd left on. *Did the neighbors have dogs?* I couldn't recall. Odd, but it looked exactly like the dog that Gran had until last year. I pulled the curtains back into place and headed for Gran's room, which would be my new bedroom. It was the larger of the two rooms, so logically it made sense; personally I'd chosen it because it allowed me to feel closer to Gran.

***

Opening the closet, I looked around for a place to put some of my clothes. It was overflowing with Gran's things. When I pushed one of her robes aside, I noticed a small storage box, filled with black journals. *Now where had I seen those before?*

My eyes flashed to the journal on the nightstand and back again. Crouching down, I looked more closely into the organizer; the journals were labeled by year. I couldn't believe that Gran kept these. Though Gran was gone, it somehow seemed like an invasion of privacy. I hadn't even opened them up and I felt ashamed, as if looking at the journal bindings was akin to reading the contents. Yet there was a part of me that realized the books could tell me more about my mother.

Without thinking, I skimmed the bindings of each book until I found the one marked 2000. That was the year my mother had died and the year that I met Calienta. Heart thudding, I sat down on the bed and began to read.

I can't believe they got to him. I wonder if he's been touched, talking about the Star Child. I had Katie from the village come over and perform a protection rite on the house the next morning, before anyone was about. Maybe I was imagining it, but I thought I saw Cabhan when I stood with Kellen on the porch.

It was the last statement that bothered me the most. Hadn't I recalled that same moment on the way to Stephen's? I thought I saw someone that night too, and I was sure that I'd seen him before and since. Who this Cabhan was or what it meant, I had no idea. I'd have to read more of the journals and try to find some other clues. When I finally managed to close my eyes, I slept fitfully, despite my exhaustion, and I dreamed of my mother, imagining her as the one on the perimeter of my eyesight last night.

CHAPTER FIVE
ADDISON

I woke up groggily at seven-thirty a.m. So this was what a hangover felt like. After sucking down some coffee, I added some of the scones that were left for me onto a plate. On the table was the package that Alistair had given me. There were things inside that I should read, but—as an exercise in avoidance—I headed up to Gran's bedroom and started immediately organizing things instead. The envelope could wait.

By about ten o'clock, I had everything sorted into “keep”, “throw out”, or “give away” piles, and further organized them by “clothing”, “personal items”, and “household items”. The room was fairly clean, but the smell reminded me too much of Gran. Opening the windows to clear the air, I stripped the bedding and bundled up the towels, taking everything with me to the laundry room.

Doing the laundry was an experience. Gran had a modern washer and dryer, along with an adequate supply of detergent, so at least I had everything there that I needed. The mechanics behind the laundry process were basic, but I wasn’t necessarily skilled in the execution. Sorting the laundry didn’t work out exactly as I planned. Somehow, Gran’s red apron ended up in the load with the bedding.

Regardless, when the load was run, the room had a chance to air out, and the fresh pink linens were placed on the bed, the room seemed more my own, though that revelation didn't bring me any measure of happiness. The pink sheets weren't helping, either.

Shutting the windows, I placed the remainder of Gran's things into garbage bags and headed downstairs. There was more to do, certainly, but completing these tasks made me feel less edgy. It also increased my appetite. Hungry, I went off in search of lunch. As I headed into the kitchen, I finally grabbed the large manila envelope that had preyed on my mind throughout the morning.

There was bread on the counter, and I rooted through the fridge until I found some baked ham slices and cheese to go with it. Marveling, I tasted a small piece of each before constructing my lunch. Everything was organic here—it was wonderful. The food probably came from the farm down the road.

I inhaled the meal; there was simply no other word for it. Then I reached for the envelope. It was warm in my hand, but that was my imagination. My fingers ran over the outside several times, unconsciously wondering what other things I could possibly need to do before opening it. There weren't any, and I couldn't put it off any longer.

Dumping the contents onto the kitchen table, several things fell out at once. Groupings of papers stapled together in separate packages and two envelopes, both addressed to me, were deposited on the aged wooden tabletop. My breath hitched as I recognized my mother's handwriting on one of the envelopes. I pushed it to the side.

Selecting the stack of documents, I noted that it consisted of Gran's will and paperwork on the financial trust that had been set up for me. There was also a copy of the deed to the house and the land. Getting up, I went into a spare room and took my time finding a file folder to store all of the paperwork in for safekeeping. This allowed me to kill a grand total of five minutes.

Next, I opened the first envelope. It contained a small key and a note from Gran. I unfolded the note as I set the key on the table and started to read.

Kellen,

When your mother died, I had suspicions that your father would destroy all of her things. Therefore, I arranged to ship many of her belongings here. I couldn't save everything, but I thought that you might like to look at what I did keep. Then you can do with everything as you please. The key is to my attic room. I kept everything locked up, in case Stephen visited.

Read the letter from your mother. You need to know her story; it was too late when I found out.

Love,

Gran

Grabbing the unopened items, I took the stairs two at a time to find the attic. It took a while, but I finally located the door in the back of Gran's closet. It wasn't a traditional attic; I think it was once a small third-floor room. With only one child who'd moved out early, they'd never needed the space. Her closet wasn't original to the house, so Grandda must have built it right over the door to the room above. There was a flashlight on the closet shelf, which I assumed was there for exactly that purpose. Picking it up and switching it to the *on* position, I pushed roughly on the door and walked up three steps into the room.

And nearly had a heart attack when I saw a lady in white.

Talk about a cliché from every ghost story ever imagined. Okay, it wasn't exactly a lady in white, but it was a white dress hung in a clear protective garment bag from a hook on one of the ceiling beams.

"Holy cow." Muttering, I tried to get my heart back in working order. I walked stiffly to the windows and pushed them open, letting in air and light. Almost immediately, the room was more inviting.

As I turned to examine the gown more closely, I was brought to a halt by the large trunk sitting on the floor beneath it. A small brass nameplate was affixed to the front of the trunk above the keyhole. The initials printed on it were ACS. Addison Clare St. James. Heart pounding, I kneeled down and slowly released the latch.

The trunk was filled with memorabilia: baby hats, baby shoes, and locks of hair. Everything was labeled in the same hand that wrote my letter. It was creepy. There were photographs of me as a child, my mother and father, Roger, Gran, and many people I didn't know. Old school chums, probably.

The final object was a small glass vial, which upon opening I immediately recognized as my mother's perfume. It was a vanilla, sugary smell and made me think of freshly baked cookies. The scent surrounded me and I inhaled deeply, taking it in, trying to imagine that she was there with me.

After I'd touched everything at least once, I sat down in one of two oversized burgundy chairs in the room and leaned into one of the many pillows that covered the chair. This was probably where Gran came to read. Although at first blush it was a little claustrophobic, with the window open I could hear the waves and smell the salt air. It was peaceful once I got over the weird dress and initial musty smell that generally accompanied attics.

Steeling myself, I looked at my mother's letter in my hand and unceremoniously ripped it open, sliding out the contents. There were more envelopes inside. The first had my name on it, but there was a second there for Roger, which I set aside. Despite our differences, I'd send it out with the morning post.

There could be no more stalling. Taking a deep breath, I began to read.

Kellen,

I know that you were probably surprised to receive this letter. I only recently discovered that you and your brother were told that I was dead. However, I'm very much alive. This is why you need to have the whole story.

First, please know that it was never my intention to leave you. I never wanted to. I love you so much and I have always wanted you, from the moment that you became a part of my life.

Although it isn't in my nature to speak poorly of anyone, I'm afraid I can't extend the same courtesy to your father. He is, most definitely, an evil man, and I can never forgive him.

When you were about five years old, I became sick. The doctors said it was cancer and that I wouldn't last long. At first your father was an excellent caregiver, but then he stopped checking on me and started ignoring me. I became very weak as a result of his neglect; one time, a whole week went by before anyone offered me food or helped me bathe. I believe he told you that I was on a women's retreat that week.

Eventually, I managed to make my way from the guest room where I was staying to my own room that I shared with your father. When I found him, he explained that I'd lived much longer than he expected, and now my care was becoming too much of a burden. Therefore, he was going to place me in a long-term care unit. I protested, but he assured me that someone would bring you boys to visit me.

I found out shortly thereafter that he wasn't sending me to a long-term care unit; he was having me committed to a mental hospital. I couldn't believe it. He'd already broken my heart but now he was taking my humanity as well.

I woke up, after what I believe was a week later, in a facility in Northern Scotland. I don't believe that anyone actually knows I have cancer here, so I'm not being treated for it. One would assume that lack of treatment would speed up my death, but that hasn't been the case.

I tried to write to all of you when I got here, but one day, when I pretended to take my medication, I overheard the nurse say that she was given orders to destroy all of my correspondence. I have no doubt that your father is behind this as well.

I was recently moved to a new room though, and it's probably the nicest part of this place. It's circular, with a lot of light, which I enjoy. It's lonely here, though. I have no roommate and, as I'm arguably the only sane person here, no one to talk to. I've gotten very good at pretending to take my medication and trying to look disoriented most of the time. Although it probably would dull the pain of the cancer, I prefer to remain lucid.

As I write this letter, nine hundred and one days have passed and I don't know if you'll ever see this message. A new nurse here is kind and brought me some paints. She's promised to get this to your Gran, though I don't know if she'll follow through with my request. I can only hope.

I would give my life to be with you every day. I miss you more than anything.

Mom

My hand was shaking as I held the letter. "Bastard. You bastard, Father!" My voice rang in the empty room. The women's retreat popped into my head like it was yesterday; I remembered her mentioning it. What type of twisted person could do that to someone else? The answer was simple: *Stephen.*

More important, was there a chance that my mother was still alive? Could she still be in the world after all this time? Unable to wrap my head around that concept, I realized with shock that it was early evening and I'd obviously not noticed the passage of time. Exhausted both physically and mentally, I fell back into the chair unthinking and, though my stomach protested, sleep won out. My eyes closed against the pain of it all.

***

In the dream, I stood alone on a weathered-brick road. Ahead of me, there was a long drive that was surrounded on both sides with open fields. After I'd walked about a half mile, a gray stone building appeared in the distance. From the outside, it seemed about four stories tall.

A cylindrical tower on one side of the building gave it the look of a castle, but the contrasting sections of the building were too contemporary to mark it as ancient. This structure was probably early 1900s. A series of wrought iron fencing framed both the building and a large yard, which appeared to be overgrowing with shrubbery. This was the hospital where my mother was a patient.

It had a derelict quality about it, what with the overgrown foliage and generally untidy appearance. Despite the fanciful tower, the building still managed to look cold and institutional. The front gates were locked, as I expected.

With a quick backward glance, I started to walk the perimeter. My explorations took me over a wide stretch of land that surrounded the place, and it wasn't long before I found a break in the gate. After squeezing through the narrow opening, I walked across a bricked courtyard before reaching the backdoor. It was also locked.

A rusted fence bordered the area, dotted with welcoming signage with the words "Keep Out" emblazoned on the front in blood-red lettering. Thin wire held them in place. I walked up to the sign that seemed to have the most deteriorated supports and yanked hard. Nothing. I braced my foot in the opening in one of the links and pulled hard. Nothing.

Placing both hands firmly on either side of the sign, I shoved my foot into the space in the fence and pulled with all I had. A metallic pop sounded the release of the sign from the fence and I came down hard on my butt. Cursing, I stood up and pulled one of the wires from an opening in the sign, before tossing the latter to the ground. I bent the wire into exactly the shape I needed. At that point, it was a small matter to pick the lock, and I was inside the kitchen.

The place was undeniably spooky. The darkened room through which I walked was lined with shadows. It appeared as though it had been looted; everything of value had obviously been removed. It was late afternoon, but the overcast weather minimized the amount of light that filtered into the place. The flashlight on one of the counters was a welcome sight.

Once I exited the kitchen and reached the main room, it was a bit brighter, with floor to ceiling windows on either side of the aluminum door letting in larger quantities of light. These walls were painted in cheerful pastels, as though someone had cared enough to brighten things up. Twin hallways, which seemed to lead to joint common areas, flanked the sides of a massive oak staircase. The wood was rich in color and tone, but the absence of carpet on the linoleum-covered steps took away any sense of hominess. As I looked up the stairs, I noticed several murals of nature scenes along the wall that ran the length of the first landing. Again, it was pretty obvious that someone had at least tried to make an effort to spruce things up.

Despite my lack of desire to remain in this place, this dream, I walked up the steps, noting the patches on the walls and watermarks on the ceiling. Searching, I walked in and out of many of the rooms on the second floor. However, there was no evidence of my mother in any of these rooms. Every room here was empty, completely cleared out. Upon reaching the third floor, I found the exact same thing: nothing.

From the outside, I could tell that there were at least four floors. However, I couldn't find the door that would take me up a level. I walked the length of the third floor again and again, searching for the steps, an elevator shaft, anything. The fourth floor could even be a façade. No, her room was round; she'd said so. I had to figure out how to get up there.

Where is her room? I was about to give up when I finally noticed the old mattress that was shoved against one of the corners on the third floor. Propelling the mattress to the floor, I found a very narrow doorway. Without pausing, I pushed through the opening.

Taking to the stairs, I counted each step as I walked. One. Two. Three. Four. Five. Six. Seven. Eight. The sun was starting to come out again and its rays illuminated the entire chamber before me when I reached the eighth and final step.

My breath hitched and I fought back the tears that were trying to force their way out of me. Frozen, I'd stopped in my tracks, only able to look around at the chamber in which I stood. It was incredible; there were no walls anywhere. There were probably walls at one time, but now it was more like one big mural covering every square inch of where a wall would be.

There was a tall ladder that stood at the foot of the bed; it stretched up to the top of the ten-foot ceiling. The circular room had three small but bright windows that looked out over the rolling hills and shimmering lakes.

Who could have painted this? However, my thought was answered when I saw my own childhood likeness painted in one of the murals, sitting in a field of flowers. A likeness of Roger sat in a tree, laughing.

This was my mother's room, I had no doubt. I remembered her painting periodically during my childhood, but I'd no idea of the depth of her abilities. It was clear that they were beyond anything that I'd remembered from my youth.

My mother lived in this room, was trapped in this room, but she painted. My mother had a gift for finding happiness in almost any situation. It would be so like her to find peace in the middle of hell. Now, however, the room was empty, and I stood alone with the realization that she was no longer in the world.

***

My eyes popped open. Transported back to Gran's, I awoke with a start and fell out of the chair. Sunlight was streaming in through the ivory lace curtains on the windows while birds chirped loudly. It was early morning and the air was freezing; the breeze blew strongly. I'd left the window open all night. Apparently, I'd spent the night in the attic chair.

Placing my head in my hands, I pushed my fingers through my tangled mass of hair as I stood up, pressing my eyes tightly shut. My stomach growled and I knew that I should've gone downstairs to get something to eat, but my legs wouldn't move. I tried to get past the oncoming rush of emotion, but to no avail.

Then my legs buckled and I sat back down again and opened my eyes. The tears came then and I hated them. They made me feel weak, a prisoner of my own grief. Yet I knew there would be no stopping them, so I leaned back in the chair and let them fall.

When the moment passed, I wiped at my face casually with my shirtsleeve. In the morning, the room was bright, with rainbow-colored dots of light glancing off every surface in the room. That was when I noticed the rainbow pattern on the ceiling. It was bright and enchanting. I identified the source as a single crystal that hung by the window. My mother loved crystals and so did Gran. Both of them claimed that crystals were magical.

My gaze returned to the rainbow and this time I followed its path along the ceiling. It ran in a thin line down the wall, where it intersected with a small framed letter. The frame held my attention for a long time until I realized that I wasn't looking at a letter. It was a framed piece of sheet music. Standing, more steadily this time, I crossed the dusty floor to get a closer look.

As I approached the frame, I identified the piece of music immediately.

Come walk with me
Along the sea
And search for shells on the sand with me
What magick we will find today
Take my hand, little one
Come and walk with me.

"Come walk with me…" I began, singing the first few bars of the melody while unconsciously reaching up to touch the glass in the frame. My voice broke, though, and I found that I couldn't continue.

It had been our song. My mother would sing it to me when we went hunting for seashells on the beach at Gran's or back home during trips to the shore. She also used the song to sing me to sleep. Closing my eyes, I listened to my memory of her voice in my head. It was still there, though the integrity of it had faded with time.

When I looked at the music again, I decided to take the frame down to my room. Placing a hand under its wooden exterior, I slid it up the wall slightly and pulled it off the hook. What I found caught me off guard.

The frame was concealing a hole in the wall behind where the picture had been placed. A skilled carpenter didn't create the opening; it was crude and looked as though someone just started hammering away. There were pale pencil marks on either side of the frame's position, an aid in the creation of the hiding place.

Peering in, I could see something white that stood out against the dark interior. Without hesitation, I reached inside and grabbed a stack of letters. My mother's handwriting stood out as they came into view. Searching the opening again resulted in finding a long thin box. Needing the exterior light, I carried it to the window, opening the box as I went.

Inside was a pendant, which appeared very old. It was made of gold with some sort of unfamiliar symbol emblazoned on its weathered exterior. I was about to put it back into the box when I noticed the small note in the box, which read simply: *For Kellen.*

Though the pendant was a nice gesture, I was unsure of why someone would have left this for me. It was my mother's handwriting, but how could she have known I'd find this secret spot? After searching for some other explanation and finding none, I shoved the pendant into the left pocket of my jeans.

My attention returned to the opening in the wall. Pointing the flashlight into the hole, I found two other large stacks of letters, which I grabbed. Many of them were addressed to me in my mother's handwriting, which brought a smile to my face.

***

With the contents of the hiding spot in my hands, I headed to the kitchen for breakfast. After taking some leftover ham from the fridge and pouring a cup of strong coffee, I walked outside into the bright backyard.

A warm sensation brushed against my leg the moment I crossed the threshold. Glancing down, I jumped when the dog from the previous night rested his head on my knee. It was a setter.

“You're real, right?" I patted him on the head.

The dog whined in response but didn't move. Not having any experience with dogs, I wasn’t sure what to do. Stroking the top of his head seemed to be working, so I kept it up. After a moment of this, I noticed that his attention was focused on my food and I couldn’t help laughing.

“Hey, buddy. You’re hungry, aren’t you?”

The dog responded with a distinct nod, so I fed him the rest of my breakfast there under the warmth of the sun.

“You’re a good dog.” I smiled as I ran my fingers through his silky fur. I didn’t feel as though I was the same person who went into the attic yesterday. I’d learned too much to go back to being the person that I was before. The most important thing was beating against the inside of my skull repeatedly and giving me a headache; my mother didn’t die when I was a child.

Walking back into the house, I got two bowls from the kitchen and filled one with ham and the other with water for the dog. The dog bestowed upon me a grateful kiss on the hand, which I accepted willingly from my new friend. We ate in companionable silence. Though I tried to persuade him to come into the house, he backed away, preferring the freedom of the outside. After a few attempts, I went inside to call Alistair.

CHAPTER SIX
THE CAVE

"I went looking for her. Before, you know?" Alistair said over the phone. He'd listened patiently before launching into his own explanation of events following Addison's supposed death. "We, both your gran and I, never quite believed that Addison had died. Somehow, I think we sensed that there was more to it than that. Maybe it was wrong to jump to those types of conclusions. However, all of my interactions with Stephen compelled me to immediately look toward foul play. We hired a private detective, but he never found anything. Your gran never told me about the letters. I don't blame her for hiding those."

There were roughly fifty letters in the stacks that I'd found within the attic room. Half were for me, the other half for Roger. Each dated note was like a journal entry, with the only difference being that the entries were addressed to us boys and not merely designed for personal reflection.

They chronicled Addison's experience in the hospital, from her admission to the day of her death. They brought me closer to her, but at the same time pushed her farther away. Alistair was as surprised as I was by all of the information. We sat in silence on the line for several moments before I finally ended the call.

"I'm going to go back to bed, Alistair. I'm beat."

"Do you want to come back and stay with me for a while? Maybe being out there on your own isn't a good plan."

I'd have to deal with what I'd learned, whether I stayed here or went to London. "Thanks, but I'll be all right. I think I want the alone time for a little while. You know, experience life without any drama."

"I understand. Call me if you change your mind?"

"Promise." Saying goodbye, I hung up the phone, walked over to the couch and crashed. Sleep began to wash over me and slowly the pain receded.

***

When I woke up, it was early evening. Gingerly, I raised myself into a sitting position, reaching for a half-consumed bottle of water that I'd left on the coffee table.

"It is about time that you woke up. I have been waiting entirely too long for you, Kellen St. James."

I jumped up. The bottle that I'd uncapped slipped from my hands and bounced on the floor. Its contents covered the carpet. "Crap." After taking a split-second to regain my composure, I let my gaze wash over the door that led to the back of the house.

And there she stood. Calienta, the girl who featured so prominently in my dreams, was staring right at me.

"Oh, this is great. I've absolutely lost my mind. I have one dream about a mental hospital and now I'm hallucinating?" I turned my back on my hallucination and started to tidy up the mess that I'd made; the impact was widespread but easy to clean up.

When I looked up again, I expected not to see her, but there she remained. Unsettled, I was convinced that this meant that I was now having imagined conversations with Calienta when I *wasn't* sleeping, which distressed me greatly on many levels.

She walked closer toward me, her simple white dress moving as she walked. "You are not hallucinating."

I took a couple of steps back instinctively. She laughed at me, clearly finding my response funny.

Letting my gaze travel over her, I noted that she looked pretty real for a hallucination. "Calienta? Is that really you?"

"It is really me."

But how could it be? "Who are you really?" Continuing to back away, I took in more of her features as I did so. She was still the same little girl that I remembered. In fact, she hadn't changed or aged at all.

"I told you."

"And you expect me to believe you?"

Fire built up behind her eyes. I'd angered her.

"What kind of welcome is this? You are the one who said you didn't want me to go. That you wanted to come with me."

"That was eleven years ago."

She ignored my response. "If you wanted to come with me so badly, why do you seem so unhappy to see me now?"

"I thought you were a hallucination then, too."

"No, you did not. If you thought I was a hallucination, why did you ask your grandmother about me? I do not believe it. Do you truly doubt my existence now?"

"Um, yeah. Kind of. I must be losing my mind or something. How do you know I asked Gran?" Great, I was talking to my hallucination. It was official. All those years of having such a messed up family were finally catching up with me.

"Kellen, I am not a product of an overactive imagination. You have known me all these years and welcomed me into your dreams."

"How do you know about my dreams?"

"I know because I was the one making you have them. If I had known that it would take you so long to grow up, I might have saved myself the trouble."

"What? Wait. You were *making* me have those dreams? How is that even possible?"

"There are many possibilities that you have not even considered, mortal."

"Listen, now I'm starting to get ticked off. I find a stranger in my house, possibly a hallucination, and now she's insulting me?"

"I have never been a stranger to you."

My brows furrowed. "Who are you, anyway?"

"You know exactly who I am."

"No, I don't. That was a dream. You aren't real." I refused to give in, shoving my hands in my pockets.

"I am real, and what I am is your destiny." She tried to take my hand.

"What you are is jail bait." I snatched my hand away. She was six years old, for crying out loud. "You're just a kid."

However, I was immediately forced to bite back my words. Instantly, she began to age right in front of my face.

At first, the changes were subtle. There was the slow lengthening of her torso as she grew in height, the tightening of her skin as the youthful roundness of her ivory face vanished. Her pale brown hair grew thicker, darker, framing her face and her wide blue eyes. In the span of ten seconds, we seemed exactly the same age.

"You were saying?" Her words were a challenge.

Backing away, I felt unsure, nervous. Who was this creature? Gran had told enough Irish legends to make me pause. Before, I never used to believe in that stuff; faerie folk, changelings, spirits weren't real to me. However, I couldn't explain any of this, and I wasn't buying that she was who she claimed to be.

Her features softened and she looked at me with tenderness. "Kellen, I am very sorry about that. However, you would have only recognized me as a child and I needed for you to remember me. I am not a hallucination and you know it. I'm really here."

"I don't believe you."

"I told you about this in your dreams. If you would only pay more attention." Her last words were stern, but her smile warmed the reproof. I found myself smiling back without thinking. Realizing what I was doing, I forced a frown. *What was I doing? Idiot.*

"Look, I've had a really long couple of days. Leave me alone." I closed my eyes for a moment and pinched the bridge of my nose.

"I am sorry that you had to find out about your mother in that way, Kellen. She was a remarkable woman." Her words were spoken with sympathy, but they angered me. What I'd learned about my mother tore me up inside. It was mine, my personal pain. There was no way that she could know about it.

"How do you know about my mother?"

"I know everything about you, but you know nothing about me. There is so much to say and very little time."

I'd no idea what was going on here, but the logical, rational side of me said that I needed to get this person out of the house. Yet there was another part, the lonely part, which screamed at me to do whatever Calienta asked, without question.

"I know that you remember me."

I stared at her, this mystery girl who'd been a part of my life for so long. Suddenly I was tired and didn't want to argue. It unnerved me to know that I wanted to stay with her; I'd been wrong. I loathed being in Gran's house alone, with only memories for company. "How could I ever have forgotten you?"

Though my voice was soft and gentle, my words had a powerful effect on the young woman in front of me. She blushed crimson and glanced down to hide her face. “Please come with me.”

Slowly, I placed my hand in hers. It was warm, as in my memory. “Where are we going?”

“I need to show you. Otherwise, you will think I am a hallucination again.”

“I suppose that’s true.”

She didn’t answer me, but she smiled back as she handed me a rough-looking knife with a black handle. “Put this in your pocket.”

“Are you anticipating that I’ll have to stab someone on the trip?” I wasn’t the kind of guy who routinely carried weapons around. More often than not, I could be a bit uncoordinated.

“I hope it does not come to that.” And before I could register that remark, I found myself running out into the night with her.

“Where are we going?”

We reached the steps that led down the cliff face. A dog howled in the night, setting an ominous tone for our journey. Calienta glanced at me for a moment but didn’t answer as she turned back to the direction in which we were heading. She pulled me close to her.

My hand burned where she held it and the air around us was thick with tension; that was how aware I was of her physically. A storm brewed between us.

There were no outside lights on, as I’d forgotten to turn them on. Home ownership was a new responsibility for me. To make matters worse, it started to rain, the long grass becoming slick and damp.

My clothes were getting soaked; Calienta, on the other hand, was completely dry. She started down the steps using the light to guide her. I followed. *Where did she get a lantern?*

This very question was just about to pass my lips when I lost my footing on the stairs. Falling, I slammed my elbow into the aged wood. It burned instantly, which told me that it was probably cut or possibly broken. Hesitantly, I stood up, taking care not to use my right arm for fear I'd cry out.

Though it seemed as though the entire staircase shook when I fell, it was now stable. We were able to make it safely to the land below. I relaxed a little then, but not much. It was almost high tide, and the waves were going to envelop us.

"What're you doing? Are you trying to drown us both?" The waves rushed in and beat against my damaged arm.

She shook her head but didn't speak, and I followed her toward a narrow opening in the rock. Calienta jumped lithely through the entrance with remarkable agility. Blinking, I remained in place, but she turned and waited for me, extending a firm hand to practically pull me atop the rock.

When I reached the top, she carefully touched my injured arm. At first, the warmth was pleasant and seemed to soothe the pain I was feeling after my swim in the cold sea. Suddenly it was too warm, hot even, and I cried out as my arm began to burn and I jerked it away.

The heat subsided after a moment. With it went any pain. It was healed.

Calienta smiled. "Sorry for the burning sensation, but any time we try to correct the past there is a price."

"What are you?" She wasn't my age, that was certain, and I was sure she wasn't human. No one could age that fast.

"In time." She pulled on my hand again and we started to walk toward a tiny crevice. Closer inspection revealed that the opening was actually quite large, though I'd never have noticed it if it hadn't been pointed out to me. Pulling myself up on top of a neighboring rock, I entered the cave.

Inside the cave, there were some crudely made stairs in the back of the main chamber. These wound their way at an angle around the walls and ended forty feet up at the entrance to an antechamber. I tried not to think about it, but I was sure that some extremely nasty things were living in there.

We didn't speak as we hastily made our way toward the stairs and began to slowly climb them. There was no railing to hold onto on the narrow set of steps, so it was a slow process. After a time, we reached a room at the very top and I breathed a small sigh of relief at being able to abandon the stairs.

As we walked into the chamber, I immediately noticed the faint hint of ocean in the salty air that permeated the space. Calienta went to light some torches that rested in brackets along the wall. With the room lit, it was much more comfortable; though I was sure I detected a sense of unease from my companion as we moved toward a larger room off to the right.

It was odd, but it seemed as though I could sense each nuance of emotion that she experienced. Her annoyance in the house, her excitement during our short journey, and now this wariness that I was unable to identify the source of—I picked up on all of it. It made me anxious to have such a connection to her, but at the same time I wanted that closeness.

We entered the next room and she repeated the process of lighting torches. Staying by the entryway, I remained ever-skeptical, fearful of what the room held. My brain was working overtime, and I started to wonder if she was some sort of serial killer or something.

As I followed Calienta deeper into the room, I expected to see corpses on the floor. Maybe this young woman's latest victim would be here. It was not long before the room was well lit, and I took a moment to adjust my eyes before I blinked.

We were inside a large circular room. The floor was dirt; the walls were constructed of crude stone. However, it wasn't the lack of décor that made it stand out; what made it unique was that every square inch of wall space was covered in drawings.

The paint was metallic; the colors used were of an extremely varied palette. Rich rusts, blood reds, and deep shades of blue covered the space in almost its entirety. Ironically, it reminded me of some of the paintings I'd seen in Catholic churches, though I was certain that no priests had created these works of art.

Calienta walked to the center of the room and turned to face me. She seemed both nervous and determined at the same time, looking up at me through hooded eyes.

"I suppose that you are wondering where you are. This place is called Fròg. It was a Pagan meeting place."

The images on the walls had me entranced. I had to force myself to look at her, which was an enormous testament to the talent of the artists.

"When the Crusaders sought out anyone who did not worship Christ, Pagan worshippers were forced to hide underground during those dark times. This was one of their hiding places."

"I thought that Pagans weren't good. That they were Satan worshippers." From my history classes, I remembered that there had been quite a bit of academic writing on this topic, disputing this notion. However, I still recognized the need to discuss the obvious stereotype.

"No. Pagans relied on the elements and charted the progress of the sun and the moon to determine future events. But I suppose that, in every religion, there are those who choose the side of good and those who choose evil."

"The scary stuff?"

"Just rumors. The Pagans believe in a single supreme being."

"If that was the case, why did they worship a sun god and a horse goddess?"

"You seem incredibly well informed for someone who did not know the basic premise of Paganism a moment ago." A smile played at her lips as I shrugged. "Paganism held the belief that there was one god, but that all of the other gods were representatives of that one being. Think about it: can you think of no other religion that has a similar structure? Saints are earth-bound representatives of one God. However, so were the Pagan gods; it was believed that they could come to Earth and interact with mortals. Their roles would be to guide them, provide them with knowledge, while still helping the being that they worshipped."

"That's where the sun and the horses come in?"

"Yes," she admitted, "though the assignments do tend to change with the development of man. For example, horses do not play the same role in this day and age."

"What, there's a god of technology now? Is that why my password keeps getting reset?" Sarcasm dripped from my tongue. Remorse made me cringe; I was too harsh with her, for I sensed that she was struggling with something.

To see the crease on her pale forehead, to know that I'd upset her mattered to me more than it should. "Look, I'm really sorry. That was disrespectful." *Way to go, brainiac*. "So, tell me more about the Pagan gods."

After collecting her thoughts, she took my hand. "Although that is an important part of this discussion, the reason that I brought you here is because I need you to know who I am. There is no time. Before we can be together, you need to understand about me and my family."

CHAPTER SEVEN
FAMILY TREE

"We just met again and you want me to meet your family?" There was no way I was ready to examine the "before we can be together" part.

"Kellen, you cannot deny that there is a connection between us. There always has been." She touched my hand.

My skin tingled in reaction and I looked into her eyes. There was kindness there, and patience, but also fear.

"No, I won't deny it, but it's confusing. I've dreamed of you my entire life, heard your voice in the air when it shouldn't be there, sensed your eyes on me when I've been alone. But I don't understand any of this."

There *was* a connection between us, and I didn't understand it. Otherwise, why would I have dreamed of her and longed for her all these years? Right, she *made* me dream of her, apparently.

She looked away from me then, but I caught her chin with the tips of my fingers and gently turned her face back to mine. Slowly, she met my eyes again. When we first met, I believed that our connection existed because she had a family, which was something I wanted desperately. Now, as I stared into her eyes, there was definitely more to it than that.

Mine. The thought that popped into my head was random, powerful, and immensely disconcerting. Withdrawing my hand instantly, I remained stationary, transfixed by her as I was. "Why do we have that connection? Who are you *really*?"

"I am afraid to tell you, afraid that you will want to leave."

On one hand, I couldn't imagine why she'd want me with her. We'd only come in contact twice, after all. Yet it also made perfect sense that she would, as though we were only waiting to come together. Suddenly I felt very old, as though I'd been waiting for her for centuries.

"And you want me to stay with you?" My words were a whisper.

"I've always wanted that."

Immediately, I was amazed at my intense need to kiss her, to touch my lips to her own. I shook it off, though; she could have been playing me for a fool.

"I'll listen and do my best to understand," I said, making the promise against my better judgment.

Calienta had a cute Cupid's bow shape to her mouth. Every now and then, I'd catch her smiling at me with her head tilted forward and her piercing eyes looking up at me from beneath the cover of her lush lashes. She showed that small smile of hers now, as she walked to the furthest corner of the room.

"Then let me show you my history and our future."

Without fanfare, she stepped forward and touched the first picture, which depicted a beautiful woman with dark hair.

"This is the story of the Mother Goddess, Danu." As she stepped away, I did a double take as a white light instantly replaced the image on the wall.

It shimmered for a moment before a movie displayed. For a split second, I noticed that the lights had dimmed minimally to allow for better viewing, but that was all that I had time to notice before the film began. Initially, I couldn't help but be blown away by the beauty of the woman in the image, yet she was clearly depressed, weeping as she gazed out over the sea.

"Many centuries ago, the Mother Goddess, Danu, whom the Celts believed to have created the Earth, was lonely and longed for children. After so many years of watching over the children of the world, she found that she desired a family of her own. She decided to create a companion for herself."

As Calienta spoke, the scene before me changed and Danu was now walking through a forest barefoot. Her woolen dress stood out against the backdrop of greenery. After she'd walked for some time, she came to a clearing and lay down upon the grass. Shortly thereafter, a man entered the same clearing. He didn't speak but stopped in his tracks. Danu stood up, prepared to defend herself, but her posture changed when they locked eyes. Both of them faced each other and took several steps forward.

The scene changed from the glen to the palace of the earlier scene once more. This time the man was with her. Calienta continued her narration.

"She took a mortal for her mate, a farmer who gazed at the stars. His name was Bilé. He was a beautiful man, both inside and out. She appealed to her creator to make him immortal, and he came to her palace in the clouds. Together they had three sons."

The screen faded on the happy, beautiful family that had flashed before my eyes. Before I could ask questions, however, she was on to the next drawing.

"Shall I continue?" She touched the next image after I'd nodded my consent.

This image depicted three teenage boys. They were taking turns throwing a massive boulder, trying to determine who could throw it the farthest. They laughed and joked with one another.

"I am the victor!" cried a tall boy, the oldest.

Calienta smiled and continued with her story as the trio played in front of us. "Her sons were Dagda, Ogma, and Cian. All three were very kind and they lived in peace for many centuries. Occasionally, when the mortals were in trouble or at war with evil forces, these Children of Danu, and eventually their children and their children's children, would come to Earth to offer their assistance and guidance."

The screen faded and we moved to the next image, which depicted a serious battle. Calienta touched the wall and a small screen came to life.

The slaughter was immense. Villages were burned, entire families killed. There were several rather tall individuals who were right in the middle of the fray. Each was uniquely beautiful, with pale skin and richly colored tresses, a patchwork quilt of colors as they fought on the brown, dying grass.

The one closest to me had possibly the reddest hair imaginable. She turned her head and her beautiful blue eyes met mine for a split second before she turned and raised her sword of gold.

"After five hundred years together, a terrible battle began amongst the mortals. Danu and her family were compelled to become involved. By this time, all of her sons were married with grown children or grandchildren, and their numbers were large. They snuck down to Earth in the night, prepared to fight for the people of Ireland. However, the opposing army was alerted to their plan by Arawn, the lord of Faerie."

When a black creature, more shadow than man, appeared on the screen, I pulled back. He floated through the air, whispering to a group of men who were sleeping in the clearing.

"When the Children of Danu arrived to aid the mortals who were on the side of good, they found that the opposing army was expecting them, along with Arawn and his army."

The beautiful women and men were attacked and overpowered. Their battle cries echoed in the room, the vibrations from the clashing of swords reverberated through the ground on which we stood.

"They were cornered and forced into the Underworld, from which they could not return. I believe your kind calls them faeries or leprechauns today. The Underworld was known as Faerie from that point on."

"I don't understand. These are the gods and goddesses that you speak of, right? So don't they have powers? Couldn't they wipe out the entire opposing army?"

Calienta took a moment to consider my question before answering. "When an immortal visits Earth, even to help the mortals, it exacts a price. Immortals were not meant to walk this planet, and therefore lose their power if they are here for long stretches of time.

"Arawn also aligned with one of their own, which gave him the strength to deplete their powers even further."

The scene changed, and a handsome young man who seemed vaguely familiar to me was running, first through the forest, then through the air and, finally, through the clouds. He ran until he reached a throne and threw himself at its feet, weeping.

"Only one immortal escaped," she continued. "Lugh, the Sun god, was able to return to the heavens."

One man appeared on the screen alone. He was fair-skinned with copper-blond hair that framed his face in curls. His hair wasn't long; it simply ended where his rust-colored beard began. The cheekbones on his proud face gave him an aristocratic appearance.

Calienta began to narrate again. "Though he was truly distraught over the loss of his family, he could not save them. He went straight to Danu and Bíle and begged for help."

"What happened? Did she save them?"

Calienta smiled, obviously noting that I was getting into the story. "She refused to interfere with what had happened, despite her own pain—afraid of the price it would exact.

"Arawn expected that Danu would seek to save her children. Our legend says that he created a backdoor to the heavens via a portal that is known as the Ellipse. He snuck in at night and murdered both Danu and Bíle. Lugh was distraught to find his family completely decimated, and he wept at the loss of them."

The murder was portrayed directly in front of my eyes. Lugh stood on the screen, powerful, enraged, now the god of destruction as he raised his hands above his head.

"Lugh went back to the site of the battle and the winning army. Once there, he unleashed a mighty flood which killed all of the opposing army, though Arawn escaped. Yet there was no triumph for him, no sense of peace.

"Revenge did not bring back his family. He tried several times to save the Children of Danu. Finally, after about half a century, he got to the point where he could free them; however, they had turned from goodness under Arawn's rule."

Caricatures of the immortals that I had seen before came up out of a hole in the earth and tried to

force Lugh back with them. He fought them off and returned home, defeated.

Calienta continued her narration. "Lugh was later visited by Síl, who came to him in a vision. He is the highest of all immortals and the creator of Danu."

Síl appeared as a mortal in this meeting, but a slight transparency to his person suggested otherwise. His eyes, a brilliant, piercing ice blue, bore into the back of Lugh's head, the latter having fallen to his knees as soon as he'd realized the significance of his company.

"It pained him to see Lugh searching for his family again and again, but though Lugh pleaded with him, Síl could not take action and could only guide."

Calienta moved to the next drawing, touching it again in a movement that I had come to expect; the flickering images no longer surprised me.

There was a different Lugh now, one who seemed older, wiser. He was holding hands with a young woman with whom he seemed infatuated.

As Calienta spoke, there was a hint of pride in her voice. I glanced at her briefly, but her eyes were on the screen. The images changed abruptly to those of lush green valleys, abundant crops; hundreds of sheep grazed throughout the land.

"At Síl's words, Lugh decided to start again. Síl created the goddess Brigid from a mortal, with the intention that she would be Lugh's mate. She was beautiful both inside and out as a mortal, and became even more glorious as an immortal.

"With the arrival of Brigid came peace and prosperity." She gestured to the images of the sun and farmland. "It was clearly a love match and they had three children together: Rowan, Cabhan, and…Calienta."

My breath hitched as I recognized the face of Cabhan. I'd seen it before in mirrors and outside of Gran's house in the night. The enormity of what she was saying started to sink in, and all thoughts of this strange young man were lost as my eyes flashed to hers and back at the screen.

The images of three young people, not more than six years apart from oldest to youngest, appeared. They were looking down on a dark blue sky filled with stars. Calienta once more touched a slim finger to the screen.

"Each of us had a job to do, since there were so few of my family left. We were given the job of making the stars shine at night, even if they would be hidden by the clouds."

"Star child," I breathed as the screen came to life. Gran's words from so many years ago were coming back to me.

"Yes, that is probably how your gran would have known me. That is the name that the mortals gave to us, but the accuracy ends there. The part of the rumor about us setting mortals on fire is utter nonsense." She smiled as she spoke. *She was messing with me!*

There she stood, on screen, with Lugh, Brigid and two other young children. I'd have known her anywhere.

"What're you trying to tell me? That you're a *goddess*?"

"Kellen."

"You've got a pretty high opinion of yourself."

"Kellen…"

"You're crazy."

"Kellen."

"No, you need to stay away from me. This is insane." I began to back away toward the door, looking for a way out.

"I suppose it would seem that way to you." She suddenly appeared directly behind me, when I wasn't even aware that she'd moved. I turned on the spot to face her, backing up a little more toward the opening through which we'd come.

Her voice was pleading. "This is my life. My normal life, as strange as that may seem. Kellen, you are free to go, but please listen to the entire story before you leave."

"Why should I stay for the rest?"

I'd been played. Though I had to admit that her AV system was out of this world, the idea that Calienta could be from a family of gods, that she was one herself, was too far-fetched to believe.

"Let's say that I believe your story. I don't understand what any of this has to do with me. Why are you telling me this?"

"You are very frustrating, do you know this? All these questions! Can you please, *please* pay attention for a little while longer?" Her change in tone was unexpected and I found myself again doing the opposite of what I wanted.

She turned to the next picture. “Lugh’s family was a happy one.” She looked back at me for a moment and glared before continuing. “Though he mourned the loss of his brothers, sisters, and parents, he had found peace again. Also, the world had changed and he recognized the importance of knowledge and education.

“Eventually he let his eldest daughter, Rowan, visit Earth. When she visited and came back unharmed and Lugh decided that it was safe for our kind to return, he planned for his son, Cabhan, to visit.”

The next drawing depicted a young man with an eager glint in his eyes. This drawing was five times the size of the others.

“I have another question. I’m sorry,” I added as she raised an eyebrow.

“Go ahead.”

“Why is this painting so much larger than all of the others?”

“Because there is more to tell.”

CHAPTER EIGHT
PROPHECY

Before I could react, I was watching Cabhan running over the hillside as fast as his legs could carry him. The landscape of the countryside through which he ran was rocky, uneven, yet this didn't seem to concern him as he sought his destination. He sprinted as though the earth beneath his feet was nothing more than a flat, cemented walkway.

As he turned the final corner, I recognized Lugh waiting for him with a smile. He seemed to fit right in, in a pair of trousers and a common work shirt. When Lugh spied his son, his entire face lit up with pleasure. He stood up, his hands outstretched as he closed the space between them. Cabhan took his father's hands in his own and smiled in greeting.

"So, how was your first trip? Hopefully you didn't get into too much trouble."

Cabhan smiled, a mirror image of his father. The only exception to their similarity in looks was that Cabhan's hair was a very pale blond, almost white, with thick curls that fell to his shoulders.

"Father, you will not believe it. You will not. I'm in love, I am." He shouted triumphantly.

"We have much to talk about. You must tell me more about her."

Cabhan launched into an explanation, rich in detail, which highlighted his time with his love. His last words conveyed his intent to marry her.

"You've known her for ten days and already you wish to marry?"

Clearly, this wasn't what Cabhan was expecting to hear. His brow furrowed and he brought both hands to his hips.

"What difference does it make how long I have known her?" Cabhan, instantly defensive, crossed his arms in front of him.

Lugh sighed and turned to sit on a nearby rock, placing his hands at his temples. "Cabhan, I'm simply asking to get a better idea of how this relationship transpired. Please don't judge some simple questions. You're my son; naturally I want to know about the girl."

Cabhan walked over and sat cross-legged across from his father on the muddy ground, his hands resting at his knees. The mud immediately started to stain his pale trousers.

"Father, I know you, and therefore know why you ask such questions of me. It is because you are trying to convince me to reverse my decision." Cabhan's mouth set into a firm line.

"You must have decided to either make her one of us or become a mortal yourself."

Cabhan didn't respond.

"You know of course that I can make you a mortal, but it is not in my power to make your woman one of us. She must be granted that gift from Síl."

Cabhan looked down and nodded. The absence of a vocal confirmation appeared to tell Lugh what he needed to know.

"That is it? You want to become a mortal, then?"

"Yes." Cabhan's voice was rough. He acted as though the idea terrified him, as though he didn't have any other choice.

"Son, I'm sorry, but I can't do it."

"It is not that you cannot, but that you will not!" Cabhan jumped to his feet. He began to pace on the spot. "You are always talking about the importance of guiding the mortals and finding ways in which we can share our knowledge with them. Is that not why we come here? All my life you have talked of Earth and mortals and their importance. How it is our job to come to Earth and share our wisdom, to guide them. I happen to love one, Father. I love her and I have made my choice. Change me into a mortal."

Lugh sighed. "Yes, it is my wish that you guide the mortals, as your family did before you, but I never wanted you to become one of them. You do not even know the girl."

"Father, I am two hundred and twenty years old. I am a man, and one who is old enough to decide for himself who he should be with." His eyes blazed.

Lugh reached out and tried to touch his son's arm, but Cabhan pulled away, acting childish. "Son, I do not discount your age, but do you realize that this action cannot be reversed? You will remain a mortal no matter what happens to your love. Do not mistake my words;

mortals are wonderful creatures and they have much to share with our kind."

"But you turned Rowan into a mortal," Cabhan insisted.

"Yes, and I have lost her. I have not seen her in years. Do you think that I want to lose you as well? Do you know that you will lose your powers and your strength? You could even become sick or wounded. And someday…you will grow old and die. You will leave us." Lugh was clearly overcome with emotion as he considered his son sick and dying.

"Yes, I have considered this." Cabhan's voice grew softer with each syllable.

"And?"

"And I cannot live without her."

"Regardless, my answer is still no, I am afraid."

Cabhan's faced instantly distorted into raw anger and the scene faded.

I sighed. "Cabhan fell in love with a mortal?"

"Yes, and my father would not help him become a mortal."

"Do you agree with that?" I searched her face.

She looked down for a moment, taking some time to contemplate my question. When she met my eyes again, her expression was serious. "I believe that everyone should be able to do whatever they wish. To have a desire so intense that you would be willing to give up your entire life for it and not have it fulfilled…I cannot imagine that."

What an unusually fascinating beauty she was. The need to believe her pressured me more and more as each minute passed. These feelings could all be part of a trick, but I'd always gone with my gut. At least I'd finish hearing her out.

Her eyes bore into mine, and I felt again as though she was waiting for something, but I didn't know what. I wanted to stay there and stare into her eyes for an eternity. I could get lost in them. However, she broke the connection by walking to the next painting.

Suddenly Cabhan was on the screen, racing across beautiful grounds, clearly irate. Lugh stood on the opposite end of the grounds, clearly waiting for him.

"You knew this would happen," Cabhan shouted. "That if you did not change me I would lose her and you could keep control over me. How could you do this, Father? Why could you not make me mortal?"

"Son, what's happened?" Lugh sounded like a normal father and not a god.

"I went to her and found her married. Married to someone else. You wanted this to happen."

Lugh's face was deeply apologetic. "Son, I'm sorry. I didn't want to lose you."

"You will certainly lose me now," Cabhan declared, and in an instant he was gone.

"What happened to him? Cabhan, I mean?" It alarmed me to find out how invested in the story I was.

"Cabhan left to live on one of the stars that we lit every night. We do not know which one he went to, for there are billions, and my father searched for him for a very long time."

"Wait, a star? I thought that stars are a collection of gases. How do you live on a star?"

She smiled patiently, as though she'd anticipated this question. "Stars are actually tiny little worlds that exist to the mortal eye as beams of light. They are completely self-contained; there is no exposure to the outside world at all."

I nodded and tried to look as though I was taking all of this in stride, but it wasn't coming off that way. I was such a geek. As I tried to shake it, some of the other more important points of her story finally started to hit home.

"That must have been terrible for you, losing your brother." I understood what it meant to lose someone. Though Cabhan certainly wasn't her parent, he was still important to her.

She didn't speak for a moment. Instead, she walked around the room, looking at the drawings on the wall and stopping at each one, placing her hand to her ear. Eventually she walked back to my side.

"He is not totally gone. After years of searching, my father has found him." But her smile wasn't a happy one. There was more to the story; I waited for her to continue.

"My family is so much easier to see on Earth, we stand out, we glow almost. You only need to look down upon the planet to see one of us. That is how my parents always kept us in check. In the heavens, though, where

there are so many brilliant things, our light cannot be distinguished from the other magick that exists there."

"How did your father find him?"

"There is an old evil that has entered our realm. We believe that Cabhan's anger, his hatred toward my father, has called it. There is a single unlit star, the only star from where light does not shine."

"You think that's where he is?"

"Yes. That is why we had to find you. The hatred is spreading, and we feared that if we did not get to you in time that it would be too late. My father is very wary of losing his family again, you see."

I absolutely didn't see and had no idea what she was talking about. As I stared at her with what I'm sure was intense disbelief, I noticed that her clothes were completely clean and dry while mine were covered in grime and soaked through. The dirt that clung to my palms from the climb was starting to make my hands itch and I brushed them against the sides of my jeans awkwardly.

"The thing is, I *don't* see. No disrespect intended, but I don't actually know what you are talking about. You've given me the last page of a book when I've only read the first." Changing my tack, I reminded her in harsh tones, "You never answered my question. What does this have to do with me?"

This girl showed up at my house, told me several stories that I wasn't sure I believed, and kept referring to my involvement in "something". What was I missing?

"You sought me out; you came to me when I was young. Why? You seem to know Gran. You seem to know me. Even if I discount this," I gestured around the room, "none of it makes any sense, Calienta."

Silent, she walked to one of the torches on the wall, removing it from its bracket. She hesitated for a moment, clearly torn between showing me something more and leaving things as they stood between us. She walked to the far side of the wall, which had the least amount of light, and placed the torch in the final bracket.

The remaining images, which came into view in this light, were faded and hard to interpret. They looked as though someone had tried to remove them and had only succeeded in blurring them. I took several steps forward before my breath caught.

The last drawing depicted a man and woman wearing matching golden rings and crowns. They were perched atop vast thrones. They, too, were large in stature, their beauty evident even through the façade created by the crude painting. At their feet were dozens of roses.

"My father found this cavern on one of his many travels to Earth. The drawing indicates a marriage ceremony, the crowns high kingship. I came here today, Kellen, because it was foreseen that you and I will be married. It was foreseen that you alone would be the downfall of my brother and the savior of my family. Of the world as we know it."

My jaw dropped. *Marriage? Downfall? Savior? Whoa, did they ever have the wrong guy.* "Gee, no pressure there."

Even if my surroundings didn't pre-dispose me to believe this young woman's tales, this drawing certainly added something to what she'd said. There was no mistaking both Calienta and myself in the picture, even with the tampering.

Yet, despite any evidence to the contrary, I had to dispute this. What she was telling me wasn't real, it was a story; she was making it all up. She knew that I'd lost Gran, inherited some money, and now she was playing me with some high-tech video equipment and an authentic-looking cave.

But there was a large part of me that wanted desperately to believe it. I'd been stumbling through my own life for so long, never fitting, never belonging anywhere. How easy it would be to take everything that she said at face value and go with her anywhere she wanted.

A large part of me wanted to know that I would never be on my own again. Yet, another part of me wouldn't give up that easily, couldn't relinquish the possibility that this was a dream or a hoax.

"There's a rather obvious solution that's staring us in the face. You painted all of this yourself, today. You must be an artist."

She seemed to choose her words carefully before answering. "While I am an artist, I did not paint these. I am much better than this." She indicated the art on the walls around her with a casual toss of her hair. "You asked why we came to find you, why I sought you out. It is because of these pictures.

"If a father finds drawings on a cave wall depicting his daughter, married to an unknown man, it is only natural that he should try to find out as much about that man as possible. That desire would be even more intense when this picture appears next to it." She took one more step to complete the circle.

I had believed that the likeness of us was the last. However, now I gazed upon a final painting. It showed me, blocking Calienta under a thunderous sky, my arm curled possessively around her; Cabhan was poised to attack us both.

"These drawings were created over one thousand years ago. They foretold of your coming, Kellen, before you were even born."

CHAPTER NINE
KING KELLEN

"Lady, I don't know what kind of line you're trying to feed me here, but I'm not buying any of it." Shock coursed through me. She'd disarmed me with her stories and I'd let my guard down around her. Now she was showing me things about myself, things that I'd neither dreamed nor imagined.

Me, *a king*? And worse, *married*? What could she have been thinking, telling me these things? I was just a kid after all, not even a man.

But you've never been "just a kid". My heart hurt as Gran's voice echoed in my head.

"What happened to 'I'll listen and do my best to understand'?" Calienta demanded, her voice rising as she threw my own words back at me.

My anger and impatience diffused slightly. She was right. As far-fetched as it sounded, I'd promised to give her the benefit of the doubt. "Look, I'm sorry. But how can any of this even be true? What do you mean, these were created thousands of years ago?"

"I want to tell you more, Kellen, but I cannot here. It is not safe for us to stay in this place. Please come with me."

Taking my hand without my permission, she glanced around uneasily before pulling me toward a small alcove. Once inside, I thought I heard a crowd of people entering the area that we'd left. Grabbing the handle of the blade in my pocket, I moved to step out of our hiding place, but Calienta yanked me back with unexpected strength.

She looked at me fiercely, motioning for my silence. She touched her hand to a spot on the wall that was covered with intricate etchings and suddenly, the floor began to move and we were being propelled upward, through several feet of dirt. Calienta grabbed my forearm as we started to move and continued to hold on, keeping me as still as possible during the ascent. We began to slow.

When our climb stopped, we were still about five feet from the opening, so it took some creative climbing to get out of the hole. Calienta had to pull me out in the end.

When we finally made it out, we were back on Gran's property and a trap door, covered in mossy grass, was slowly closing in on itself. After a few moments, the door simply shut on its own, having been pulled back down again, it seemed, by an intricate lever system. It was now invisible, having blended into the surrounding blades of grass.

Before I could comment, Calienta pulled at my arm and urged me toward the house. We were almost there when she stopped, held her hand in the air, and pointed to the right of the house, where there was a wooded area.

Trying to figure out what she was up to, I squinted in the direction that she was pointing. Slowly at first, dirt started to fly up in the air, shooting every which way. It looked as though an animal was digging a small ditch from under the surface. Only the sound of moving earth filled the air as a small opening was created.

Calienta turned and I realized that she was guiding the creation of this path. She extended her delicate arms until the path formed an arc in front of the house and effectively surrounded it.

A snap of her fingers and the void in the ground was filled with water from the natural spring that ran by the house. It wasn't a lot of water, but it was enough to fill the opening about a quarter of the way.

She shrugged. "They will not cross it." Abruptly she was pulling on my hand again and leading me swiftly to the house.

"Who won't cross it? What's all this about?"

Once we were inside, she locked the door and closed the curtains. These tasks completed, she seemed relieved. I'd have to find out why. The fact that there was more to the story would be obvious to even the dimmest of bulbs.

Without a word, I went to put on a pot of coffee. I'd sort of assumed that I wouldn't be going to bed anytime soon, despite my oppressing exhaustion. Calienta paced in the small dining room.

After a few moments of silence, which I would've normally preferred, even I needed to speak up. "You show up, take me into this hole in the earth, put on some home movies, and excavate my front yard. I'd continue the conversation, but I feel like you might be up next, what do you think?"

"I have already told you about my family. You now know what we are, but you think this is all something I have made up, or maybe even a dream."

"Of course I think it's a dream. You probably know that I got some money. It would've been easy for you to drug me, maybe get your hands on some of my inheritance."

Her eyes narrowed and my empty coffee cup exploded in my hand. However, before a single shard could touch me, the pieces changed direction in mid-air, returning to their original design. The cup was whole once again.

Forcing myself to remain standing, I nonchalantly raised an eyebrow. Her anger pulsed within the room and I found myself feeling a little bit afraid once again. "Or not?"

My brain was laboring for an alternative explanation about what I'd seen and heard, but was coming up empty. Glancing at the cup in my hand, I decided to play it safe by choosing another from the cabinet. Gingerly, I sat the survivor in the sink. I poured myself a cup of the good stuff from the still brewing pot into the new cup, scalding the burner in the process.

"There are other creatures out there that would do us harm. However, they will not cross the water. I connected it with the spring to protect the house," she explained.

Taking my coffee, I walked into the living room without responding, turning on more lights as I went. Not having directed my cleaning efforts at the downstairs yet, I found that I was pleased that Gran's things were still here. After the strange turn of events that my life had taken in the past few weeks, seeing these familiar things calmed me now as I walked over to the fireplace and opened the flue.

"I thought I'd light a fire." Without looking at her, I turned around to direct my search to the kitchen to get the matches. After rummaging through a few drawers, I finally found them sitting on top of a small stack of back copies of the *Irish Times*.

Grabbing a four-year-old edition from the aged wooden countertop, along with the matches, I headed back to start a fire. However, by the time I walked into the living room, there was already a blazing fire, and Calienta was sitting on a blanket in front of it, warming her hands.

She'd changed into some of my clothes. She wore my faded gray sweatpants and my old Oxford pullover. Those clothes suited her, and it pleased me that my clothing graced her skin.

My eyebrows rose again. "You're pretty resourceful, MacGyver. Do you want to use some chewing gum and twine to make us some hot chocolate and break us out of the compound?"

There was that crinkle between her brows again that was starting to get to me; my eighties references were lost on her, though technically they should be lost on me as well. There was so much we didn't have in common. Would I even be able to relate to her? I wasn't sure where to begin.

We'd managed conversation up until this point, but we came from different worlds. Then when you added to the mix that she was a beautiful girl and I was…well…*not* beautiful… You get the idea.

"I'm very sorry. Please, won't you tell me the rest?" I took a seat beside her, keeping some distance between us.

"But you do not believe me, Kellen, and if you cannot believe what I have told you, there is little point to the rest." She sounded sad; I was disappointing her. I picked up on the letdown that I'd been the cause of.

"Even you have to admit that this is a lot to take in. I didn't even know that you truly existed before this night."

She nodded in agreement, and we sat in silence for a time as I waited for her to speak. The fire crackled, warmth spilling inside the cheerful room with its wooden beams and rustic wood floor. Only the floral couch and chair made the room appear slightly modernized.

"I forget that you do not really know about me, that I am a stranger to you," she admitted.

I said nothing, preferring to let her speak, to listen to her dulcet tones as she told her story.

"I have known about you for years. Before you were even born, it was foretold that you would come here. I have dreamed about you and who you would become. I have waited to speak to you for so long–"

"What did you want to say?"

"I wanted to hear you talk. I have felt such a connection to you throughout all of these years. It is not the same when you are not here."

"You could have come to visit me in New York," I told her. "That would have meant a lot to me."

"I cannot really see you clearly there. It is only when you are here, closer in proximity to my home."

I nodded, not sure that I understood but suddenly wanting to give her my support. I hadn't meant to upset her; I didn't like it.

"You aren't the only one. I tried to find you after that first day. I asked Gran about you. I didn't know how to get to you."

"I know, Kellen. My father went to your gran and told her everything. She has watched over you all these years, knowing that one day I would come. All of this would have been so much easier if she were here. I doubt you would have struggled half as much with this information."

Laughing, I shook my head. "No, I think I still would have struggled with it." I found myself again getting lost in the depths of her eyes.

She seemed blurry to me, out of focus. There was something bigger than the both of us drawing us together. Something was waiting for me to give in and believe in this girl, this *goddess*.

There was an almost tangible connection here. I'd waited my entire life not having someone special in it and now I did. It was that easy. All I had to do was believe in her.

She looked into my eyes, which I was sure portrayed my newfound understanding, and smiled. I returned her smile. What did I have to lose after all? *Everything*.

"Tell me more about what's happening with your brother."

Once she was certain of my commitment, she began to talk. "My brother blames my father for the loss of his love. He has had years to ruminate on all of this."

"What's this evil that you spoke of?"

"We do not know, but we can sense it and know that it is powerful. We also know that it has control over my brother."

"Did your father always know this about Cabhan? Did he always know that he'd turn, uh…" I searched for the most appropriate words. "…to the Dark Side?"

"He did not know until he came upon the cave one day during one of his many early attempts to rescue his family. And he still did not know what any of it meant until I was born, when it became clear to him that the images that he saw were not history but prophecy. After Cabhan left, he brought me to the cave. He wanted me to know."

"But where do I fit in? The picture on the wall, the two of us, what does it all mean?"

"From what my father was able to find out, it appears that my brother will gain enough power to rule Earth."

"Earth, as in the entire planet? Man, can't this guy get over it already? People get dumped all the time."

She smiled, clearly finding my perspective amusing. "For us, the change—the impact, if you will—that love has on us is permanent. Once we fall in love, it cannot be undone. It is painful being away from those you love once you fall in love with them."

Scratching my head, I tried to take all of this in, all while thinking longingly of breakfast. Here she was talking about the destruction of the planet and all I could focus on was my stomach.

"What is it that I'm supposed to do to stop your brother?" I was hoping for some planet-saving tips. Not having much experience with evil forces, unless you considered my family, I'd need all the help I could get.

"No one knows."

Damn, I was afraid of that.

"The reason that I came here, to tell you all this, is because you are destined to stop Cabhan. I do not know why and I do not know how. I only know what has been foreseen."

For some reason, I believed her. That didn't mean that I knew what to do with the information she was giving me. "And you're somehow destined to be with me?"

She nodded. Calienta was as confused about all of this as I was, didn't ask for this, and wasn't looking for any of it.

Before I knew what I was doing, I pulled her to me and pressed my lips against her own. Her mouth was hot and it seared my skin as if it was burned. Kissing her was incredible, unbelievable, though my experience was definitely limited. She tasted like sugar cookies and summer all in one. I never wanted to stop; yet our lips had only met when a loud crack of thunder broke us apart.

Calienta rolled her eyes. “My father,” she muttered. “He is so interfering.”

“Is he this way with all the guys you date?” That was intimidating, although I didn’t want to admit it.

“I have not dated anyone. When you are immortal, your options are limited.”

This scrap of information made me happier than it should have. I waited until she moved a little away from me before punching my fist in the air triumphantly. *Yes!*

She grabbed a pillow from the sofa and laid her head upon it.

Grabbing my own pillow, I rested my cheek against the soft fabric. Waves of exhaustion hit me, but I didn’t want to close my eyes for fear that she’d disappear. “Who was after us tonight? Was it the Children of Danu?”

“I believe so,” she said, “although we now refer to them as the Sídhe, as their motives are no longer pure. It is dangerous for me below ground, as that is their territory, and I am not sure that they would have been welcoming to you, either. I believe that they may have sensed our presence.”

“And the moat, the knife, all of that?”

"Basic precautions to protect against the inhabitants of Faerie. I did not want to take any chances with your safety." She closed her eyes then and within minutes her breathing slowed, became heavier with sleep.

Moving closer, I wrapped my arm over her, taking care not to disturb her. I was so grateful not to be on my own. In seconds, I fell asleep on the soft quilt or, more accurately, I fell into a dream. I was definitely dreaming, as the environment that I was in was so very different from my own.

***

I stood, shielding Calienta, gripping a sword, as we clung together in a patch of fog looking out into the gray distance. I wore a white shirt, which was soaked through, and the same jeans that I'd just changed into. Around my neck, I wore the silver pendant that my mother had left me. Looking up, I met the eyes of the warrior. I smelled my own death, could foresee it in the half-crazed glare that he directed at me.

"You shall not be allowed the chance to destroy me, mortal. I know of the prophecy and I will overcome it. I will reign over this world when you have been destroyed. My father will pay for his mistakes."

My eyes closed, wanting to block out the visual, but I immediately forced them open. I wouldn't die with my eyes closed, a coward, but instead with them wide open and aware of my ever-approaching fate. The black

mist clung to my skin as I welcomed death in the fading light.

***

"Wow." I hadn't meant to say that out loud, and I woke Calienta as I snapped out of the dream. I glanced at the clock. Seven a.m.

"What is it, Kellen?" Her voice was thick.

"I can't talk about it right now." I muttered the words before I noticed her expression. "I'm sorry, that was rude. I'm just not ready to talk about it yet."

"When you are ready to discuss it, I will listen."

For a moment I hesitated, but my stomach had other ideas. Shocker. It started grumbling at full volume. Embarrassed, I changed the subject. "Uh, do goddesses eat breakfast?"

She smiled, radiant. "It depends on what's on the menu."

"Eggs, ham, some bread? Coffee?" Whether she wanted those things or not didn't matter to me; I planned on eating regardless.

"That would be lovely."

CHAPTER TEN
FACE IN THE MIRROR

We spent the day together, the two of us. For the moment, the prophecy was forgotten, but it was only a temporary interlude. On such a bright and sunny day, it was tough to remember that Cabhan was out there, seeking to destroy the world. In fact, it was incredibly easy to delude myself into thinking that nothing was wrong.

We walked on the country roads and through the town, talking. Calienta asked me countless questions about my childhood, where I grew up, about my parents.

"Don't you already know the answers to these questions? You're mythical, after all."

"I'm not mythical. I'm very real." She crossed her arms and pretended to pout, but I'd discovered in a short time that she was never angry for long.

Changing the subject, I asked, "What happened with Rowan?" The name had come up repeatedly when I listened to the prophecies. I was curious. It seemed as though she hadn't been in the picture for quite a while. "You haven't mentioned her much. I wondered what happened to her. Is she on a star too?"

"No, Rowan married a mortal and chose to become mortal."

"I know that Cabhan said that could be done, but I'm surprised that she'd make that choice."

Calienta looked at me thoughtfully. "People make many interesting choices in the name of love."

"I suppose they do." I thought of my own parents.

Mulling on that, we walked in silence for a time before she spoke again. "Rowan was visiting Earth and met a man, a musician, who was very charismatic. He was exactly what she was looking for. She became mortal for him."

"So, do you see her often?"

"Sadly, no. Mortals normally are unable to travel to our world; we can only choose to visit mortals. Time passes so differently for us that many months or years will go by before we chance to visit. I think she would be around sixty now."

"So, you miss her?" Brushing my fingers along her cheek, I waited for her answer. She nodded, her eyes never leaving mine.

"What do you think she'd think about me?"

Calienta blushed and smiled. "She would like you, I think. You both have a great love of reading."

"Do you like to read?"

The questions were off and running again. It was only when I got to the subject of her powers that she paused. "Why do you want to know?"

"Last night you made a cup explode, if I recall. What other things might I expect if I'm not on my best behavior?"

She laughed at this, the musical sound carrying across the air. "It's simple. I can control the elements and I can fly."

"Oh, well. Is that all?" *Nice one. Let's try and be a little smoother.*

"Yeah, your normal everyday powers."

"Your speech is changing. You sound more like me now."

"That's something we do to blend in. We assimilate with the current culture when we visit Earth."

"It's odd."

"What about me isn't?" She smiled.

"Huh." I liked her more and more every moment that we spent together. "Why don't you want to tell me about your powers?"

She looked away for a moment. I could tell she was considering this and I didn't press, though the possible answers intrigued me. I felt her nervousness again and wished that I could alleviate it.

"Last night you didn't believe me. I was afraid that you'd think I was making everything up again. I want you to believe me."

I stopped walking and placed my hands on the sides of her face. "Aren't we past all that, Calienta?"

"Are we?" she asked.

"All I know is that when I kissed you, something changed for me and I can't change it back. All I had to do was let go and believe."

"You're saying that you believe now?"

"Yes, I believe in you." I kissed her again. This time I got a little farther before it started to rain.

Laughing, we ran to the house, which was a good quarter of a mile away. The rain came down in sheets, plugging my ears and blinding my vision, but I kept running and tugging Calienta's hand. Despite the weather, I'd never been this happy. Then it hit me. *I loved her*. How it had happened overnight, I didn't know, but love her I did.

The moment we walked into the cottage, Calienta was instantly dry and wearing new clothes. Not having those abilities myself, I decided that a hot shower was in order. "I'll be back. I have to clean up the old-fashioned way."

I'd no sooner walked into the small bathroom than I cried out. The face in the mirror wasn't my own. The face that stared back at me was the face of a bronzed god, as chiseled and handsome as a work of art. I may be a guy, but I couldn't miss these details.

"*I am watching*." The voice reverberated in the small room as the face began to fade away and mine began to return.

Crap. I'd recognized Cabhan from the cave, so there was no mistaking him. This was all I needed. Some revenge-seeking god wanted to take me out and appeared in my bathroom mirror, which was a little too stalker-esque for me.

"If you're watching me, I hope you at least close your eyes while I take a shower." My words were directed at my own reflection as Cabhan faded away.

Thunder rumbled as I stepped under the spray and tried to get my heartbeat under control. To my credit, I managed to take my shower without freaking out. However, I was pretty close to running downstairs.

***

I walked back downstairs and had taken Calienta's warm hand in mine. "How is it that your brother can see me?"

The surprise on her face told me that this was something that she hadn't expected me to say. "How do you know this? What did you see? Was it your dream last night?" Her voice was urgent as she spoke, but not fearful. I tried to see this as reassuring.

"Actually, he made an appearance in the bathroom mirror to let me know he'd be watching me." I witnessed the concern as it played across her face.

"I didn't expect that. He must know about the prophecy, then."

"I didn't want to talk about it, but he was in my dream. Just as he was about to kill both of us, I think, I woke up. It was about ten different kinds of freaky, let me tell you."

I released her hand and went to make myself something to eat. Calienta followed me into the kitchen. After some searching, I settled on ham on rye. I wondered thoughtfully how long ham actually lasted before it went bad.

Watching Calienta's face carefully, I filled her in on the additional details of the dream, or at least what I remembered. The memory was fading fast.

Needless to say, I was doing my best not to take all of this personally. Most guys my age would have graduated high school at this time and only have to worry about the lazy days of their last summer as a kid.

Me? I got to graduate from college, find the eternity-mate that I never knew existed, get singled out as some sort of high-king-god, and finally would have to kill some deranged evil god that was the brother of said eternity-mate. Oh, did I forget I'm supposed to save the world somewhere in there?

Without speaking, Calienta took my hand again and pulled me through the back door. We headed for the steps that led to the cove.

The dog that I'd fed some of my dinner to a few days ago instantly greeted me. Sprinting over in my direction, he seemed to be smiling, and brushed up against my leg for a pat and a chance to sniff my pocket for food.

"Oh, please, we don't have time for any of this." Disdain was inherent in Calienta's tone.

"Geez, what are you, some sort of animal hater? I thought you all came to Earth to look out for us and guide us? Give the dog a break." Bending down, I gave the dog a big hug, kissing him on the head. I fed him the rest of my sandwich, which he ate greedily. When he was finished, the dog looked up at Calienta and let out a small whine.

Calienta smiled slightly as I stood up. "I do love animals, Kellen. Just not when they overact their parts and waste a lot of valuable time."

"Sorry I wasn't timely enough for you, daughter," a deep male voice said.

I turned to the right of where I stood only to see that the dog was no longer next to me. In its place stood a tall man with bronzed skin. He was naked.

"Ah!" I yelled.

"Father, do you mind?" Calienta asked, looking him in the eye.

"My apologies." The man laughed. Instantly he was clothed in torn jeans, loafers, and a tight-fitting t-shirt.

Lugh's looks hadn't changed at all from the time I'd first met him all those years ago at the cove. If anything, he looked as cool as he did then, the dad that everyone wanted—the dad that I wanted.

"You're the *dog?*" I stared at him, trying to figure things out.

"Yes, someone had to look after you." He smiled.

"You ate my sandwich."

"You gave me bad meat. I think we're even."

"Don't mention it." My brow furrowed as I contemplated the proper greeting that one should give to the father of a young goddess that he was supposed to marry.

Lugh was perceptive and instantly put me at ease by holding out his hand. He practically crushed my palm.

"You may shake my hand, Kellen. It is my wife you'll want to bow to." A hint of an Irish brogue clung to his speech.

"Is this some sort of god and goddess hangout? Seems like an odd place to reconvene."

"One might think that, Kellen St. James, but the cove and your gran's land is an area that was once revered by the Pagans as holy land. They used your gran's backyard as a place to hold their rituals and perform worship services. Plus, it's out of the way. We don't attract much attention down here."

"You mentioned the Pagans. That brings up a really interesting question..."

"Go ahead," Lugh said patiently.

"They worshipped all of the gods and goddesses, but isn't there only one god and heaven and hell and all that? I guess I don't know how it all comes together." This was a question that I dreaded asking because I didn't know if I'd hear something that I didn't believe in or couldn't agree with.

"Kellen, think of every religion that you know of. Almost every one of them has a supreme being that is guiding the people. Many religions also have emissaries of their god."

"And that's what you are?"

"Basically, yes."

"What makes each religion unique, then?"

"The debate isn't usually about one supreme god, but instead about the diversity in worship and how the one supreme being came to power. The name of the religion doesn't matter, Kellen. They are all special and unique. The only thing that matters is whether they focus on good or evil."

"And you're on the side of good, right?" Better to check one more time.

"Always." He was serious now.

"And Cabhan?"

Lugh sighed and looked at the ground. That was the only answer that I needed. Parents could make choices for their children with the best intentions, I supposed, but who knew how they'd turn out?

"We were coming down here to look for you. Kellen saw Cabhan in the mirror and in his dreams," said Calienta.

Lugh's eyes snapped back to mine.

"Yes." I wasn't sure what else to say.

"I guess that means he knows about you and the prophecy. He must be working with someone who knows about it too."

"But who?" Calienta asked. "One of the Sídhe?"

"They definitely know, but Arawn would never set them free. They're trapped."

"What about this Arawn, then?" I wished I hadn't spoken at first. Calienta met her father's eye. I'd hit a mark.

Calienta's face betrayed her alarm. "How would Arawn be able to breach our lands?"

"I don't know," Lugh admitted.

"All this over a girl?"

Calienta's eyes flashed.

"If only I'd made him mortal. Now his heartbreak has turned him. He isn't the same as he once was. He's not thinking the way he should. What makes matters worse is that he probably hates you almost as much as he hates me."

"But I've never met him and he hates me. How does that make sense?" I ran my hands through my hair.

Calienta spoke up. "You've never met him, but remember, Cabhan has dwelled on his hatred for so long. If he's seen the Pagan drawings, he'll know about the prophecy."

"What're you looking for me to do? You've obviously been watching me, seeking me out. You've been visitors here since I was a child, perhaps longer. You say that I'm supposed to help you, but how? I'm not a fighter. I have no skills in battle, no abilities that would help me fight your kind." I walked away from both of them and began to pace back and forth.

Lugh threw up his hands. "Kellen, all I know is that the two of you must be together for this to work. I'm sure of it."

I turned to face him. "That's another thing. You seem all too ready to pass off your daughter to me, a mortal, when you didn't want your own son to meet the same fate."

"I'm not 'passing off' my daughter, as you say. However, this is a different situation. Your life together has been ordained. I cannot dispute what has been foretold. Besides, the drawings show the two of you together, married and united. Your bond is a strong one. We will need that strength to beat Cabhan."

Why should I risk my life to stop Cabhan? But the answer was there, in my mind, before I could speak the question. *Calienta. I'd risk my life for Calienta.* I'd have done so when I first met her as a child. That reality freaked me out enough. Her father, however, was another matter.

Then Lugh spelled it out for me. "If it is Arawn behind this, his power alone won't be enough to rule the Earth. However, with Cabhan's power, the two of them could take me. They will unleash the Cwn Annwn and every evil creature in his command. The world as we know it will be lost."

"What's the Cwn Annwn?"

Calienta shuddered. "They are the Hounds of Hell, the spectral dogs of the underworld."

I'd no idea what the deal was with spectral dogs, but no good could come of it.

"They are basically Arawn's lapdogs. He is the reason that I couldn't save my family," Lugh explained.

This wasn't new information. It had been told to me in the cave already. However, I was interested in Lugh's point of view.

He continued. "I fought Arawn in combat for their release, but he didn't fight fairly and turned my family, or what was my family, on me. I escaped with barely my life and returned to the Green Lands to heal."

"Greenland—like the country?"

"The Green Lands are what we call our home," Calienta explained.

Lugh smiled affectionately at his daughter. "If Arawn is behind this, he and Cabhan could overcome me. Together, they would have enough power to challenge me, and an army at their disposal to help destroy the world."

"But you're a god. Can't you destroy all of them with a wave of your hand?"

Lugh shook his head. "No, I won't destroy my son. As for the army, you can't kill them when they are already dead."

I must have looked slightly horrified, but if anyone noticed they didn't comment. "When will they attack?" If I was going to play my part in this, I'd better have as much information as possible.

"I don't know that yet," Lugh admitted.

"But he knows about me. How can we be safe? Why doesn't he attack now?"

"I imagine that if it is Arawn that's involved, he's trying to figure out whether it's worth the risk. You're an unknown to him, so I can only guess that he is considering his options right now."

"He is, Father," a new voice answered. We all turned as Cabhan appeared. He was wild, unkempt, not at all the love-struck young man I was first introduced to in the cave.

His eyes were fierce, the rims red, his pupils appearing to glow a pale red. "And now that we know your warrior king is nothing more than a confused and frightened young man, I think Arawn will agree that it is worth the risk."

Before any of us could react, Cabhan lunged at his father. When they hit the ground, both of them disappeared from sight.

"Father!" Calienta's cries fell on deaf ears as we stared at the empty space.

CHAPTER ELEVEN
KIDNAPPING

"What the heck just happened?"

"This is worse than I thought. I'd no idea that he'd take action this soon." Calienta's wide eyes conveyed her horror.

"What do we do? What's the plan?"

Her eyes welled up with unshed tears. "Maybe I shouldn't have come here. I told you all about the tales of my family and our stories, our challenges, but I am nothing to you. If it wasn't for the prophecy I would never have come here. We wouldn't have met. I shouldn't have dragged you into the middle of all of this. It wasn't fair of me." She turned and started running toward the steps.

I stared after her for a moment, contemplating what she was saying. I didn't like the sound of it. Positioning my hands around my mouth, I yelled after her, "You're not 'nothing' to me. Are you actually thinking of leaving?"

Bolting after her, I lunged for the first step, stumbling as panic coursed through me. I couldn't believe the words that I was hearing. She'd sworn that she couldn't stop her brother without me. Now she was willing to leave me behind?

She stopped at the head of the staircase and turned. "I think it's best if I leave you alone and go and find my father on my own." Her voice sounded disengaged as she turned away from me, running again in the same direction, though more slowly.

None of this was making sense, unless she was trying to protect me. I ran after her, increasing my speed (she wasn't running at her full capacity) then reached out and grabbed her arm, whipping her around.

Her eyes blazed. There was a small explosion to my right; turf flew up into the air.

However, I wouldn't be deterred. "I feel it too, you know. Don't push me away when you need me the most." My words were soft and sincere, but she simply looked on as I spoke them.

"You don't have a choice. None of us has a choice in all of this. We're connected by more than a prophecy." Her hair whipped around her in the wind caused by the turmoil of her own emotions.

"You know," my voice broke, "you may not be able to protect me if I go with you." Her eyes flashed to mine; now we were hitting on it. "But I can't protect you if I stay here. There's no easy way out for either of us."

This time a look of tentative hope crossed her face. "I know, Kellen. I'm afraid, not only for you and my family but for the entire world. You have no idea what could be unleashed on mortals if my brother is allowed to succeed."

"Now that that's over with, what do we *do*?" I was hoping she had some idea; I was coming up empty.

"You'll need to come with me." She grabbed my hand.

"Always." My word was a promise.

***

Movement caught my attention and I looked to my right, back in the direction from which we'd come. A woman had appeared. Her hair was a dark burgundy color. It fell in a cloud of waist-length curls that framed her face, which was a picture of worry. Her skin was fair, with a blush at her cheeks that projected her angst as clearly as if she'd picked up a megaphone and announced it.

"That's my mother." It was a whisper on Calienta's lips. As soon as both women saw one another, they were at each other's side in a flash.

Calienta's mother held her close, stroking her hair. They both fought to get their words out in a rush.

"I was hoping you were all right. I escaped just as Arawn arrived."

"I'm glad you came, Mother. Cabhan took Father. I have no idea where."

Thunder shook the ground as the weather began to turn. I moved forward to take them by the elbows. "Let's get inside."

No sooner had I spoken the words than it started to rain. I suddenly realized that my feet were no longer on solid ground. Both Calienta and Brigid had taken one of my arms and we were flying through the air.

My stomach dropped as we ascended into the air at a rapid pace. I'd only ever flown on an airplane before and had hated it. I was afraid of heights, so this experience should've made me feel nauseated, but the result was exactly the opposite.

We reached Gran's cottage in a quarter of the time that it would have taken us to run. Making my way inside the house, I shut the door against the wind. Soaked through, I dried off; both of the women had already "changed" into dry clothes.

I looked at Calienta. "You really weren't kidding, were you? You *can* fly!" Despite my fears, there was no denying that the experience was cool.

"I told you." She winked, but then the light quickly faded from her eyes as concern for her father seeped through.

Brigid turned to face me. "Greetings, Kellen. I am Brigid."

Remembering Lugh's words, I bowed slightly. She laughed, but didn't correct me. Clearly, this was the level of greeting that Brigid was used to.

"Hello, ma'am." I was unsure of whether or not it would be appropriate to use her name. Normally when meeting new adults, I'd add a "Mr." or "Mrs." to the front of every greeting. However, I didn't know if she had a last name, or if Calienta did for that matter.

"What do we do now?" I'd been asking that same question the entire afternoon.

"*You* are not going to do anything. This is not a fight for mortals. You will die if you go near Cabhan."

This last part clearly saddened Brigid. I couldn't imagine that she'd have wanted this fate for her only son.

"Mother, I want him to remain safe as well, but the prophecy–"

"The prophecy was written many years ago. I am not convinced that it tells us the truth."

Calienta's face showed no emotion, but she took my hand and pulled me closer. "One part of the prophecy has already come true: we have pledged ourselves. However, there is more to this, as you are well aware. Kellen needs to be the one to stop Cabhan, he needs to see this through. You should know better than anyone not to stand in the way of fate."

Although I appreciated Calienta's backing, I wanted to speak for myself. "I'm not going anywhere unless she goes with me. I promised that I would help her. Just let me keep that promise."

Brigid stared at me. "Kellen, I do not doubt your sincerity, truly I do not. I have been with you when you suffered over your mother's death and from your father's cruel ambivalence. I have often thought of myself as a surrogate mother of sorts. I have always been with you."

That sentiment caught me off guard. My impression of the gods in mythology was that they were a little self-involved. I didn't know what the appropriate words were in this situation, but I decided to take a gamble.

"Thank you. That's more than I ever could have hoped for. However, your daughter was meant for me–I believe that now."

She considered my response for a moment before speaking. "Fate's loom weaves many connections." She seemed amazed. "So be it, then. If you are truly bound, then into battle you must go. Kellen, I am so sorry that you had to get involved in this. However, I will be forever grateful that you have chosen to stand beside my family."

Although Brigid looked resigned, she didn't argue further with either of us. I was still reflecting about the part where I might die.

"You had better be going then. There is no time to waste and we have already used some of it." Brigid clasped my hands in her own for a moment before turning and hugging Calienta.

Once their embrace ended, Calienta turned to me and rattled off a list of items that we should take with us. It wasn't a long one and I was easily able to commit it to memory. After searching the house, I managed to collect the black-handled knife, as much iron as I could find, and a container of salt. My list mostly consisted of food, none of it healthy and all of it designed to keep my blood sugar level up. These items, along with my iPod music player, were added to a small backpack.

For some reason, I remembered something at the last minute. Sprinting upstairs, I reached into the pants pocket of a discarded pair of jeans on the floor of my room. Instantly, my hand clasped around the pendant and I pulled it out. Resolutely, I put the chain over my head and tucked the pendant under my light sweater. Grabbing my bag, I headed back downstairs.

When I returned to the living room, Calienta was having a disagreement with her mother. "It's the only way. He'll know that we're coming, otherwise. We'll have no chance at all."

"No. It is too dangerous for both of you. We do not even know if the rumors are true, if a back way exists. What if both of you make this foolhardy journey and find yourselves trapped there for eternity?"

"Father would argue that a back way exists," Calienta insisted.

"Yes, isn't that how Arawn got into the heavens and murdered Lugh's parents?" Both women turned and looked at me, clearly annoyed at the interruption. "Okay, I'll be quiet now."

"You have a good memory, Kellen. We have, over the years, been told tales of another path, another way to the heavens. But we do not know if it is still there or if Arawn destroyed it, even if it truly exists," Brigid answered me before turning to Calienta. "If your father lives…" She trailed off, taking a moment to gain her composure. "He will not be able to get you out. We have tried that. He already attempted to reason with Arawn when the Children of Danu were trapped. What salvation will there be if you do not get through?"

"More salvation than if we *don't* proceed and are all destroyed. This is not a child's quest, Mother. If we don't save Father there will be no sunlight, only darkness. We cannot let Arawn win. You and I both know that we have a greater chance of stopping him if we surprise him."

"How do we do that?" Breaking open a Snickers candy bar, I bit into the candy hungrily. I knew that I wasn't going to like her answer.

"You have to find the gateway. It is called the Ellipse," Brigid explained. "All beings may enter the Underworld willingly, as long as they know the way in. There is no guarantee that they will be able to get back out. There are stories and legends of mortals wandering into the Underworld and leaving what they feel is only a few days later, to find that hundreds of years have passed and their families have all died. Time stands still there and advances here. There are also several creatures that could stop you from passing through—faeries and demons, creatures who would seek to end you."

"But aren't those 'creatures' your family?" Even though I didn't have a high opinion of family, I thought her situation was a little bit better than my own.

"It would be better if they didn't know me as such," Calienta explained. "They have never forgiven Father for surviving, for remaining in the light while they were exiled to the dark. The dark has turned them and they aren't the same."

"What you're saying is that we have to go through this crazy Underworld, and that leads us to Heaven?"

"Not Heaven as you would know it, but it's in the same realm," Calienta clarified for me.

"That is if you get past Arawn. I think it is too dangerous, Calienta. You put yourself and Kellen in great danger." Brigid looked at her daughter pleadingly.

"Yet he'll be in danger regardless. Don't you see, Mother? If I take him with us, he'll die; if I leave him here, he'll die; if we go below, he could die. There's no one option that's better than the other." Calienta was almost yelling now.

"Not that anyone's asking me, but I think the only way that gives us a shot is to go the creepy, spooky Underworld way. Cabhan won't be able to see you there, otherwise Lugh would have been able to find his family easily, right?"

"That is a good observation, Kellen," Brigid said. "You might be right—you could be safer there than here."

Calienta smiled, I assumed because of my impressive intellect. *Not*. "Kellen, more important, Cabhan won't be able to see you once you are below ground. You'll be safe from him even though you are with me. However, there'll be many dangers that will come your way. We must take as many precautions as possible."

Brigid placed her hands on my head and pure heat traveled through my body. It wasn't painful, and actually felt pleasant when compared with the feeling of dampness that seemed to permeate the house. We only had a moment of contact, but when she stepped back and removed her hands from my head, Calienta gasped.

Curious, I looked past Brigid and into the mirror on the wall behind her. At first, I noticed only its gilt frame and couldn't process the likeness within it. It was only when the figure moved that I realized I was staring at myself. I jumped.

My hair was a long shock of red against my nondescript cotton pants and a thick beige sweater. On my feet were work boots, which clearly had seen better days. This all seemed very odd as I stared at the mirror through turquoise-blue eyes, a distinct departure from my normal emerald color.

"Why did you do this to me?" My tone was deliberately calm, but inside I was freaking out. There was not one feature in the mirror that was familiar to me, which was both unexpected and unsettling.

"Do not worry, Kellen. You will need protection on your journey. This change is only an illusion and it will give the impression that you are the same as any creature that you encounter. The spell will allow you to act, in effect, as a chameleon. You will be able to tell friend from foe because you will only change your appearance when you are in danger."

Looking at myself again, I made a face at the image before me. Calienta chuckled.

"I hope that you play your part well. They are very suspicious," Brigid added.

"Don't worry, I'm pretty good at acting," I promised.

Brigid smiled.

I had the distinct impression that I was being laughed at and shoved my hands into my pockets. "Hey, where's my candy?" I'd expected to find my multiple

Snickers candy bars in my pocket and they'd apparently not transferred to my new pants.

"Kellen?" asked Calienta.

"Look, if you expect me to go into some underworld and risk my life, I need some food. Where are my other pants?"

Brigid tried to hide a smile as she pointed to the pile of clothes on the couch. Trying not to sulk, I went to the couch and grabbed the goods from my pockets. There was no way I was fighting evil without my chocolate caramely (yes, that's my own word) goodness.

"When do we leave?" I held out my hand to Calienta, who took it at once.

"Immediately." Brigid gestured to the sky outside. "The night is their daytime and many of them will come above ground until the morning. You must use this to your advantage."

I nodded and extended my hand to shake hers politely.

She ignored my hand, choosing instead to hug us close. "I love you both." In an instant, she vanished.

I looked around for Calienta and found that she, too, was gone. However, before I could panic, she reappeared. "She gave me a gift too, Kellen: the gift of invisibility. Whenever we encounter someone who is not a friend, I'll disappear from view."

"Cool." I sounded way immature. However, she smiled in response, so she must have thought it was "cool" as well.

We walked to the door and I grabbed my coat from the hook, briefly touching Gran's work coat as I did so. Taking Calienta's hand, I opened the door to begin our journey. I looked around Gran's cottage for a moment and wondered if I'd ever see it again.

Be brave. Gran's voice was there again. As I listened to the words on the wind, I hoped that bravery would be possible, for I had no idea what lay ahead.

***

We traveled on foot as we made our way away from the cottage, following the tree line past the woods. Neither of us spoke, but that was mostly due to our unsettling surroundings. It was eerie, like a million tiny eyes were watching us, though physically there was nothing but trees.

Calienta had become transparent, so I was not able to hold her hand as I'd have liked to. Only her occasional touch, her scent, and light steady breathing gave away her presence. Then she took my arm and I relaxed at the connection.

We walked at a fast pace, past sleepy houses and lonely fields, staying out of the woods and restricting ourselves to the more populated areas, mowed fields and country roads.

Suddenly she pulled me sideways into a field, and we continued again, this time through high grass that pressed against me from all sides. I could tell that

Calienta wished to go faster but we kept pace, all the while with her gripping my arm.

"Where are we going?" My voice was low.

"Cahercommaun."

I'd heard of that place; it was a stone cliff fort in the Burren. Though the term "barren" would have been more appropriate, as there was little sign of life in this rugged land.

The way became steeper as we moved onward. Weathered stones barred our way as the climb continued. I found myself stumbling over rocks and into ditches in the landscape, but neither of us spoke. At first, I looked at my watch about every fifteen minutes or so, but then after a time I gave up.

When Calienta finally came to a stop, I glanced at my watch. It had taken us roughly four hours to arrive at our destination. We were about fifty feet from a small mound in the earth. Though the site was quite popular on the tourist path, it would have been difficult to find within the craggy system of gray rock unless of course you knew what you were looking for.

"Is this a rath?" Gran had warned me about these as a child. I'd never seen one.

"Yes, it is a faerie fort, or rath."

Stay away from the woods, and for goodness' sake, don't go climbing into any holes in the ground. The memory of Gran's voice echoed a long-forgotten warning in my mind.

Calienta whispered into my ear. "When I pinch your arm, you must say 'leannan'. That will grant us entrance. That way we don't need to sit here and wait for them to find us."

Did goddesses get scared? Was it possible to have all of that power and be afraid of anything? I didn't know, but I was afraid, so how could she not be?

"Hey, let me see you for a moment," I whispered. As she reappeared, I pulled her to me, hugging her close and closing my eyes as I held her.

Her hair smelled like rain: clean, pure, and calming, her skin like the scent of cinnamon. It was a warm, homey smell that soothed me. I never wanted to leave this place, to go anywhere else, with anyone else, despite the life-threatening circumstances.

Her dark eyes met mine. This time any trace of fear was absent in them. "It's time."

"Leannan." That was the last word I uttered before we were sucked into the hole and out of sight.

CHAPTER TWELVE
INTO THE UNDERWORLD

"Whoa! Oh," I cried out as we were pulled through a waterfall. It was almost like taking a shower with one of those elephant-sized showerheads and stepping directly into the spray.

Drowning was at the forefront of my mind and I held my breath in the overwhelming onslaught of wet. However, when I began to get concerned about passing out, the water subsided and we found ourselves completely dry and standing in a wooded glen in the middle of the day. It would have seemed normal, like a public park, except that the grass and the leaves were fuchsia-colored.

Looking back behind me, I saw that we'd traveled between two tall pine trees with nothing but a narrow opening between them rather than the raging waterfall I'd been expecting. Calienta squeezed my arm, which was our unspoken signal. I was reminded that we were unwelcome here; silence was our cloak.

After a brief glance around the glen, I started heading down the path to our right. It was a dirt path, covered with rocks in shades of purple and turquoise. The rocks would make the journey uncomfortable, but the path seemed well traveled, and I remembered Brigid's warning to blend in.

Walking confidently, I did my best to appear as though I was not having any trouble whatsoever. The landscape seemed gloomy despite the beautiful colors and the faint glimpse of sunshine overhead. The trees pressed so close together that there was very little space for the light to filter down. We were trapped.

Although I enjoy the quiet as well as anyone, this was certainly more than I was used to. It allowed me to focus too much on the magnitude of what we were attempting, and my mind began to dwell on negative thoughts. I didn't like that.

The rocky path got steeper as we continued. Higher and higher we walked until the path ran alongside a precipice that overlooked a sea of pine trees.

In that instant, the enormity of what we'd taken on completely overwhelmed me. I wanted to bury my head in the dirt or curl up in a ball and go to sleep. Anything but continue this quest. How could I have put myself in this position?

Do it. Just jump. You don't need to go on. Perhaps it was because I was so used to hearing voices by now that I noticed that this one was different, or maybe it was because Calienta's posture suddenly mimicked mine. Whatever the reason, it dawned on me that we were both leaning slightly toward the sheer drop with one foot outstretched over the edge. Abruptly, I grabbed her and slammed us both back against the rock wall.

Bag, bag, I thought, *what's in the bag?* It came to me. I reached into the backpack, pulling out the packet of ordinary household salt that I'd collected earlier, and

sprinkled it around us in a circle. Instantly the emotions vanished. All of my senses had been turned off and they were suddenly restored. Sound and thought hit me all at once. I was struck by what had almost happened. Calienta was herself again, but she was angry, shaken.

"What was that about?" Catching my breath, I placed my hands against the sides of my face; it was cold and clammy. My heart started to pound as I realized how close I'd come to the edge.

Calienta grabbed my arm and tugged. We ran quite a distance away from the bluff, neither of us speaking for several moments. It wasn't until we were back on open land that she spoke.

"It was a Glacadóir Anam. It means Soul Snatcher."

I didn't know what a Soul Snatcher did, but I could guess, and I didn't like the sound of it. Not one bit. "What do they do?"

"Exactly what their name implies. They depress you and try to force you to end your life. When you do, they take your soul."

"That's disgusting." I looked around, back down the road that we'd taken. The weathered path seemed foreboding, certainly, but I didn't see anything.

"You saved us, Kellen. How did you know what to do?"

"Gran. She said that salt was a ward against evil, a purifier, and she always put it around the perimeter of the house. I have a knack for remembering things, I guess."

"Thank you for saving my life."

"Aren't you immortal?"

"I am, but if I were to die here, life as I know it would end though I'd continue to live. They probably know we're here now, at least some of them anyway."

"Did I give us away?"

"We both did. Most of the creatures in this land have no fears for the Glacadóir Anam to play upon. It is only in the mortal world that they can wreak havoc. Down here, they are soulless."

Seeing my expression as I berated myself for my own stupidity, she said, "Kellen, it was unavoidable. We could have been taken. You did the right thing."

Soul Snatchers were too much for me to process. "Let's get out of here." Our stay couldn't be extended.

We continued to walk again, encountering a host of animals in all shapes, sizes, and colors. All were apparently tame, since none of them chose to attack. The animals were almost as strange and diverse as the landscape. It wasn't every day that you passed a pink cow or a chartreuse pig. What was worse was not being able to comment on such an oddity.

When we first laid eyes on a purple cat, I learned my lesson. "Loo–"

"Shush." Calienta slapped my hand.

"Sorry," I replied, which led to another hand slap.

We continued on and the landscape began to change as we made our descent down the mountain. Slowly, the wooded forests gave way to boggy marshland. Fortunately, there was an overgrown footpath to walk across the landscape, but that didn't make me feel any easier about it.

I'd made it to the end of the path when two things happened at once: The first was that I suddenly found myself in new, rather tight-fitting clothing, sporting a red coat and a hat. The second was that an animated human skeleton appeared in the middle of the road. It seemed unbelievably authentic and smelled of rotting human flesh. I started to cover my mouth and Calienta stopped me. It looked like Brigid's protection was kicking into gear.

"What do I say?" Nothing had prepared me to actually speak to a one of them.

"Leave it to me." Calienta's calm voice was a promise. "Far Darrig, I command that you show yourself. I am not interested in your petty practical jokes."

My voice sounded impatient, so I did my best to take on the stance of someone who seemed both ambivalent and annoyed at the same time. I crossed my arms in front of me as a loud popping sound rang through the air. The skeleton disappeared, only to be replaced by a little man in a red cap and coat, who couldn't have been more than three feet tall.

"I have business here." My voice was stern though fear permeated my skin. Although in my human form I was three feet taller than this little man, he had powers that I didn't understand. I was intelligent enough to know when I was outmatched. What if we were found out? My heart was slamming against my ribs, and it seemed to me as though everyone could hear it.

"Come with me, my friend, and we will find the mortals. They will give us good sport this day," Far Darrig cried in a nasally voice. He raised his hands to perform some sort of magick, and I wasted no time improvising. I hoped that it was the right way to go.

"It is I, your master. You will leave this place at once or suffer the consequences." *There, take that, punk.*

The little man put down his arms and started to shake in his boots, but he didn't move from his spot. He seemed rooted in place.

"I have business here."

And then with a bow and a pop, the little man turned into the rotting skeleton again and skipped down the path, giggling to himself, no doubt searching for his next victim. I breathed gently, taking air back into my lungs as I returned to my previous height and disguise.

Calienta's words were a whisper. "We mustn't linger here."

"Good. Those leather pants were pretty tight. Nice job with the creepy voice, by the way, I had no idea what to say."

Exhaustion began to plague me as I suddenly wondered how long we'd been at this. I looked at my watch. It was three o'clock, but I didn't know whether it was a.m. or p.m. I assumed a.m. However, as Calienta had pointed out, time was different here in this world below my own, so it could have been a week later for all I knew.

The bogs gave way to forest again, but the trees were more spaced out, easier to navigate. The sun was out, or what I assumed was the sun, though we were underground. Learning from our earlier mistakes, we kept fistfuls of salt ready in our pockets and walked in tense positions, hands at the ready in case we needed to protect ourselves. We wouldn't stop to rest, and I didn't ask about it. Calienta would want to keep going. So onward we went.

After a time, the woods were overcome by darkness, and the odd shapes and sounds started to give me the creeps. This impression I kept to myself; I was a brave warrior, after all. When she produced a small lighted lantern from who knew where, I tried not to let my relief show. I took the lamp from her. The path wound familiarly in front of me.

In a heartbeat, I found myself lying flat on my back. Although the path seemingly continued on for miles, the way was blocked. Upon closer inspection, it appeared as though a glass window was preventing us from going any further. Anxiously, I looked at the path through the glass. The path was visible but we were unable to follow it.

Calienta whispered, "There is a password. I don't know what it is, but we must wait for others to come whom we can follow in." My own concerns were put on the back burner at the tone of frustration in her voice. She pulled me behind a tree that lay off the path.

"Do you think we should guess?" I suggested.

"No. A wrong password could take us somewhere that we definitely don't want to go."

Slowly, we sat down on the soft grass. The events of the day were catching up with me and I was sorely tempted to go to sleep. However, I was very concerned about Calienta. What must she be feeling, wondering if her own father would live or die?

"I want you to know that I do realize that you didn't have to come with me." Slowly she reappeared before me until I could plainly read the worry on her face. Her eyes burned into mine. The only sound was that of her quiet breathing; I was holding my own breath.

"Yes, I do. Don't take offense, but that's a ridiculous statement."

"No, it's not. We barely know each other. We've only met and yet here you are. You could have stayed behind." She looked down at the ground, not meeting my eyes.

Lying down, I propped myself up on my side, leaning against my elbow in the cool, damp grass. With my free hand, I pulled her down to the ground to mirror my position. "It is ridiculous, because I love you."

She stared at me in disbelief. Words seemed to have escaped her.

"Wow, I thought it would be much harder to tell you that." The words were always there; they were only waiting for me to say them.

"You love me?"

"You must know that I do."

"When did that happen?"

"I'm not sure, but it did. All I know is from the moment that we first met I didn't want to be apart from you. Not ever."

"But we've planned out your life for you. As I watch you make this journey I realize that, while I may live, it could cost you your life." She was insistent, leaving no stone of doubt unturned.

"Yours would be a worthy cause to die for."

She started to cry; quiet tear tracks streaked down her face as she let my arms envelop her. She felt so right there; my arms were made to hold only her.

"And would you grieve for me if I were to die during this journey? Would you feel the same devastation that I'd feel if I lost you?"

She didn't speak for a moment and I worried that I had asked too much of her. I was mortal; she was a goddess. *What if I'd imagined there was more between us than there actually was?*

"I would lose part of my soul. I've always known that there could be no one else for me."

My heart was trying to pound its way out of my chest. "Even without the Pagan prophecies?" This had been a silent fear of mine from the beginning. We were really laying it all out on the table now.

"The prophecies paved the way for us to be together, but I wonder if I'd have found you even without them." Tenderness colored her words.

"You've no idea what you've given me. Before you came into my life, I was on my own. The world was gray and unfeeling. There was no sense of belonging for me, no welcoming home. Only Gran's home was a refuge and one that I rarely had the privilege of seeking. I met you that day on the beach, and you brought light and warmth into my life. I wanted you. You gave me this incredible sense of belonging. I can't explain it."

"You don't have to. I understand."

"You're everything that I could ever have imagined for myself and more." I thought briefly about the journals and drawings that I'd dedicated to Calienta. When this ordeal ended, I'd show them to her and give them to her as a wedding present, if I had the opportunity to marry her.

Suddenly, we were kissing as though every second could be our last. In the brief periods where our lips were apart, we spoke.

"You kept me going," I told her. "You helped me to become who I am in so many ways. You and Gran, you both saved me."

"Saved you from what?"

"From becoming my father." I tried not to sound bitter.

"No. You don't understand. You were never going to become him."

"How could you know what I'd become?"

"Because too many things have happened to you; terrible, horrible things have happened. Yet you always chose the path of goodness and you didn't let these things change you. I think it's because you have much of your mother in you. Even if you had never met me, even if

you did not have your gran, you would have become the man you are."

CHAPTER THIRTEEN
THE TROOPING FAERIES

Before I could respond, there was singing and the pounding of what sounded like a herd of wild horses. As I cautiously looked out from around the tree, I was shocked to see a large group of small men and women in green jackets riding tiny white horses across the wood.

"Trooping faeries," whispered Calienta.

Though I stared at the tiny crew transfixed, my attention was pulled away by Calienta's quiet laughing. I guessed that my appearance had changed again.

Turning, I looked at my reflection in the shaded pond behind us. In the water, I looked about two feet tall and was clothed in the same riding gear of a hunter: green vest and pants. Across my face were speckles of glitter, and my now violet eyes almost glowed with excitement.

I must have been leaning too close to the water, because Calienta called my name in warning. It was no good, however. Two claw-like hands reached out of the water and pulled me in. I fought back, kicking and punching, but the creature started pulling me to the bottom.

The small pond was pitch black even in the breaking light of the early morning, and I could see nothing except for a pair of red eyes that were peeking

out at me from behind the underwater plants. I continued to fight but I was running out of air and energy.

A new pair of hands grabbed me and pulled me upward, toward the light. As my head broke the surface, I gulped air, letting the hands pull me to the shoreline.

"There, there. You should not have gotten so close to the water. Are you all right?" Expecting to hear Calienta's voice, I frantically wiped at my eyes when the words were spoken in a high-pitched, almost girlish voice. Sputtering and blinking on the bank of the pond, I tried to gain my bearings. It was a challenge not to cry out when I finally raised my lids, for before me stood a troop of little people. Their expressions ranged from indifference to hostility to concern.

"Greetings, and thank you," I heard myself respond as I was hauled out of the water.

"I am Dagné," said the faerie that had first spoken to me.

"Hi, Dagné. I'm…Manuel." It was the best I could come up with on short notice.

A blond faerie gave me the once-over. "Manuel, an unusual name, certainly. You have lost your troop. Please come and join us at our home for a feast." Though the last sentence was an invitation, the tone of voice made it a challenge. I could tell already that some of them didn't trust me. There would be no choice but to go with them.

"It would be an honor." Unsure of the appropriate response, I bowed to him. I realized that may have been

overdoing it, but what could it hurt? Several of the faeries smiled in approval so I must have been on the right path.

One member of the troop, a girl by all appearances, winked at me from the back of the group and blew me a kiss before conjuring another white pony from thin air.

"Thank you." Smiling, I climbed on the back of the animal, wondering how I was going to get out of this one.

"Eat or drink nothing." Calienta whispered this in my ear as we started to trot the animals toward the glass barrier. My eyes widened as I searched my peripheral vision for her, but I gave no additional sign that I knew she was there. Calienta had made herself invisible when the faeries arrived so I doubted it was safe for her.

"Cali." A little man in the front of the group spoke. Would Calienta have been able to hear that?

Instantly the glass vanished and the troop began to pass through. As I took the opportunity to ride in with them, I only hoped that Calienta, in her invisibility, was behind me. There was certainly no way that I'd be able to look for her without being conspicuous as we passed through the glass and out into an open field. There were high blades of grass dancing in the wind, which had picked up into a cool breeze now. The air smelled of lavender and some other scent that I didn't recognize.

The scene should have been calming and relaxing, but it did nothing for me. I needed to think about a way out. Closing my eyes, I tried to sense whether Calienta was with us. So in tune was I with her emotions that I was certain I'd know it if she wasn't with me. I kept forgetting to ask her why that was.

Nothing. She wasn't there. Suddenly, my world came crashing down as I realized that I was alone with the faeries. They seemed benign enough, but they'd turn on me if given the slightest inclination.

"We will go to our palace and have a feast, Manuel. You must tell us how you got here." The blond man on the horse in front of me had spoken. There was suspicion in his tone and I wondered how I was going to answer his question.

"Si." God, I was such an idiot.

We continued across the fields. In my memory, I couldn't remember ever having been this hungry or exhausted. The tension was making my body ache. I wondered at first if this was because I'd shrunk in size, but then I remembered that this was only an illusion; I was still really my normal size. Looking down at the small white pony on which I rode, I noted that he seemed more winded than the other horses.

Our group cantered through the field until the female who'd fussed over me finally spoke. "Welcome to our home."

An open field spread before me. There was no house there and absolutely nothing remarkable about it. Yet the group dismounted and walked briskly in the direction of nothing. Dismounting as well, I walked through the tall grass, which came to my shoulders.

Oh, geez, I've got to believe. It was a scene straight out of a movie. The thought struck and debilitated me all in a matter of seconds. Certainly, I'd seen many things since meeting Calienta that I never would have thought possible. However, if I didn't find a way to believe now, I was in a lot of trouble.

"I believe," I whispered. *What a lame attempt.* Listening, I closed my eyes for a moment and tried to absorb my surroundings.

With my eyes closed, the environment was entirely different. Magick was everywhere. I didn't understand its source or whether it was good or bad, but there was no denying it.

Help me believe, I thought to myself. *I want to believe. I need to believe.* Slowly, I opened my eyes. The air in front of me was hazy. It seemed to shift and bunch in the twilight. Determined, I continued to think *I believe* again and again. After a few moments of true effort, I finally saw it.

Directly in front of me stood a palace of generous proportions, though instead of looking like any palace I'd read about as a child, this place had the look of a timbered lodge. The structure seemed to consist of several massive oak trees on top of which the home itself had been built. Large open windows dotted the bows of the trees and I could see that immense bedrooms had been constructed in hollowed-out portions of the trees themselves.

Connecting the various parts of the home were a series of wooden bridges and spiral staircases that defied gravity, seeming to go straight up into the heavens. A large front door stood open and the faeries were practically running through its opening. Wanting to blend in, I started to do the same, but came to a halt once I crossed the threshold.

Here was the marble palace that I'd expected to see, complete with gilt-framed mirrors and a winding staircase. The faeries were everywhere, their little riding habits standing in stark contrast to their luxurious surroundings. Each faerie looked unique and beautiful, but there was a quality about every one of them that made them seem fierce. This did nothing to qualm my nerves.

"The feast is this way." Dagné steered me by the elbow.

Thoughts of Calienta plagued me as I followed Dagné warily into the dining hall with its dark wood-paneled walls. I'm ashamed to say that all of my worries temporarily vanished when I glimpsed the food that covered the many long tables within the room. There were so many of my favorite foods and I couldn't wait to try them all.

It was after I started to fill my plate that I remembered Calienta's warning against eating or drinking. My stomach growled unbearably as I looked around. But that all changed when I stared down at a roast chicken only to have it suddenly change in front of my eyes from a piece of poultry to a pile of rocks.

Looking down the length of the table I saw, instead of tray after tray of luscious foods, plates and bowls filled with peat and rocks. *It's an illusion*, I

thought. None of it was real. It was all an illusion, like my disguise.

Disgusted, I replaced a serving spoon and lowered my plate to the table. As I did so, I noticed that the one faerie that had questioned me before was watching me. He hadn't introduced himself, but I noticed now that his hair was even longer than I'd thought originally and flowed from beneath his hat. As I continued to stare at him, the vision shifted and he was suddenly an ugly little man with a wart on his nose.

Trying not to give away what I'd seen, I turned to Dagné, who was seated to my right. I suppose to some, Dagné would have seemed very beautiful with her dark hair and periwinkle eyes, but I only had eyes for another.

"Do you have a place where I could rest?"

She looked at me with concern on her face, but if she seemed surprised by my request, she didn't let on. Instead, she nodded and beckoned me to follow her, which I did, out of the hall and up the grand staircase.

Together we walked in silence to a grand bedchamber. The bed hangings and covers were made of red silk and hung on a massive bed that was part of the tree. Branches grew down on either side and provided a convenient step for getting in and out of the bed.

A large window had been flung wide open and the air smelled of dirt and grass. A small chair made of rich fabrics sat in one corner and a table with a simple basin of water on it in another.

"Sleep well, Manuel."

There wasn't an opportunity to reply as she turned without another word and left the room, shutting the door roughly behind her. Carefully, I walked over to the window and looked down. It was easily one hundred feet or more to the ground. Shaking my head, I walked away from the window and turned to look at the bed.

Thinking longingly of food, I rummaged through my pockets for a Snickers candy bar. They were in there somewhere. After minutes of searching, I was reminded that my snacks were probably in my other pants. This was getting very inconvenient.

A scowl transformed my face as I lay down upon the bed, the sounds of the feast echoing dimly in the background. My heart was pounding, aching for Calienta. Her confessions at the pond had changed things again between us. It was one thing to say you loved someone, but it was another thing entirely to hear that they loved you.

Now that I'd found out exactly what I meant to Calienta, I didn't want to lose her. Despite her powers, I wanted to protect her, and I'd done a rotten job so far. Against my will, my eyes closed within seconds. My own worries followed me straight into sleep and I dreamed almost instantly.

In the dream, Calienta wandered alone through the wood, searching for me. I could see no one around, but I had the intense feeling that she was in grave danger. She seemed to sense that she was not alone and her eyes scanned the area, searching. No matter where she went, she was unable to find what she was looking for. The

feeling that she was being stalked remained throughout the dream.

When I awoke, I was sweating. I looked down at my clothes.

"Awesome. My own clothes for a change." I shoved my hands in my pockets for my Snickers candy bars and a can of Pepsi from the jacket.

Although I was shaken by the dream, I couldn't trust it. There were too many creatures in this place to influence my mind, my thoughts. I'd remember what I'd dreamed, but I'd have to remain calm if I were going to get out of here and find Calienta.

Suddenly, I noticed that the palace was eerily quiet. There was literally no sound, which stood in stark contrast to the sounds of music and merriment that I'd fallen asleep to earlier.

Cautiously, I walked to the door and opened it.

And found at least twenty-five faeries waiting on the other side, their faces menacing, their teeth bared. That was when the faerie with the golden hair spoke up.

"I placed a reveal charm on the bed so we could see him for what he is. He is not one of us."

Great. Looks like Goldilocks sold me out.

"I can explain." What was I going to say? That I was trying to make it through their world in secret to find a backdoor portal to the heavens and destroy the source of all evil? Hello, movie of the week.

"We want none of your lies." The group started to press in on me, making me feel nervous.

Slowly, I checked to see that the knife that Calienta had given me was still in my jeans pocket. It was. I needed to get out and fast. I jammed my hands into my jacket pockets and hit the play button on my iPod, which queued up "The Hunter" by my favorite band, Everybody's Mother. The sound traveled through the speakers embedded in the iPod case and the room was soon filled with the sound of the hunting horn that graced the song's opening notes. The faeries immediately perked up, turned, and charged out in pursuit of the hunt.

Every one of them left. I stood in amazement for a moment, completely unable to believe that I'd cleared out a roomful of mythical faeries with garage metal. I turned to look for a way out. Who knew if they'd be coming back? Rather than wait around, I ran over to the window, pulled out my knife, and jumped out. I'd hoped that because I was in the Underworld there was no gravity, but I was wrong. Falling, the ground came at me faster and faster until suddenly my knife caught onto one of the large trees that supported the house.

Relief washed over me but it was short-lived as my knife began ripping the tree literally into two halves. The word "rip" was most appropriate, because it felt like I was cutting into a bed sheet with my knife, such was the consistency of the tree.

It was a prop, not real, merely a stand-in. Yet there was nothing more beyond it. Behind the tree, the rest of the house should have been visible, yet there was only a black void. The tree itself seemed blurred and insubstantial, like a watercolor painting that had gotten caught in the rain. It appeared as though my surroundings were nothing more than a colorful canvas that I'd ripped a hole into.

Once I reached the ground, I turned at the sound of the Trooping Faeries on horseback charging at me. Without thinking, I ran directly toward the black hole where the tree once stood and jumped in. And I was falling again.

The blackness seemed to have no beginning and no end. There were no points of light, only the darkness. Everything was blacked out. It was like being covered with a blanket. The fall seemed to go on endlessly and I began to fear that there was no end. Why did I choose this particular escape route? *Did I mention I'm afraid of heights?*

Something was off. Plus I was even more lost than I was before. I tried to let myself feel calm, but that's difficult when you're plunging through a black void at forty miles per hour.

Finally, I could take it no longer. I wanted out of this place. "Stop!" In seconds the world went blacker than black.

***

After coming to, it took several moments for my eyes to adjust to the glaring sunlight, but once they did, I saw everything around me for what it truly was. The Trooping Faeries, the woods, the palace—it was all gone.

Instead, I was in the middle of the desert. I was really and truly lost now. How would I ever find Calienta here?

At first, I was relieved to see the sun. I'd traveled through the blackness for so long that I began to despair of ever seeing light again. However, this way of thinking was short-lived. Within minutes, I became conscious of both the scorching sun and my thirst. My last drink was a can of Pepsi, and that wouldn't hold me long.

Standing up, I brushed the sand off me. I didn't know where I was going, but I had to keep moving. There was no other choice if I wanted to survive.

The landscape was barren, with seemingly mile after mile of sand dunes, but there was always a chance that this was an illusion too. There was very little vegetation and what did exist was mere ground cover. Nowhere was there a sign of shelter or a safe place to rest; the entire area was completely void of life.

After I'd walked for several miles, I started to hear a faint rumbling sound. It reminded me of thunder in the distance. It was worrisome to me because it kept increasing in volume. I kept turning to look around, to figure out where it was coming from.

Finally, when the vibrations were causing the very ground beneath my feet to shake, the cause of the noise appeared on the horizon. Then all of the air was sucked straight out of my body, rocking me.

A pack of enormous wild dogs pounded across the desert and headed straight for me. I started to search frantically for somewhere, anywhere, to take cover. There was nowhere. I was trapped again.

I didn't see the bird until it was too late. It opened its large mouth to swallow me. My feet pounded on the hot sand as I tried to make my escape. Yet with each step, I sank deeper into the sand; I was getting nowhere fast. The large pelican swooped down out of the sky and scooped me up in its beak before taking off again.

The dogs howled below, their red eyes glowing hungrily after us. Realizing that I faced a new type of danger, I struggled in the bird's beak. However, I was not as rough as I could have been, as it was a long way down.

"Hollonasec. Hollon," said the bird.

"What? I didn't understand a word you said."

"Yourrin mymouf. Hollon."

We flew a bit further. Then the bird landed, opening its beak so I could climb out. "Sorry. I cannot talk with me mouth full."

Blinking, I took in the enormous bird. He was beautiful, with shining feathers of white and gray that seemed to sparkle in the sun. His eyes were large and kind, amber in color. The animal was roughly the same size as the Audi that Stephen had given me.

"Why do you not 'op on me back and we can speak easier. I cannot have much of a conversation with something in my mouth, ya know, boy-o?"

Looking around, I scanned the area for options. There were none.

"They're coming for you, you know. You can't be stayin' here."

After hesitating shortly, I ran forward and jumped onto the pelican's large back. The feathers were soft and comfortable. They also seemed cooler than the desert around us, so I instantly felt better despite the strong smell of salt and fish that clung to them.

"See, I did not eat you, so you can trust me." The pelican nodded as he spoke.

My arms wrapped around his large neck and he began to take off again. The ride was unsettling, and I feared that any sudden movement on my part would send me falling to the ground.

However, I soon got the hang of it and found the proper position for my legs and hands. Only then was I comfortable enough to talk. "Thanks, but you said they're coming for me. Who's coming for me?"

"Did ya not see the mighty great beasts that we flew over? Are ye blind?"

"Yes, but what are they?"

"The Cwn Annwn—the Hounds of Hell. You could say they keep the peace around here."

"The Hounds of Hell were coming for me?"

"See, it is a bit hard to remain incognito when pretty much everyone already knows that you're here." The bird tilted his head back toward me and winked.

"Everyone knows we're here?" I swallowed. I'd expected as much from what Calienta had said earlier, but to have it confirmed was unnerving. So much for maintaining a low profile.

"You tell me, but I know that everything is out of sorts and it is all because of you and your girlfriend coming down here and tearing the place up."

"My girlfriend? Do you know where she is? I've been looking for her everywhere."

"I do not know, lad. I do not have the foggiest idea."

I was afraid of that. "I need to find her. Do you have any idea where I should look?"

"There are many different dimensions here and she could be in any one of them. I do not know if I would even know where to start."

"Could you *please* help me?" I was certain my voice sounded weak and I hated that. Regardless of the tone, however, it must have worked because he consented.

"Of course I will help you, lad. Everyone likes a rebel, after all." He laughed.

"How do I know I can trust you?"

"I saved you, did I not? Not *all* of us are on the side of evil, after all. I myself quite like mortals. My name is Ghárda, Kellen St. James."

"How did you know my name?" Skipping the pleasantries, I asked the blunt question.

"There are those of us who have known for many years that you would come. You are the one who will keep the light from vanishing from Earth."

Yeah, that's me, I thought. However, I said nothing as the ground swept past us below and the landscape changed yet again from the desert to a richly colored forest. I hugged the large bird tighter and tried not to think of my quest or what lay ahead. There was no point in fearing these things; being afraid wouldn't change what I had to do. Instead, I tried to put it out of my mind.

"Why are you helping me?"

"My family has long been charged with helping those in need. We are protectors in this land and we look after the humans that find their way down here, either by accident," he looked back at me, "or by design."

I processed this for a moment. "How many are in your family?"

"I have twenty children, one hundred and nineteen grandchildren, and two hundred and thirty great-grandchildren."

"Huh." He didn't waste any time. "And you're all protectors in Faerie?"

"We call this here place Faerie. To answer your question, yes, in one way or another."

As it turned out, Ghárda was a wonderful storyteller who shared tales of his family and their life. Whenever I asked him to explain how he ended up in the desert, he happily changed the subject. I shouldn't trust him, but I wanted to. I needed to trust someone; it was all too overwhelming otherwise.

Scanning the ground, I looked for Calienta but I didn't see anything but the forest. "Where are we going?" I meant this more as a "Do you know where you're going?" sort of question, but I didn't want to seem pushy when the driver had the ability to let me drop hundreds of feet to the ground below.

"We must travel through all of the dimensions of Faerie to the place where your girl must be. See the light ahead?" He indicated a rainbow on the horizon with a flick of his beak. "That is the portal between our dimensions."

"How many dimensions are there?"

"There are seven. Discovery, Inquisition, Knowledge, Contentment, Transition, Desolation, and there is one more. I do not wish to speak of it, though."

This wasn't going to get me anywhere good, but I asked anyway. "Why not?" I fully expected him to buck me off.

"Because it is the darkest place in our land; nothing but evil dwells in that place and we do not speak its name." The bird's tone contained a finality to it that indicated that no further questions on the matter were welcome. I decided to comply for the moment, but I was willing to bet that was the one that I'd need to go to.

"Where did the portals come from?"

"Let me think about how best to explain it." The wind rushed past us for a moment as he considered. "Years ago, when the Children of Danu were exiled here, they started to turn. Some became evil; some did not. Others chose to walk the line now and again. There was no way, with such varying beliefs, that everyone could get along, if you will."

"They decided to live in different parts of Faerie?"

"Faerie decided for them. Their fighting was so fierce that the land was split apart into different dimensions. Everyone went their separate ways. Though they did learn to travel between their own little worlds, few chose to."

"And you were a Child of Danu."

"No. My kind came after that epic battle." Changing the subject, he gestured with a nod of his head. "We are heading straight for the first portal. As we pass through each one, tell me if any of them speak to you. If you think there is one place where your mate might be, let me know."

"Okay."

We crossed into the first dimension. Mountains capped with snow and dotted with endless pine trees filled the landscape. Mentally, I shut down my own worries and focused on sensing Calienta, the way I'd been able to before.

"We have entered the dimension of Discovery." The bird's wings beat furiously as we moved through the air.

The cold air blew ceaselessly, chilling me, causing me to shiver. Closing my eyes, I thought of my love, calling to her with my mind, but I received no reply, no feeling that she was there.

"She's not here."

"You are sure?"

"I can't sense her here."

That was enough for Ghárda and onward we flew, once again toward the rainbow that signified the gateway to the other portals.

"We already know that she is not in the portal of Inquisition."

"That's where we came from, isn't it?"

"Yes," answered Ghárda. "They will be looking for you there. It is not safe for you to return there, at any rate."

We searched through the portals of Knowledge, Transition, and Desolation, with no success. It was incredibly discouraging and I was afraid that Calienta was in the portal that Ghárda wouldn't name—the scary one that contained all the evil. Or worse, what if we searched like this forever and I *never* found her?

"If she is not in the dimension of Contentment, I very much fear that I will not be able to take you any further."

"I know. I wouldn't expect you to." If Calienta wasn't in the dimension of Contentment, then I would go on alone to search for her. I'd never stop looking for her, no matter how long it took.

Once we entered the realm, however, my senses came alive again, every wrong made right, every fear destroyed. She was here.

"This is the one, this is the one. Please land, please land!"

Ghárda chuckled, beating his large wings as we slowly descended into a dense forest similar to the one Calienta and I'd first visited. Once we touched the ground, the large bird lowered its wing so I could climb down.

"It is all right, my friend, here we are." He laughed at my enthusiasm as I scrambled off of his plush feathered back and ran around to face my chauffeur.

When I looked up to thank him, he looked much older than when we'd first started our journey. His wings were wilted and part of his beak was missing. His feet were curled and aged, while his eyes had a world-weary look about them.

"Why do you look so old all of a sudden?" It was a very direct question but I felt we'd bonded.

"I am not the same age as I was when we first met. In this dimension I am much older." The bird stood there, completely unfazed by his current state. After a time he shook out his ratty feathers, which now appeared to have taken on the consistency of an old, filthy feather duster.

"Will you die?" My throat was rough. I didn't want anything to happen to this creature that had saved me. Where would I be without him? Most likely dead, or trying to survive in the desert. Certainly, I wouldn't be here, so far away from where the faeries had taken me.

"Probably not, although that idea is amusing." He laughed out loud and the warm chuckle filled his body and seemed to change his entire appearance. "No, I cannot die, but I am out of sorts. I do not belong in this dimension, you see, or in this time. The journey back should be intriguing."

"I hope it's a safe one."

"Goodbye, Kellen St. James." He turned and shot into the air.

In an instant my friend was gone, a single feather floating to the ground in his wake. I picked it up and pocketed it, feeling a sense of loss. I'd miss him. I let my

fingers explore the smooth texture of the feather inside my pocket and hoped that it would bring me luck.

With resolve, I turned away and headed toward the oppressing silence of the forest. To some it might have seemed like I had a plan, though in truth I had no idea where to begin.

CHAPTER FOURTEEN
CHASING CALIENTA

As I made my way forward, the tall trees closed in on me again from every side. *Ooh, who wants to go into the spooky forest now? Um, not me, that's for sure*. However, I sensed that Calienta was in there, so there was no other choice for me.

I'd only taken a few steps when a wave of depression attacked me once again. Several yards to my right, there was a fast-moving river that I'd have sworn wasn't there before.

Staggering toward it, I was overcome by my own cruel doubts. I'd never find her. I was doomed to roam this land alone forever.

Suddenly I found myself standing along the bank of the river, staring into its dark depths. I remembered not to get too close after my experience with the pond, however the running water was mesmerizing and I was lost in my own worries.

One of the quirks that I couldn't grow accustomed to in this strange place was the odd passage of time. Here time responded jerkily, like a sports car running on poor quality gasoline: For a moment, it would speed up, gain incredible mileage, only to pull back like a heap of scrap metal.

After an indistinguishable period of time, I became aware of the negativity that hung in the air. The morose power that the Soul Snatcher held over me was not real. Once I caught on, I was pretty ticked off.

"Stop it." I rose to my feet. I didn't see anything in front of me; no creature rose to the occasion, but it was there nonetheless.

"I command my own thoughts." Maybe it was the choice of words that I used or perhaps my own resistance, but an invisible fog lifted from my head. I was now seeing everything clearly once more. Before I could react to this, however, a shadowy form appeared before me.

What it was supposed to look like, I didn't know. However, ill intent rolled off of it in waves. I looked down to see if my appearance was at all changed, but I looked the same as when I'd started out on my journey, so this creature must not be a friend.

You cannot escape me, young mortal. The creature's voice echoed in my head, making the forest seem even eerier than before. *You have escaped me twice before, but you cannot escape me a third time.* And with that, a strong burst of wind took the creature away and with it any sense of calm that I had.

"Manuel, you are truly a powerful warlock to banish the Glacadóir Anam. I bow to you."

"What? Who?" Startled, I jumped and spun around to find Dagné, the Trooping Faerie, on her hands and knees. She was the last person that I expected to see. Abashed, I suddenly remembered the horrendous alter ego I'd given myself. As I glanced down, I noted that I'd reversed into my Trooping Faerie ensemble.

"No, please, you mustn't bow to me. I am no warlock. Please, Dagné, get up."

"He remembers my name." For a moment, I believed she felt honored, but I quickly caught on. She was making fun of me.

"How did you find me?"

"Oh, I followed you." There was something about her expression that put me on edge. I didn't feel as though I could trust her for a second.

"Dagné, what happened when I jumped out the window?"

"You entered a time portal. When you went through the window, you journeyed to another time and place."

"A time portal."

"The entire land knows about it. The Hounds are after–"

"Yes, I know." I didn't need a reminder that everyone hated me, wanted to kill me, or at the very least steal my soul.

"You are angry. What right do you have to anger when you have damaged the fabric of time? Who are you?"

Her eyes blazed a brilliant green. I noticed that she now wore a pink riding habit trimmed in white fur. A pink beret sat upon her head and her now red hair was tucked up inside it. Again, I was outmatched, despite this creature's stature; I'd need to distract her.

"The fabric of time?" That explained the ripping sound, but how did I manage to tear it? My fingers closed around the rough edges of the knife handle in my pocket. I had to cover myself.

"Who are you?" she repeated the question.

"I'm a traveler passing through. I'm far from my troop, but I told you that already."

"Regardless, you have torn the fabric of time and our world has been damaged."

"I'm sorry, I didn't realize. I was never taught properly. I don't even know how I did it." That wasn't entirely untrue. After all, I'd had no clue what I was doing at the time. I wasn't sure if she was buying it, but I needed her not to hurt me while I found a way out of this place.

She crossed her arms over her chest. She wasn't buying it.

I again tried to divert her. "What happened when I tore the fabric?"

"When you jumped, you separated yourself from the time we were in. You have moved into the light of the future."

"How do I get back?"

"That is your quest, great Manuel, not mine. However, with your powers you will find a way." The sarcasm in her voice wasn't a good sign.

I didn't have any powers but I'd been able to find this realm by trying to sense Calienta. I'd need to do the same again if I was ever going to find her. The only sound was the wind in the trees.

All of a sudden, the forest seemed to come alive. The rustling of the leaves overtook my senses, while a million different scents assaulted me. Closing my eyes, I inhaled. Pine, moss, mushroom, heather, lavender…Calienta. I smelled her scent before I heard her voice. *Sugar cookies*.

"Kellen, where are you?" The voice was faint.

My eyes shot open and I turned again to Dagné. "Why are you away from your troop?"

"I have not left my troop." She said this sweetly but my sense of unease increased. They were tracking me.

From somewhere behind me, there was a rumbling sound again and I could only surmise that either Dagné's troop or the Hounds of Hell had located my whereabouts. Regardless, they were coming for me and I couldn't hang out here any longer.

Looking around, I found that I was in a small clearing. To my right, there was a young birch tree that came to my shoulders. I took note of its location and height. I didn't know if Dagné had told me the truth and I'd really traveled through time, but if I could… Well what did I have to lose? Maybe I could cut into the fabric of time again and travel to this same spot in another time?

Unsheathing the knife in my pocket, I held it up in front of me. Trying not to think too deeply about what I was about to do, I drew back my arm and stabbed the air, pulling the knife downward. The scene in front of me took on the consistency of canvas again and tore easily.

Taking my time, I began to cut a slim opening about my height.

My theory was simple: If I jumped across instead of falling vertically, I should remain in the same place but reappear at a different time.

Without a backward glance at Dagné, I looked into the opening in front of me. This time instead of free-falling, I'd lunge forward. Giving myself a running start, I launched myself through the opening.

Focusing all of my energy on jumping across a divide worked, and I landed on an invisible ledge. Choosing not to look down, I reached out again and cut into the air. I stepped out into the exact same glen that I'd left.

Pleased that I'd guessed correctly, I looked to my right for additional confirmation. The small birch appeared several inches below my shoulder height. Did trees grow the same in Faerie? I didn't know for sure, but this was the only comparison point I had.

As I looked around, I noticed that it was early winter. The ground was dead; the trees were bare. Closing my eyes, I tried to sense Calienta. She seemed stronger here, but not strong enough.

"Calienta?"

"Kellen?"

My efforts were validated when her voice echoed within the space. It did sound closer though it was still muffled, like it was coming through an old speaker system. Not quite there, I guessed. Without hesitation, I reached out and performed the same cutting motion again with the knife.

Yet again I jumped and was propelled across the black divide. Once more I landed on a slim ledge where I again used my knife to cut into the air, slicing the fabric of time.

"Please let me find her." When I stepped into the clearing again, it was fall. Leaves were coming down around me everywhere. There was a crisp quality to the air that told me winter was on its way. I could practically smell the snow. When I looked for the birch tree, it appeared even shorter. Still a young sapling, it showed nothing of the magnificent foliage that it would grow in the future.

Again I closed my eyes, willing my senses to find Calienta. As I'd experienced before, I heard her voice, but now it was no longer muffled. Now it was clear. I'd found the right time at last.

Before I could begin my search, there was the most wonderful sound in the world, one that I couldn't have conjured up in my dreams if I'd tried. Up ahead was the sound of a raging waterfall. Suddenly conscious of my own overwhelming thirst, I stumbled through the dense undergrowth, searching for the water. Finally, I found it.

It was a glorious place. Water fell from three hundred feet up into a small round pool below. Then it went…nowhere. There was no river, no outlet, nothing. The water fell into a circular pool and it looked mouth-watering. I couldn't remember the last time I'd eaten or drank anything, so I raced to the pool's edge. I'd scooped my first drink into my palms when there was a ferocious barking and snarling. The growling and howling grew louder as thunderous footsteps approached with ever-increasing speed.

Despite the bad luck that I'd had before with water, I had no choice. Jumping into the pool of water was my only option if I wanted to live, so I took the plunge, sinking a couple of feet below the surface. The water was ice cold and I was soon soaked to the skin and shaking.

Swimming to the top, I broke the surface, not knowing what to expect. The hounds were tearing down the path straight toward me. They were spectral-looking, semi-transparent in nature, with gleaming red eyes that glowed in the filtered light. Each was the size of a grizzly bear, and they dominated the space around them. They made huffing sounds as they ran, which made them sound more like a herd of caribou than anything else.

I took a deep breath and went back under the water. As I looked around below the surface, I realized that what I'd initially mistaken for a shallow pond was about one hundred feet deep.

Following my instincts, I decided to swim deep below the surface. The hounds couldn't be trusted and I feared that they'd either smell or sense me. Down into the depths I started to swim, praying that I didn't run into anything worse.

When the animals appeared at the surface and began drinking the cold water, my heart started to slam against my ribcage. It was over now, that was certain. But looking down at my hands, I saw that Brigid's protection had morphed me into some sort of water plant. It was a very odd sensation to look down at your hands and see leaves instead, but I wasn't complaining; at least I was safe.

Safe or not, however, this facade was merely an illusion and my lungs burned as I hungered for air. My chest might explode at any moment, a match waiting for ignition. Turning in circles, I looked for a way out, but the pressure from the waterfall was so intense that it was next to impossible to see behind it, to identify an escape route.

The great beasts lapped greedily at the water and I prayed that they'd finish soon. The black around me began to turn blacker and I was on the verge of passing out. The heads suddenly disappeared from the surface. The beasts had gone.

Barely hanging on, I allowed myself to float to the top, permitting my face to break the surface so that I could take short, uneven breaths. Several moments passed while I caught my breath before I peered over the edge of the bank.

From my hiding place, I saw the animals return to the path and reassemble their pack. A cloaked figure dismounted from a black horse and walked forward to another transparent barrier I hadn't realized was there. Cocking my head to one side, I listened for the password that I knew I would need to pass through to the other side. The animals, refreshed from the water, wanted to run and they whined impatiently as they waited for their leader.

"Alaunos," the cloaked figure whispered and hopped onto his mount again so fast that I couldn't believe my eyes. Both he and the ghostly animals vanished through the opening.

For a moment I remained in the water, feeling fairly freaked out. Yet it was too cold to stay in the pond, so I scampered out and did my best to dry off by dancing around and wringing out my clothes. This really did no good at all, but it would have to do.

My thoughts returned to Calienta. If I listened closely, I could almost hear her calling my name. Tentatively I took a few steps, first to the left, then the right, trying to gauge her direction. The closer I got to the barrier where the hounds had gone the clearer she sounded. It was no use. I was going in.

With only a small amount of hesitation, I walked up to the glass barrier and whispered the word that the cloaked figure had spoken. "Alaunos."

The glass rippled and I passed through. When I reached the other side of the glass, there were Christmas trees. Not two or three, but hundreds upon hundreds of brightly lit decorated trees.

Falling from the sky in slow motion, like large tufts of cotton, were the largest snowflakes I'd ever seen. They were so large in proportion that they reminded me of the department store decorations that magically appeared back home immediately after every Halloween.

Unsure of what to expect, I put my arm up in front of me to protect myself, but the flakes melted against my clothes. These simple snowflakes weren't a danger to me. They didn't seem to have any effect on my clothing as I glanced down, examining myself.

What was strange, though, was that as damp areas appeared on the worn material they immediately dried again, failing to chill me. It was every child's dream, a snowy day that never had to end because you got too cold. Oddly, that seemed to be the case as I didn't feel cold at all. Instead, it seemed as though it was sixty degrees outside and I was taking a pleasant stroll, alone, through an underground world where dogs were chasing me while I passed through time portals.

Glancing down at my shoes, I stopped walking. "Wait a minute. I look like *myself*." Sure enough, I had on my worn jeans again. The faerie costumes had gone on hiatus, it seemed. This must've been a safe place for me.

I didn't know to whom I was talking, but I found that I was so unnerved by my appearance that even the sound of my own voice was comforting. The only reason that I would have changed into myself was if I was safe or possibly dead—the latter being a concept that I didn't want to explore. Yet I couldn't imagine being safe in Faerie; there was danger at every turn.

"I must be dead."

"You're not dead, my son." The voice was oddly familiar.

"Who's there?" I whipped my head around and started looking behind each tree, beneath every branch. Yet there was no one. It was too quiet as I searched for the source of the voice that I felt certain I recognized.

"I'm here, my darling."

This second pronouncement caused me to fall backward onto the snow-covered ground. I would have known that voice anywhere. "Mother?"

I stayed on my backside in the snow, gaining my bearings as I looked around again and prepared to get to my feet. Then I could do nothing. I couldn't stand, I couldn't even speak, rooted to the spot as I was. Pain punched me in the gut like a prize fighter.

My mother walked toward me and it was as though not a single day had passed. Her dark hair fell past her shoulders in shiny waves like the night sky. Yet if her hair was the night, her skin, the sheer paleness of it, was the moon. Fair to almost translucent, her skin seemed to shimmer, and her green eyes, exactly the same shade as my own, were smiling, laughing.

What an idiot I was. This was a trap, a total set-up. I should have known better than to believe anything in this place.

"Who're you? I'm sick of being your toy. You people have dragged me through all types of crap. How low would you stoop?" My voice cracked on this last sentence. I couldn't bear this. Showing me my mother was too cruel; it was torture.

"This isn't a trick, my son. I'm here. You've found me at last."

"I don't believe you." I crossed my arms in front of me, a petulant child.

"Look to your heart, Kellen. Ask yourself if you truly believe it is me. Would you look like yourself if it wasn't?"

"How do you know about that? How do you know about anything?"

"I know because I'm on your side. I'm here to help you."

"That's exactly the type of thing that you'd say if you were my enemy, too. I'm sorry, but my mother is dead." It pained me to say the words. It cut me to the core, but it was true. There was no way that this woman could be my mother.

"You're exhausted. When was the last time you slept?" There was reproach in her tone, and I was reminded of the time when I'd climbed the oak tree in our back yard. I'd almost made it to the first branch when I fell, skinning my knee in the process. She scolded me, but there was a twinkle in her eye then as well. Stephen cut down the tree the day after my mother died.

"That tree was always way too tall for you. You could have broken an arm or leg. How could we have played then?"

Horror washed over me as I realized that this woman could read my mind. "Get out of my head. Who are you?"

"I'm your mother, Kellen."

"Prove it then. I've been messed with way too much in this place."

She seemed to think for a moment before closing her eyes and singing. I'd known somehow that she'd sing this song, that this would be the first to pass her lips. "Come walk with me along the sea, and search for shells in the sand and see…"

There were goose bumps on my skin and a heavy anxiousness at the pit of my stomach. There was no way it could be her, but how could the faeries know about our song? Could this be real?

"How can you be her?" The last traces of my reserve were fading. I wanted to believe what I was seeing and was only kidding myself if I acted like I thought otherwise.

"You're right, Kellen. I'm dead in a sense. But in Ireland, many believe that when you die you go to the faeries. That's where I am now. We are in the realm of Contentment, but I call it Heaven."

And as though she'd been there all along, Gran stepped out from behind a tree and clasped my mother's hand. She looked exactly the same as I remembered. I couldn't be mistaken about this, could I? I had to take a chance and trust them. I needed this too much. I *needed* to believe in something.

"Mother?"

She opened her arms wide and I stepped into them, letting her hold me close to her thin frame as she did when I was small. Tears streamed uncontrollably from my eyes as I stood there and let myself be held in a way that I hadn't been in more time than I could remember. However I was still seventeen, and I found myself pulling away much sooner than I would have liked. But she pulled me closer, hugging me as though I were her life force.

"Sshhhh." She held me close, rubbing my back the way I remembered from my childhood. Gran squeezed my shoulder, and I touched my hand to hers as I inhaled my mother's sweet fragrance.

How long I sat there being comforted by my mother and grandmother, I'll never know. But there in the snow, I shed silent tears for every moment of pain and loneliness; every micro-second away from her was relived before it could end. And then, as quickly as it all began, it stopped.

Somehow this was what I needed. I needed to say goodbye to them, to let them know how much I cared for them. "I'm sorry we never got to say goodbye." I wasn't sure which pair of eyes I should look into first.

"So am I, Kellen," said my mother. "I'm sorry you had to find out about pain and betrayal so soon. I wanted to come and find you, but I couldn't. I've missed you so much."

"It's okay." I wanted to put her at ease.

"No, it's not. None of this is okay. What I wouldn't give to go back in time, to leave your father and take you and Roger with me."

"But you could come with me. This girl— Gran, it's the girl I told you about, remember? Calienta. I'm trying to find her." And suddenly it all came back to me: what I was trying to do, Calienta, the prophecy.

"We know, Kellen. We've always known," said Gran.

"You know about her? Do you know what I'm supposed to do?" Both Gran and my mother nodded their heads almost in unison.

"Lugh came to me when you were six," Gran explained. "He told me about the prophecies and he asked me to have you come and live with me. He didn't know that I'd been trying to get custody from your father. Naturally, he wouldn't let me have you. The best I could do was to get you to that boarding school in England so Alistair could check in on you.

"Yet I didn't know about your mother. Both Alistair and I hoped that there was somehow a mistake, that you wouldn't be needed. When I saw your mother for the final time and I learned the story, it was clear that there would be no other path for you."

"Kellen, listen to me," my mother pleaded. "The hounds know where you are and they're waiting for you. We've come to warn you and protect you for a little while, but they're hoping that you'll lead them straight to Calienta."

"How do they even know where to find me? I keep changing my appearance, not at will I might add, and I've been on the move since I got here. How could they possibly have found me?"

"You've angered many a creature in this land by disrupting the flow of time," Gran cautioned me.

"I didn't even know I was moving through time. The first time was an accident, but I learned that it was the only way to get back to where I needed to be."

"It was an easy mistake to make. You've been lost for over four years, looking for your love. You were desperate." My mother's eyes were compassionate.

"Four years?" I stared at my mother as the enormity of her words sunk in. Four years. I'd been gone for *four years?* I was never going to find Calienta now. How could I? Yet I wanted my mother to reassure me, to tell me that everything would be all right.

"I'll never find her, will I?" I stared at the ground, tears pricking the backs of my eyes. I'd no idea how to solve this and not a clue as to how to find Calienta.

I stared into my mother's eyes. "The funny thing is that they don't really need me. I have no special powers at all. There isn't anything remarkable about me." I smiled then, looking at my Gran, who was shaking her head.

"That's where you're wrong, Kellen. You can do anything that you set your heart to and you will." Her eyes bore into mine.

"But how can I save her when I don't even know where she is?"

My mother smiled. "That's precisely why we're here. The Hounds of Hell are unable to stand the realm of Contentment. There is too much happiness, too much love here. However, they will come looking for you anyway."

"We're going to slip out the back door?"

"Something like that," said Gran.

"Take my hand," my mother said, reaching for my fingers.

"Wait. You won't be coming with me, will you?" I already knew the answer.

"I can't go with you, my son, but you must know that I love you with everything that's in me."

"Will I ever see you again?"

My mother smiled and hugged me before stepping back to let Gran hug me as well. "In dreams, my son, you'll see us in your dreams."

With my grandmother and my mother gripping my hands firmly on either side, the scene before me disappeared and I found myself hurtling through the air toward a feather-light rainbow suspended under the husky glow of a setting sun. It was probably one of the best moments of my life.

CHAPTER FIFTEEN
FOUR YEARS

When I finally landed, surprisingly unscathed, I looked around in wonder. If I didn't know better, I'd have guessed that I'd arrived at a farm somewhere in the midwestern United States. The climate had changed to that of late autumn. The placed looked so American, so normal to me that I was instantly at home.

"What's this place?"

"It is a safe place. You'll find friends here, I think." My mother gently touched my cheek.

"You have to go." It was a statement, not a question. My mother, who'd seemed so real, so solid before, now appeared more transparent. It was only a matter of time before they left me. Both she and Gran nodded, almost in unison.

My arms went around the pair of them and I hugged them both, trying to savor the feel of them. I wanted to commit these few seconds to my memory so that I'd never lose them. Not a hard feat for me, but one I paid special attention to anyway. "I love you, Mom."

"I love you too, Kellen." Her voice was wistful as she slowly faded before my eyes.

It was almost harder to say goodbye to Gran than it was to my mother. My mother had been gone so long that I'd long ago learned to live without her. Gran, on the other hand, had only just left my world. I hadn't had a chance to really deal with her death yet, so it was still too raw, too painful.

"Kellen, I want you to do something for me," Gran said.

"Anything."

"You need to trust Calienta. Stop letting your head do the leading all the time. Start letting your heart take the reins more. Calienta is who she claims, so you need to trust her." The intensity in her words startled me.

"I do trust her. She was always meant for me, but I think you knew that all along."

"Your old Gran does know a few things after all, see?"

"I guess so." I was teasing her.

"I also know that you don't trust easily. You're young, but you've never truly been your age. You've an old soul. Now be off with you. She's waiting for you in that house at the end of the lane. Go to her." And both Gran and Mom were gone. I was alone again.

Turning to look in front of me, I found myself at the end of a long gravel drive, fields of green surrounding it on either side. The land, this place, took my breath away with its beauty. There was a red barn, which stood out against the ripe, rich green of the surrounding farmland. To my right, a generous farmhouse in shades of white and gray sat welcomingly.

Someone had grown a small garden in the front of the home that practically spilled over with brightly colored flowers. Giant trees dotted the landscape, ancient protectors, keeping the place safe. Near an orchard at the top of the hill, a small herd of miniature goats ran freely, chasing one another across the field.

There was a sense of *home* here that I could feel down to my bones. It was everything that I'd ever thought a home could be as a child. Unlike the cold stone mansion of my youth, this place was the epitome of the word "home". It was simply breathtaking. Though it was late summer, it wasn't so hot as to make things unbearable, but rather the perfect temperature.

This place encouraged the visitor to stop and to rest forever. This, I thought, was probably one of the reasons that mortals were so drawn to the faeries, and many spent lifetimes trying to breach this world. For those who made the journey, it was probably one of the reasons that they never returned above ground.

But what was even more compelling to me in that moment was the lone figure that awaited me at the end of the lane. Her dark hair blew in the warm summer breeze. She looked as wonderful as I remembered, but even more so because I'd been searching for her for so very long.

I don't know when I started running, maybe it was in the first moment that I glimpsed her, but run I did. Nothing could stop me, not even the odd feeling of running through cobwebs that I experienced as I charged down the lane. I needed to get to her, and suddenly our separation seemed like it had lasted for hundreds of years. I couldn't get to her fast enough.

My arms were around her and I started hugging her, never wanting to let her go. The urge to kiss her was so great, so intense that it seemed as though there could be nothing in the world that I wanted more than her lips upon my own. At first, I hesitated because our relationship was new and I wasn't sure if she wanted what I did.

Then I didn't care. My mouth found hers anyway. I'd never kissed anyone this way. In that moment she was the only thing keeping me going in my life, my only source of warmth, of light, of love. She welcomed my kiss, my touch, with the same warmth that I felt. *She's mine*, I thought greedily.

"I'll never let you go again." I made this promise as I kissed her eyelids, her lips, and her cheekbones.

"I know."

"I didn't know how to find you." Tears unwillingly pricked the backs of my eyes.

"I know."

"I didn't think I would ever find you again. I thought you were lost."

Innumerable moments passed as we stood there entangled in one another's arms, heat pulsing through our veins. Prophecy or not, this was the woman I'd waited for all my life. I wouldn't be apart from her again.

"Hhmmmp!" There was a grunting noise behind us, causing us to jump apart.

A little man stood behind us, beaming from ear to ear as he rocked back and forth on the balls of his feet. I glanced at my clothes and took a peripheral glance at my hair to confirm that I hadn't morphed into anything else. I glanced at Calienta, but she seemed relaxed and her emotions seemed calm, so I sensed that we were safe.

The man was quite petite in stature, roughly three feet tall. He was dressed in a kilt, an off-white fisherman's sweater, and a tasseled fuchsia-colored beret. From the angle at which he was leaning against a nearby fence it appeared that his black shoes had spikes on the bottoms.

"Welcome to my farmland, child." He burst into a series of giggles. In fact, the joviality emanating from him was almost tangible. I couldn't help but smile back.

"I am Dillion. I am a member of Calienta's family. This farm belongs to me. I call it Dei. You are a welcome guest in my home." He smiled again.

"Dillion, I'd like to introduce Kellen St. James." Calienta gestured to me.

The color drained from Dillion's face. Almost immediately, he dropped to his knees. "It is an honor to meet you, your majesty." He bowed his head repeatedly until I intervened.

"That's okay, I'm not a king yet," I reminded him, holding out both hands in front of me. "It's nice to meet you." I extended my hand. Dillion looked at it but didn't accept it, instead turning to Calienta as he slowly climbed to his feet.

"You never told me that it was he you were looking for. Why did you fail to disclose this information?"

Calienta seemed to consider this momentarily. "Because I did not know at first if I could trust you, and I'd not endanger his life."

Dillion nodded, his brightly colored beret bobbing awkwardly on top of his head with each nod. "I suppose that I would have done the same in your position."

Calienta let go of me and walked over to Dillion, placing her arms on his shoulders, gripping him urgently. "Uncle, the time that was foretold is upon us. Kellen is the one who will save us, I am sure of it."

"This is really the one that prophecy decreed?"

"Yes, it is he."

Dillion gave me a quick once-over. "He does not seem very powerful."

"Hey, what happened to all of that 'your majesty' business?" I was offended on my own behalf.

Dillion, ignoring me, pivoted on the spot and started walking down the lane. We followed him. "You are not a king yet!" he cried.

As we started walking, I held Calienta back to give us some distance between our host and ourselves. Wrapping my arm around her waist, I leaned toward her ear and whispered, "How can he be safe? I thought all of Lugh's relatives were bad news. I'm sure you know what you're doing, but I'm still concerned."

Calienta shook her head in response. "Most of them are, but not all."

Dillion stopped his procession to turn back and look at us. "I do not expect you to know the difference, so I do not take offense to your questioning my hospitality. You are a mortal after all. There is much that you cannot see in this world or your own."

He addressed me as a small child or at least a slow and dim-witted adult. I tried not to take offense at his patronizing approach and instead simply nodded. Better to blend in with the locals.

"Dillion," Calienta said, "I think you'll find Kellen far more intelligent than most mortals that you've encountered." There was laughter in her voice.

The man looked at me and shook his head before continuing on. Apparently, he was not in agreement.

She raised her voice to get his attention again. "Now that Kellen is with me again, he'll be in need of rest, food, and some information. Can you provide those to us?"

He stopped and looked at her before responding sarcastically, "Of course. Follow me. Nothing but the finest here." Almost immediately, he began sprinting down the path.

When he reached the end of the drive, Dillion turned back and looked at us. "What are you waiting for, Manuel?" He looked pointedly at me before giving me a wink and a smile.

"Manuel?" Calienta said questioningly, her lips curving into the slightest of smiles.

"You don't want to know." And, taking her hand in mine, we walked down the lane to the farmhouse with its curious garden. I wondered silently if we'd ever leave this place. I realized that I didn't want to, but I kept that information to myself.

Dillion's home was as welcoming on the inside as it was on the outside. There was a small entryway with faded floral wallpaper and a distressed bench of aged oak. The carpeting was worn but still cushioned my feet as we entered. The whole place looked oddly mortal to me.

In the small sitting room, the walls were covered in rich mahogany, with built-in bookshelves that were simply crammed with books. I was immediately drawn to those and I realized that for the first time in my life I couldn't remember the last time I'd read a book.

Calienta had that effect on me. When I was with her, I forgot about the things that were part of my normal routine. Being with her was so all-consuming that it was hard to think of anything else. This should concern me, but it didn't. Right now, nothing mattered but her and the prophecy.

Continuing my perusal of the room, I noticed that trinkets of all shapes and sizes littered the side tables. An additional set of shelving contained books that hinted at an interest in exotic travels. Curious, I looked at the spines, expecting to see titles like "Your Journey to the Foremost Nether Regions". Instead, there were titles such as "San Francisco on a Budget" and "Exploring Canadian Wine Country". Just like Dillion himself, his house was surprising me.

Two leather chairs and a settee dominated the room, inviting anyone to come and rest by the fireside. As tempted as I was to immediately accept this strange one's hospitality, I had one burning question that I needed answered.

I looked directly into Dillion's blue eyes as I spoke. "I need to know how close we are to the Ellipse." There was shock and surprise his eyes when I finished my question.

The little man started to shake and ran to hide behind a small sitting chair. Only the tip of his beret peeping over the top gave away his location. "You must not go there. You will never survive. They will destroy you."

He was afraid, I got it, but we needed information. "Look, I know it's going to suck, let's face it, but it's the only chance that we have, Dillion."

He peeked over the chair and looked me in the eye, his piercing blue ones meeting my own.

"Her father could be dead right now," I continued. "We can't let Cabhan win. This is her father here. Your family."

"I know we are talking about my family." The little man ran around from behind the chair. He pointed a plump finger at me. "I have been trapped down here for years with no one. But do you think I would see her die so easily? You are not the only one who loves her."

Shame flooded me as I realized that I'd never considered what such a thing would mean to Dillion.

"You do not know what you are up against. You have no hope of winning," Dillion said earnestly.

"Look, I'm sorry. This must be done, though. It's our only hope."

"Thank you." Dillion acknowledged my apology. "I know that you are right. Of course it must be done. That does not mean that I like it."

He went to sit down in one of the chairs by the fire, defeat evident in his features. Calienta and I followed him, taking seats across from him.

"You are trying to get to the Ellipse? I do not know if there is much point in that now." The little man seemed sad.

"I saw my mother," I said, turning to look fully at Calienta.

"Your mother?" She didn't speak again after I nodded my confirmation. Instead, she simply took my hand in hers and squeezed. As I looked into her eyes, no words were necessary. She understood what this had meant to me.

Eventually I let my gaze drift back to Dillion's. "My mother told me that I have been traveling for four years. It's too late now, isn't it?"

Dillion looked at his shoes.

"Dillion, please answer me," I implored.

As he looked up a shadow passed over his face and my suspicions were correct; we were too late and we were trapped here. Too much time had passed and he was telling us we were too late.

He spoke after some hesitation. "The Ellipse is not much farther, but you will not be able to get to it. We have tried. It is beyond the Upside-Down Ocean and that in itself is littered with the Sluagh."

Calienta gasped, obviously showing a concern that, in my own ignorance, I didn't have.

"Who or what's the Sluagh?"

Calienta hesitated. With a chill, I realized that this must be the part where I could die—although I believed that there'd been quite enough opportunity for that already.

Finally, after being silent for so long, Calienta spoke up. "The Sluagh is the name given to the collection of hosts of the unforgiven dead ancestors of the Celts. It has long been known that Arawn claimed him for his army."

"Yes, and the hounds will be there as well, along with, I am sure, many others waiting for you." A tear graced the little man's plump cheek.

"Dillion, we have to get through somehow. There must be a way. Arawn and Cabhan have her father. We've no choice."

"No, you simply cannot go. I will not allow it." Dillion crossed his arms in front of him.

"Is this a trick then? Why won't you tell us how to get there? Are you trying to keep us from leaving? I've been told that faeries trick humans into staying down here. The jig's up, old man." Standing up for emphasis, I found myself about a foot tall and wearing a pink tutu. Admittedly not my best look. I glared at him.

"I am sorry about that, lad, but you seem to have an anger management problem." Dillion giggled at his own humor.

Instantly I was myself again and blushing beet red.

"He's not trying to keep us here. He's trying to avoid telling us that it's too late, that my father is already dead." Calienta's last words radiated with such agony, I found that I could barely look at her.

Instead, I reached out and took her hand in mine, finding it cold. Her hands were never cold; she was always warm, like she'd been sitting by the fireside. Did this mean that there was no hope for us?

In the silence, Dillion and Calienta maintained eye contact, staring one another down fiercely in the cozy sitting room. Dillion restored me to my previous state, sans tutu. "Aye. Cabhan and Arawn have destroyed your father."

Lugh was a stranger to me, yet I couldn't imagine the world without him. Without a word, I pulled Calienta into my arms. She didn't cry, as I thought she would. We stood that way for a few moments.

Absentmindedly, I glanced in a mirror that hung on the wall to my right and looked at myself for the first time in…years, taken aback by my gaunt frame and haggard appearance. This was far from what I'd expected. My clothes were dirty and torn, my hair long and past my shoulders in a hornet's nest of black. I'd never noticed that it had grown.

My eyes gleamed with a spark of wildness. Part of my shirt was torn, and I could see my ribs pushing against my pale skin. I stared at myself for a moment before turning back to face Dillion.

"This is some sort of mistake. If I've been here for four years, how have I been able to survive without eating hardly anything?"

"Things do not work the same way here in Faerie. Surely you have realized that by now? You have really only been in our world for a few months, but time passes differently here. It has been four years in your world, not ours." Dillion seemed almost embarrassed by my lack of knowledge.

Four years, I thought, amazed, wondering what had happened back home. How was the house? What had happened to Gabe? Suddenly I was flooded with homesickness. Even though I didn't have too many people in my mortal life, it was still my life.

"What's been happening?" Calienta finally asked him.

"How about I let you see for yourself? I do not know that I can do the situation justice." Dillion turned to a small table on his right and grabbed a remote control. With the push of a button, a small screen on the wall came to life.

"You have a plasma TV?"

"I am not living in a cave after all. I use the Internet, too."

I was starting to wonder where the FedEx packages were sent, when the first image came up on the screen. We were looking at Gran's village, but a run-down dirty version of the original. Each building was covered in soot. The beautiful flowerbeds that complemented the tiny yards in front of each of the houses were torn up. Only bare soil remained. When I'd walked through town on my last visit, all of the windows were open and many of the townspeople sat on their porches, waving as I walked past. Now everything was locked up tight, with each house appearing more unwelcoming than the next.

At first I didn't see them, but then my attention was drawn to the two people walking along the street. They were dressed in gray, as gray as the village itself, with sour expressions pasted on their faces as they trudged along. One of them, a woman, looked around nervously, as though she expected to see something. Taking a right, they turned onto the walkway that led to the most depressing of the cottages. Two flower boxes had broken and hung askew at both of the front windows, giving the house a lopsided appearance.

The pair had made it to the entrance of the small cottage when a man came bursting out of the house across the street. He was balding and heavy-set, with stains on the front of his olive-colored cardigan. With each step he seemed more off balance, which was concerning since he carried a rifle in his hand.

He shouted something at the couple, but when the pair started to speak, he raised the rifle and fired two rounds, taking them both down. The couple collapsed to the ground. It wasn't clear what the argument was about, but it was made more horrific when the gunman then turned the gun on himself and ended his own life. The last scene depicted three pairs of dead eyes.

In an instant, we were immediately watching a full-scale battle in a different location, though I couldn't name it. Tanks charged down the street while fighter planes dove through the air. My mind immediately came to the conclusion that we were watching a movie or even a video game, because by now I recognized Times Square in New York City. The lighted billboards and TV screens were destroyed as a bomb dropped from the sky, showers of sparks raining down on the streets below. The camera panned over a destroyed city. Historical landmarks were reduced to ash. Rubble flew everywhere as the few people that were on the streets ran for cover.

Then in an instant, we were in the street with a young soldier who'd taken a hit and was unable to stand and make his escape. A section of building was leaning precariously in his direction and he was sweating profusely as he looked around frantically for help.

Spying another soldier running in the opposite direction, he called out, "Help me. Help me, man."

The soldier stopped and looked at the wounded man on the ground. With a look of purest loathing he walked away without a backward glance.

The show continued with many similar scenes, each more depressing than the next. As I looked for some sort of pattern, some sort of rhyme or reason, I only noticed that the sun was missing, which I suppose was the most telling piece of evidence that there was.

Dillion must have read my mind. "This is what the world looks like these days. When Lugh was killed, the sun was covered in clouds. People need the sun. They gain strength and energy from its light.

"The unsettling darkness that you have seen in every image is a constant. There is never any light. To make matters worse, Arawn has infused them with a general sense of anxiety. Everyone is afraid to talk to everyone else. Most people will not trust, let alone help their neighbor. It has destroyed any sense of goodwill and has been the cause of several wars."

"We can do nothing to stop this, then?" My heart ached for Calienta. She met my gaze and held it. There was uncertainty there that told me that she could not answer my question. Gulping, I realized that I would need to take the lead. "Surely there's another way?" I looked to Dillion.

"There is. I've been told of a way to turn back the clock, but it is very dangerous. It is possible to do the world more harm than good, you know."

"What could be worse than what you've shown us? People killing each other, homes destroyed, war, narcissism, apathy…"

"Very little, I imagine," Dillion agreed.

"We've come this far, Uncle. We must try, whatever it is." Calienta's voice was pleading.

After a long pause, Dillion nodded his head. I could tell that we'd finally convinced him. "First, we need to feed your young man here." He inclined his head in my direction.

Starving, I longed for food, but we were getting somewhere and I didn't want to stop and eat. "Food isn't important."

"Kellen. Kellen." Calienta was shouting my name and I felt her warm hands against my face as I blacked out.

***

When I came to, I finally realized how hungry I was and how long I'd gone without actually eating anything other than candy. I also smelled. Bad.

"Do you have a shower?"

"Glad you asked," said Dillion, his merry eyes twinkling. I guess it was no secret how bad I reeked.

"Thank you."

Following him, we walked into a very modern-looking bathroom.

"There are some towels by the sink for you. I'll work on getting you something to eat."

"Thanks, Dillion."

"Sure, lad."

With Dillion gone, I looked around as I undressed. The floor was a dark-blue slate, which appeared weathered but at the same time maintained a quality of newness. In one corner there was a walk-in shower and in another area a small sink. It was amazing to see such modern amenities in this place. Flat screens, the Internet, now a walk-in shower. It was more updated than Gran's house.

The warmth of the hot spray was incredible. It had been such a long time since I'd experienced anything so wonderful. There was an elephant-sized showerhead with several dials on it to adjust the pressure. How bizarre. The shower itself resembled a home remodeling showroom. I moved the knob to the most intense massage level and let the water beat down on my sore muscles. When my back started throbbing, it was time to get out and find food and a nap.

After I'd cleaned up, I wandered out into a large bedroom that I hadn't noticed before. On a table next to the bed there were several covered dishes and a tankard of something thick and creamy. Practically drooling, I started looking through each of the offerings. A large roast turkey surrounded by bowls of mashed potatoes, endless gravy, and macaroni and cheese were a few of the comfort foods within reach.

Grabbing a fork, I didn't bother to scoop anything onto the empty plate that sat at the table. Instead I picked up each serving dish individually, eating a little here and there. The table across the room went ignored and I chewed standing up. I remembered the warnings that Gran had given me about not eating food from faeries, but I was too hungry. I had to trust Dillion; I'd starve if I didn't.

I ate until I could eat no more and then crawled into the massive bed, exhausted beyond belief. Intending to close my eyes for only a few seconds, my eyelids soon shut and wouldn't open, and I slowly fell asleep.

***

The dream seemed to begin at once and I found myself on a grassy plain. I'd never dreamed of such a place before and I looked around, trying to figure out where I was. At the other end of the field there stood a young man. Cabhan. In his hand was a sword, which he waved in front of himself, taking a few practice swings as he approached.

When he got close enough he spoke up. "Your journey will prove futile, Kellen. You can't save my father and you can't protect my sister. There is nothing that you can do to beat me."

Then I remembered what I held in my hand. I glanced down to see a sword resting against my palm. Raising it in front of me, I stared at it closely. It was light, easily wielded, which was unexpected for its size.

Looking back at my nemesis, I spoke: "It's not up to you to decide the outcome, Cabhan. There's more at stake here than the two of us." My voice sounded almost bored, my calm exterior seeming to come from someone else.

"You speak of the prophecy."

"Among other things." I looked at the sword again once more before I woke up.

***

When I looked out the window, it was dark outside; I had no idea how long I'd been asleep. Then I remembered what Dillion had told me and it hit me that I was spending my time eating and sleeping when Calienta's family needed my help. Launching myself out of the bed, I looked around, panicked.

"Ssshhh." Calienta got up from a nearby chair and came over to me, taking my hand in her own. She curled her fingers around the hair at the base of my neck and gently squeezed my fingers, filling me with warmth.

The physical response that I had to her was intense, but I tried to be cool about it. Slowly, I placed my hands on either side of her face and drew her lips to mine. I was hot, practically sweating all of a sudden, and overcome with an intense desire to get as close to her as possible.

Don't get me wrong, this had been with us all along, through years of searching, but there hadn't been a sense of urgency then. Now that we'd lost, our closeness was a reprieve and escape from the pain and disappointment.

"Calienta." I sat down on the bed and pulled her onto my lap, kissing her roughly, fisting a hand in her hair. No longer was this a young love; ours was one of desperation and I clung to her, wanting nothing but her forever.

"I love you. I want to marry you, even if it's too late. We can figure out what to do about it together." Wow, I'd done it. I'd proposed. True, I didn't have a ring and I wasn't exactly sure of what I was proposing, but there we were. I was scared, but this was so right, a joke that everyone got but me and I'd only now caught on.

Which was probably why my worst fears came true when Calienta started screaming and sobbing at the same time. “Dillion. Dillion! What did you do to him?”

Dillion came bustling into the room, clearly out of breath. His chest heaved as he made his way over to Calienta.

She jumped up and pointed a finger at the little man. “Did you kill him?”

Dillion waved his arms in front of him in protest. “No, of course not. It is a spell.” He continued to take large breaths, catching up from his sprint into the bedroom.

“He looks pretty transparent to me.” Calienta was furious and I was enjoying it. Hey, I was a guy after all. Then I caught a glimpse of myself in the mirror.

“Things really keep getting worse for me, don’t they?” I looked down at the floor and realized that I was hovering above my own body. “What’s with your family changing me into different forms? That is an abuse of power.”

Dillion stared Calienta down, ignoring my words. “And you want to get him through the Upside-Down Ocean how, exactly? A human would never survive. We can hide you but we cannot hide him. His only hope is to blend in.”

“Blend in?” She looked at me, one eyebrow raised.

Dillion studied Calienta with concern creeping into his eyes. “I guess you have a point there.”

The little man scratched his head and scrutinized me as if I might have another persona stashed somewhere. "Could you do anything to look, well, more unpleasant?" There was a hopeful note in his tone. Both he and Calienta looked at me expectantly.

Thinking about every bad cliché of a horror movie, I let out a low growl. I thought it was impressive.

"We don't stand any chance. That will certainly not convince anyone." There was a frustrated note to Calienta's voice.

I caught her eye and raised my eyebrows questioningly. She tried for a weak smile but it came out as more of a grimace.

"Hey, I'm the great Manuel. Have a little faith. Surely a little confidence in me wouldn't be that hard to drum up."

Dillion shook his head. "It will have to do. That is all there is to it. Just do me a favor and at least try to look unforgiving."

I sighed. "Thanks, that really narrows it down. So, what's the plan?"

Dillion grimaced. "It will not be easy."

When our eyes met, I read his concern and doubt there. "Like any of this has been easy so far?" When he shrugged, he was close to caving, so I pushed. "You have to help us. We can't figure this thing out without your expertise."

"There is this one thing. Just a small one…"

"What thing, Uncle?" asked Calienta.

"I do not know how to get through the Ellipse. There is something that you have to say, but I do not remember what it is. Without the words, you cannot get in."

Calienta blew out a puff of air and sat down.

I wasn't sure I believed Dillion. "Don't you have any information at all on the Ellipse?"

"I do, I do. No instructions, though; just a picture in a book."

I turned and walked back toward the library that I'd passed on my way to the kitchen. It was rather extensive, loaded with books of every size, shape, and color. The walls were made of smooth stone, the books sitting within carved bookcases that were built into the wall.

Dillion came up behind me and I looked down at him, resting my hand on the doorframe. "Where's the book?"

"Oh, all right already. But I want you to know a poor idea this is indeed. You will not be coming back to me, that's for sure." He seemed too confident in my eminent demise. It was simultaneously upsetting and annoying.

Dillion bustled into the library and raised his hands into the air. A stack of books flew off of the shelves from random places and landed in neat stacks on the floor. There were about fifty in total, so we sat on the hard floor and started grabbing books, looking through them for more information.

When my fingers passed through the first book, ghostly, unable to grab hold, I looked at Dillion, a single eyebrow raised. He caught my eye and in a snap changed me back from ghost to mortal. Without hesitating, I reached for the tattered green book that rested on top of the stack.

After about the twentieth book, I started to feel discouraged. I doubted that anything I was doing was helping. Suddenly, page thirty-nine of "The Darker Times" caught my eye. "Dillion, what's this?" I held up the page.

"That is it, the picture that I was telling you about. Does it have any more information?"

I simply stared at the image on the page. "I know this picture."

"Kellen?" Calienta came to stand beside me.

"This picture is in Stephen's study." I'd never forget it because it had frightened me as a child. So much so that I ended up looking at the floor whenever I passed it.

The image itself was disturbing and there were times that I thought it was whispering to me, although I always rationalized later that it was my imagination. There was silence for a moment while everyone digested these details.

"There are words that appeared in the original painting. It is a shame that you do not remember the words."

Dillion's assumption was incorrect. "Actually, I *do* remember them, but I don't know what they mean. Do you have something that I can write with?" I glanced at Dillion.

He was staring at me, clearly taken aback that I'd remember such an obscure piece of information. After a moment, he went to retrieve something I could use to capture the words, returning with a quill, inkbottle, and a piece of parchment. *This ought to be good*, I thought as I started writing the words down on the page from memory.

The words were written in Gaelic or at least a derivation of it. When I finished transcribing the words from memory, I turned to Dillion. "Can you translate this for me?"

After only a brief hesitation, the little man started to translate the words out loud.

Through the forest ye shall go
To the sea where no soul rests
Have caution, ye who seek the light
For the path is barred with terrible things
Let the beam of light be your compass
Should you cross the sea and still have breath
Then the doorway waits on the island's end
Unlock the door with a piece of the past
From the ones who have lost all.

Dillion spoke the words and I transcribed them. After I'd captured the last line, I looked up to find him staring at me.

"Your father had this?" His eyes were questioning.

"Kellen's father is…interesting," Calienta said gently.

"But you know that the other half of the prophecy—"

Calienta cut him off. "Uncle, he collects things."

Glancing from Calienta to Dillion, I felt an unusual desire to defend Stephen. "He was an academic. He had a very large book and art collection. This was on the wall in his study and is still there, I believe."

Dillion didn't comment any further, though I could tell that there was more that he wanted to say. Yet it was Calienta that I wanted to ask, not Dillion.

The latter stroked his long white beard for a moment. "You cannot go on your own. You will need help."

"Who'd help us here?" I didn't think I could trust anyone in Faerie again, despite the trust I'd placed in Dillion.

"There is one other that you can rely on, but he will not be easy to find."

Calienta and I shared a glance. This was obviously news to her. "Uncle, how do we find him?"

Dillion took a fortifying breath. "You will proceed through my fields to the forest. It is there that you will seek the white stag. The journey will not be an easy one and you may become trapped during your search yet again.

"When you find him, you must fall to your knees and beseech the beast to grant you the power to make things right. If your gift is granted, you must run over the bridge made of wood and down the hill to the Upside-

Down Ocean. You must travel straight through to the other side until you come to the Ellipse."

"What happens if he doesn't grant our request?" Naturally I had to point out the obvious.

Dillion's face was a picture of desolation. "He will take your life. The stag brings life as well as death. You must ask sincerely and with kindness in your heart." He gestured to the back of the house. "Come, my friends. The last part of your journey begins."

We'd be leaving immediately. I was already mourning this warm and cozy house, knowing that I'd never return to it. We reached the back door when panic hit mc. This was really it and we could both die.

"Dillion, will the Hounds of Hell know where we are once we go outside?"

"My spells will hold, but only until you reach the border of my property. I will keep you in my thoughts, girl." He touched Calienta's cheek.

She nodded in response and took my hand firmly. With my heart in my throat, we set out on what would be the final leg of our journey, chasing a portal that might be fictional, with love and courage our only weapons.

And I didn't even have a Snickers candy bar to carry me through.

CHAPTER SIXTEEN
WHITE STAG

In seconds, we said our goodbyes and were walking out into the dark night. The air had grown cold and I found myself already missing the warmth of Dillion's country kitchen. It reminded me of Gran's kitchen, a safe place. The woods that we were walking toward were anything but, and I wondered if I'd ever feel that way again.

Wanting one more look, I glanced back at the farm, but it was gone. "The house—where did it go? Where's Dillion?" I continued to try to look behind me.

"Dillion's home is only a haven for those he invites in. Should we want to return to it, he'd welcome us again." I caught Calienta's sadness in her words. "But it's time to move on now. If it is meant to be, we will meet him again. And I know that we will. I can feel it."

Her loose gown flowed around her in the wind. The moon shone hazily through the dense clouds, giving her skin an almost angelic glow.

"Where's this forest we have to look for? It seems like we couldn't move any slower if we tried."

"I don't know. We need to keep moving in this direction. I think it's time we started speeding things up." She performed another one of her quick changes, but this time we both ended up in a new ensemble. I touched my hand tentatively to the fleece outerwear that I was now garbed in.

She grabbed for my hand and before I could speak, we were in the air and I understood the reason for the fleece. The wind chilled me, but the excitement of flying with her again outweighed my discomfort. I wouldn't look down and instead chose to look at my pilot.

"What happened to maintaining a low profile?"

She turned to me, a look of mischief in her eye. "We've spent enough time lurking around here and it's not done us any good. What's the point in hiding? We might as well move a little more quickly."

"Are you saying my mortal pace is slowing us down?"

She laughed out loud, which was refreshing given our circumstances. I expected her to deny my statement, to stroke my ego a bit. "Yes. We don't have all day."

She was teasing me, so I smiled at her as I said, "Thanks so much, princess."

"I'm not a princess."

"Oh, I forgot—goddess."

She rolled her eyes at me and we continued the rest of the way in silence.

Before I met Calienta, I'd hated flying. Yet there was something about flying with her, soaring into the night with utter abandon. Every moment with her was magical. I was so tuned in to Calienta that it was no time at all until the landscape changed.

When we'd left Dillion's, the forest was dense with trees that I'd have expected to see in the woods back home—maple, oak, pine, even cherry. Now the trees had changed. The place reminded me of every haunted forest in every book I'd ever read. What made this one stand out, however, was that each tree was white and bare of leaves, giving the forest a chilling, skeletal look. It was difficult to tell if I was looking at the same species of tree. Each was crammed practically against the other, so they appeared as though they were blocking any visitors from landing. There was no open space anywhere, so we stayed airborne.

Calienta broke the silence. "You know, you were impressive back there, remembering the picture and the text. If you hadn't, we wouldn't know where to go."

I blushed at Calienta's compliment. How humiliating. "You may not want to thank me when we get there. It sounds like this Upside-Down Ocean place sucks bad. My question is how do we know where to look?"

"We don't. We look for a white animal, a stag."

"That will be a piece of cake with this landscape." That was the end of our conversation for the time being and I returned to staring at the ground, looking for any sign of the ally that we sought.

After what must have been hours in flight, we decided to land in the first clearing that we came upon. The forest was covered in frost and shrouded in darkness, but the strangest part about it was the silence. There was not an animal in sight, no sound of any creatures stirring in the woods. As my feet touched down upon the cold ground, it started to snow.

Calienta pulled on my hand and we began to walk. "We need to keep moving."

The search began again on foot. It wasn't as rough going as it seemed from the air. The trees were far enough apart that we could walk side by side. There was barely enough light until Calienta held up a lantern. Its bright light helped guide us, rendering the dark less intimidating. The only sound was from a small silvery brook that ran alongside the path. Though we could have taken a different direction, there was an unspoken assumption between us that the stag would come to the brook to drink. We stayed with the brook.

"How are you doing?" It was a lame question, perhaps the worst one that can be asked when someone loses a father. I didn't know what else to say, though, because I hadn't missed Stephen in years. Decades.

She understood my meaning. "I can't think of it. I can't see it as real." She didn't look at me when she spoke, keeping her gaze trained on the land around us.

"Obviously I have no idea what you're going through."

She stopped then and touched my arm. "Kellen. You don't see it but you know what I am going through. It was you who lost his father before you were even born. You were denied the hope, the chance for a father. You know."

A safer topic was needed now. "Will the Glacadóir Anam find us here?"

Calienta opened her mouth to speak, but I didn't get a chance to hear the words. My legs collapsed underneath me and I felt myself starting to fall toward the ground. Bound like a rope had been wrapped around me, I was unable to move my arms or legs and my chin slammed into a flat rock on the snowy ground. Blood seeped into my mouth from the spot where I'd bitten the inside of my cheek. Its rusty flavor made me sick.

Stupid. I'd been stupid and careless talking about the creature out loud. I'd probably alerted it to my presence simply by speaking its name. Calienta was standing beside me, staring off into space; the creature was impacting her. Whether it was because I'd fought off the Soul Snatcher before or out of sheer luck I didn't know, but somehow I still had my head and suddenly I could move my limbs. It probably wouldn't last long.

Taking advantage of the situation, I grabbed the knife from my jeans pocket and lunged forward. The knife had helped me so far; would it work to destroy the Snatcher? The creature hissed at my attempt but nothing changed. If anything I'd angered it more, made it more determined to take me out. Anticipating the Snatcher's actions, I reached into my pocket before my legs started to go numb, and threw a handful of salt blindly up into the air.

For a moment, there was nothing as I fell on the ground. The shrieking began after that, and I was able to see, for an instant, the shadow of a decaying man hovering in the air. It stared into my eyes with hatred, which scared me even more. What looked like steam began to emanate from all parts of the shadow, like someone poked holes in it and its contents, all of its substance, was escaping. It howled with rage as it evaporated directly in front of me.

This action was enough to shake Calienta and we rebounded. Grabbing my hand, she took us back to the sky, the cold wind rushing past my ears, chilling my body. My stomach contracted in revulsion as we removed ourselves from the presence of the damaged creature.

Calienta sounded ill as well. "Normally, they are too afraid to come to this part of their world. This is known as a sort of holy land. They are getting bolder and that's not a good sign."

"I'm not surprised. That one had a bit of a beef with me. I ran into him before." Then her words caught up with me as I looked at her, looked anywhere but at the ground. "A holy land buried in Faerie, huh?"

"In every place of darkness, there is always some light. There is always both good and evil."

"That's an optimist's viewpoint. Some people are just evil; there's no good in them."

"You speak of your father."

"Who else?" I looked ahead, not wanting to think of Stephen anymore. I was still kicking Calienta's earlier words around in my mind and I wanted to think of something else besides my dysfunctional family and imminent death.

"But yet your mother fell in love with him. Even he must have some good in him somewhere."

“That I’d like to see.” I’d wondered about that myself. There were the letters that my mother had written that I’d barely had a moment to look at. Maybe they contained an explanation for the choice that Addison had made in Stephen…although there was little point now in discussing any potential merit that Stephen might possibly possess.

The snow continued to fall at a persistent pace, the wind whipping it this way and that as we carried on in the darkness. Again we decided to land in another clearing, north of where we’d encountered the Soul Snatcher, but still close to the brook.

The landscape sloped here to form more of an incline, and it was not as easy going as it had been initially. The woods became thicker as we pressed on, closing in around us to the point where it began to feel claustrophobic. We had to walk in single file to pass through the thicket of ghost trees.

“Where could he be?” Calienta didn’t try to hide her anxiety.

“I don’t know.” I was haunted by the growing concern that we’d never find the stag in this wintry maze. Yet my eyes never strayed from our search.

We’d walked in close quarters for days, possibly, when we were both taken aback. The pair of us happened upon a clearing that was about the size of an American football field. Stepping out from behind Calienta I walked around, savoring the openness of this place and inhaling the crisp, clean air.

Here the snow didn't fall, though it lay on the ground like a fluffy white blanket. The air was still in the darkness. The moon, large and translucent, shone in the sky above. A small pond lay tranquil in the clearing. There was no other sound except for our breathing as we looked around, our fingers still entwined.

Calienta let her breath out in an audible huff. "I feel as though we will never find our way out. My powers are mostly useless here, we've been tricked at every turn, and my father is already dead. I'm not sure what more I can do." I sensed that it cost her to admit this to me, even though we'd grown so close. She didn't want me to know that she had any weaknesses.

"We can keep searching, that's what we can do. The stag is here. We have to keep searching." My words weren't getting through to her and I was thrown off by this discouragement; it was so unlike her. I wasn't sure how to catch this curve ball. "Don't be afraid of letting me see what you're feeling. You aren't the only one who's afraid."

She pivoted on the spot. "I'm not afraid. Goddesses do not fear anything."

"You're lying."

Showers of blue sparks shot from her eyes.

I rushed my words to try and repair the damage. "You don't have to pretend with me. I've felt your every emotion since we met again. I know you're afraid."

"You what?"

"Why is that, I wonder?" I'd wanted to ask her since that first day but never got around to it. "Do you feel all of my emotions too?"

Her face was a picture of astonishment. "No, I don't. I can guess, but I don't actually feel what you're feeling."

"Do you know why I can feel that with you?"

She shook her head. "No. I don't think it will hurt us. Though I am a bit jealous."

"Don't be. You're kind of moody." I feared the admission would cost me, but she laughed at my words.

"It's simpler for me not to let my fear, my weaknesses show. I usually only acknowledge it when the challenge, the experience that caused my fear, has ended. That's my way."

"I guess it's mine too." As we looked around the clearing, I searched my mind for our next course of action. "Maybe we should take a moment and ask for guidance."

"Like a prayer?"

"Yes, well, I guess like a prayer. There must be something greater than all of us in this world. We can ask for wisdom, for strength. These are things that we all have inside of us." I was so stupid. "Look, it was a dumb idea…"

However, before I could say more, she'd gone down on her knees and looked up at the sky. I knelt down and joined her, taking her hand.

Neither one of us spoke our wish aloud. Instead, we kept our thoughts and concerns internal, choosing to mentally ask for help.

Show us what to do. *We are lost*, I thought. In my mind, I repeated the mantra over and over again: *Show us what to do. We're lost. Show us what to do. We're lost. Show us what to do. We're lost.*

Time was not important; I didn't know how much of it passed. We knelt there in the darkness as the snow began to fall again, this time covering the clearing. After a time, I figured that we'd probably gotten the message across as best we could. Slowly I opened my eyes and looked to the far end of the clearing. Standing there was the most beautiful creature ever to appear in my sight.

It was larger than any deer that I'd seen in real life, with antlers in a pale pine color and a nose the shade of damp tree bark. Most animals would have been skittish, but there was an unusual aura of calmness about this one. Boldly, I looked directly into his piercing blue eyes, unlike any I'd ever seen. The eyes that I met told a story of glory and despair, a story of triumph and tragedy.

My logical mind told me to hide, to flee from this large beast whose antlers were certainly longer than the length of my legs. Dillion said that this beast could kill us if he chose to. Yet I wondered if that was just propaganda, something shared among the Children of Danu to keep them from seeking help, from trying to leave. I believed the stag was too kind, too patient to take a life on a whim. It was intuition that spoke the loudest and it told me that I was not to fear this gentle creature.

He approached us slowly, almost as if he feared us. Despite our nervousness, Calienta and I bowed our heads in respect and continued to genuflect, although my head remained raised as I followed the animal's progress. I listened for the crunch of hoof against snow as it made its way forward, but only the soft rustling of the steadily falling flakes disturbed the quiet. The stag held its head high, with the air of royalty. Though it was tentative, it was also proud.

At last it came to a stop several yards away from us. Its eyes held sadness as it looked down upon us. Once again, I was struck with the impression that this animal wouldn't hurt me.

"You have sought me, my children," the stag addressed us.

Calienta raised her head. "Yes, great one."

"You may speak." His voice held a note of authority and I wondered if I hadn't been too bold in meeting his eyes.

"We came to this place to save my father, and we have become trapped here for far too long and we are lost. Both my father and brother have been destroyed."

"Yes, I know of this. What do you ask of me, young one?" The stag inclined its head to the side.

"Excuse me, please, but we came here to find the back way into the heavens, to save her father. He's been destroyed and the world has been plunged into darkness. Only we can stop what happened."

The stag listened but didn't interrupt, so I continued. "We need to go back through time to four years ago so that we may travel through the underground ocean to the Ellipse. We must save the light before it is too late."

"You speak the truth. The state of the world since Lugh's demise saddens me. The evil that has arisen in his son has become so great that he cannot be stopped even by all of the angels in heaven. Only the one that the prophecy speaks of can end this."

Calienta looked to me. "Kellen is the one from the prophecy."

"Yes. That is why I will help you. Only a great warrior can stop him." The stag looked from Calienta to me.

"Unfortunately, we're a little short on great warriors at the moment." My voice held no small amount of sarcasm.

The stag smiled and asked, "Are we?"

Warmth started to spread throughout my body. It was a welcome feeling after traveling through the snowy landscape for so long. My body began to float up into the air until I was suspended more than ten feet above the clearing. The hunger disappeared, as did my aches and pains as my body filled with energy. I'd morphed into the best version of myself—the one who got a full night's rest and plenty of Snickers candy bars.

This transition lasted only a moment. When it was over, I found that I was clad in armor; one hand gripped a sword, the other a shield. I was transformed into a warrior. I looked up at the stag and shook my head, disbelieving.

"I'm no warrior. I keep hearing that I'm going to save everyone, that the fate of the world rests on my shoulders, yet those gifts which you speak of aren't in my possession."

The stag seemed to ponder this for a moment before speaking again. "Things are not always as they seem, Kellen St. James. When the time is right, your gifts will reveal themselves. You must have the courage to try and the patience to wait for them." Looking to Calienta he warned, "We will not have much time when we get to the other side of the ocean."

"You can help us?" Relief flooded her face.

"I can only take you to the end of the ocean. Once you get there, you will be on your own. It is your destiny to finish the battle. You may call me by my name: Crísdean."

Calienta bowed her head in deference once more. "Thank you for agreeing to help us."

"Please rise. We must move quickly before they learn of our plan."

We stood, and Crísdean beckoned for us to follow. As a precaution, Calienta abandoned her lantern. Leaving the clearing behind, we once again moved through the darkest part of the woods as the moon receded behind the clouds.

CHAPTER SEVENTEEN
UPSIDE-DOWN OCEAN

It was slow going on Crísdean's back, even with the brisk canter he was taking. My arms had a firm grasp on the coarse fur around his neck and his breath appeared in visible clouds in front of us as he ran. Calienta's arms were wrapped around my waist, and though this was a distraction, my mind wandered back to something I wanted to ask her about.

"What did Dillion mean about the other part of the prophecy?" For a moment, I thought she stiffened beside me, but then dismissed the concern.

"It was nothing. He was overreacting."

"Still, I want to know. What's the other part of the prophecy?"

After some hesitation, Crísdean spoke on her behalf. "There is another part of the prophecy that says a new evil will come after the darkness is vanquished."

Calienta cut across Crísdean's words. "And it has nothing to do with us."

I stared at her, wanting to ask her what she meant, but then I began to hear the windy sea. The sound increased in decibels as we continued on, and the climb became steeper. Eventually we were forced to dismount from Crísdean's back to struggle up the steep embankment. I slipped as I tried to gain purchase on the snowy surface.

Who knows what I expected of the Upside-Down Ocean, but when I reached the top of the hill, my breath stopped and all of my courage flooded out of me. This we'd never get past. This we'd never be able to conquer. I pulled Calienta to me, knowing now that there could be no future for us. To even think of fighting this was futile.

"Have faith, Kellen." A glance to my left showed that Crísdean was smiling at me. "There is nothing like a good adventure, and you are about to have the adventure of a lifetime."

"I'd rather leave that to the movies." Looking away from the intense eyes of the stag, I wondered dimly if I'd ever see a movie again, ever hang out with friends again, or ever live a normal life again—if you could call my life normal.

The three of us crouched below the ridge of the embankment, hiding. However, it was tough to keep cover when I couldn't believe what was before my own eyes. My mind kept telling me that what I was seeing was impossible; my eyes claimed otherwise. This wasn't a normal ocean. Where the sky should have been, there was water. Where the water should have been, there were clouds that made way to some sort of dark abyss.

The water was black as night and it was dotted with white-capped waves lapping against the surface. The surface appeared above our heads, where the sky should have been. The waves crested several thousand feet high;

they could easily surge down to where we were and suck us into the churning sea.

Progressing rapidly, the tide was taking over the surrounding land, seemingly to swallow all of Faerie whole. The narrow strip of beach that remained consisted of a thick carpet of bones strewn across the water's edge. I wondered how many had died to contribute to it.

"What is that sound? It's horrible." This was meant for Crísdean, though he didn't respond.

The sound was coming from the ocean itself. My eyes kept being drawn back to the waves, and it was only upon closer inspection that I finally understood what they were.

The white-capped waves were actually spirits. If you pictured a ghost in your mind, you'd probably conjure a transparent, white-colored shadow, like the kind that they showed on "Scooby Doo" or "Ghostbusters". These creatures did not disappoint. They were white, skeletal, and opaque in their consistency. Rolling in the ocean, they appeared to have no control over their direction, no sense of free will.

The temperature had dropped since we'd reached this area and it was unbearably cold. I couldn't imagine that these lost souls couldn't feel that; it was a part of their eternal damnation.

Now I understood Dillion when he asked me to look unforgiving. I never would have been able to pull off the disguise that he'd planned for me. Those churning souls in the black sea were the spirits of both the mortal world and of Faerie, of those who'd committed atrocities so vile that neither heaven nor hell would have them.

After only moments with the ocean in view, the pain and suffering of these beings began to permeate the corners of my mind. My bones began to ache and my heart was pained, a broken thing inside me. I could only compare the feeling to that of losing my mother one hundred times, one thousand even.

"You cannot save them." Crísdean looked at me with dark, understanding eyes. "I have tried, but there is no turning back." He walked over to me and touched his warm muzzle against my arm, trying to comfort me, I realized. As quickly as the intense emotions began, they ended. He lifted his head and turned so that he could look at both of us.

"When we turn back the clock, there will be very little time for you to reach your goal. You must pass through the doorway as quickly as possible. You should climb onto my back again."

We did as we were told and climbed onto the wide, strong back of the white stag. This time, Calienta sat in front of me and I reached around to hold the stag's neck.

"Whatever happens, you must never let go until I tell you to." Crísdean spared us one last look over his shoulder before trotting up and over the hill to the rocky beach below.

Gripping the neck of the stag fiercely, I pulled Calienta back against me. There was an unexpected coldness to her skin, so I pulled her closer, wanting to warm her. "We're in this together, until the end. I love you," I said.

Wanting her to understand that I wasn't going anywhere, I let go of the stag with one hand and tipped her chin toward mine and kissed her. It might be the last time. Who knew what we'd have to face?

Her answering smile was brilliant, despite the circumstances. "I can't believe that I've only found you and I have to leave you."

"Who says you have to? We can get past this."

Her smile didn't waver, though her next words told me she wasn't confident. "Kellen, you're the one who has to get to the Ellipse. So no matter what happens, you have to go on."

"What do you mean, 'no matter what happens'?"

"Just promise me. If something happens to any of us, you need to go on."

"I won't leave you, no matter what the damn prophecy says. Others have controlled me for far too long. Now it's time to make my own choices and I choose you." This was my choice now; I would not be controlled by a bunch of dead Pagans.

She nodded, seeming to consider this. I wondered if she was thinking the same thing that I was, wondering what our lives would have been like if we were both mortal and we'd met under different circumstances. I'd have asked her to dinner or a movie. We'd have had all the time in the world to get to know each other.

"We'd better succeed then, hadn't we?" I lifted her hand up and kissed it, watching her blush lightly. I gripped the back of Crísdean's neck again. "We're as ready as we'll ever be."

"Very well, but before we go on, I must caution you. The emotions that you felt when we first arrived will be nothing compared with what we will face in the ocean. Keep love and light at the forefront of your mind at all times. These are the only things that can destroy these creatures; they are your only true weapons."

And with that, we began to move forward. It was odd. One moment we were riding on Crísdean's back across the beach, and the next we were upside-down, looking at a vast ocean ahead of us.

Once we reached the water's edge, it took only a second for the lost souls in the black sea to sense our presence. A tsunami started to form and it was both terrifying and exhilarating at the same time.

A sheer wall of water the height of the Empire State Building was heading straight for us. It was disgusting; a churning wall of rotting flesh and bone that circled around and around like a twisted merry-go-round. The souls' hunger seeped into my very bones, penetrated my thoughts with their anguished cries. The lot of them wanted to absorb us into their masses, wanted to end our lives and turn each of us into one of them.

Fear started to overwhelm me and I looked around, frantically searching for somewhere to run. There was nowhere. The darkness was everywhere; the water, filled with lost souls, swirled straight at us.

Crísdean's words knocked me out of my reverie. "Do you believe in the power of the light, Kellen?"

I frowned; this wasn't the time for philosophical questions. Then I remembered his words to me only a few moments ago. I'd already discarded them like an empty candy wrapper. "Yes, I do."

"Do not stop." It was a simple command, but I understood it absolutely.

Crísdean lowered his head and charged forward, powerful beams of light shooting from his antlers. The brightness was more powerful than any I'd ever seen, even at the night football games at the Yale Bowl.

The wave instantly dissipated and the moans turned to a violent shrieking, reminding me of a wounded animal. I longed to cover my ears and make it disappear, but I couldn't.

Crísdean clearly planned to jump directly into the water, but it had a life of its own. Immediately the water started to surge up again, preparing to overtake us. I could see individual faces staring back at me from the large wave. These were people once, with lives and homes. What had gone wrong?

Despite their bravado, Crísdean jumped in and the water began to part; a pathway was being cleared for us. The souls of the unforgiven, unable to bear the light, were granting us passage and moving aside, though probably more out of fear than courtesy. The water rose up on both sides of us forming two unfathomably high, seemingly rigid walls. Skeletal hands shot out to grab us, to pull at our hair and our clothes, but we pressed on. As the water parted, a thin sheet of ice formed beneath our feet.

After a few moments, I realized that it was Crísdean himself who froze the water with his breath. Short, frigid huffs of air were pushed from his lungs as we sped along the ice. We were almost flying now, speeding along the surface at a rapid pace like an Olympic speed skater. It was absolutely intolerable in the cold.

In an instant, a hand reached up and snatched at Calienta's hair. Crísdean slowed and we were almost forcibly dismounted. Instinctively, I slammed my shield down upon the hand and Calienta was released as cries of pain pierced the night.

"What happens if they get one of us?" I thought I already had the answer to this question, but it made sense to put it out there. Better to be prepared.

"Instant death." Crísdean shared this without missing a beat.

"Fabulous." At least I had something to look forward to after this high-speed nightmare.

"This is going to take us quite a while. Hold on tight and do not let your guard down for even a moment."

I hadn't imagined the Upside-Down Ocean would be the size of a real ocean, but it was. There were two primary challenges that we faced: First, if we weren't careful, we could be unseated at any moment. My knuckles were throbbing, my fingers locked around the hilt of my weighty sword. Second, the need to sleep was a dead weight on my shoulders, threatening to push me off my mount at any moment. The time that we spent traversing across the ice was agony, and I couldn't wait to get as far away from this place as possible.

The only sounds now were the occasional cries as I fought off greedy hands, and the pounding of Crísdean's hooves on the ice. There was no mistaking it when, after a time, I started to hear a roar. At first it was faint, like the roar of a crowd from a distance. Yet there was no denying it. Chancing a glimpse behind me, I was nearly sick.

The Sluagh, outraged that we weren't vanquished instantly, began to regroup. The same large wave once again began to build strength.

Crísdean increased speed, but I noticed that his light had grown dimmer and he held his head lower. This worried me, as we'd be done for if we couldn't get through the sea to the other side. Again, I'd no idea what awaited us on the other side, or if there even *was* an "other side".

If we made it to the Ellipse and it wasn't there, I had no idea what we'd do. At least, I didn't want to think about it too deeply. I could only assume that the "instant death" factor Crísdean mentioned would kick in.

Though we ran upside-down, we unconsciously adjusted our perspective so that we were running right side up. The sky churned, parting to show the dark abyss below—or above, depending on how you looked at it—blacker than the blackest of nights. I was looking into hell and it was more horrifying than I could have imagined. There was a groaning from the abyss. It was alive, its own entity.

I shivered and steeled myself to look straight ahead. None of us could speak, so our trio continued on, with me keeping my sword pointed out in front of us, my left hand holding tightly to the stag, prepared to fight whatever came our way.

At first I thought the light in the distance was only my imagination. We'd been crossing the distance in near darkness for so long that it seemed a mirage, a trick of the mind. Yet the light stood out like a sunrise on the horizon.

"We are nearly there, young friends. You must watch the light. Do not take your eyes from it."

I could hear a tentative note of triumph in his voice that gave me a lift. I wanted to dance and shout aloud as relief started to creep into my veins.

Crísdean cautioned us. "When we reach land, I will turn the clock back four years. The creature will immediately try to attack me, so you will not have much time. You must find a way out."

I nodded, though Crísdean couldn't see me. Both Calienta and I did as we were told and looked straight toward the light, which was shining on a beautiful coastline that must surely be only a quarter of a mile away. Yet as much as I was focused on our goal, I was still distracted by the growing roar behind me.

It might have been my focus on our target or Crísdean's words, but I let down my guard for a second and something grabbed my armor. I gasped for air and yelled "Crísdean!" as I grabbed onto one of his flanks. I didn't have a very good hold on him and I'd be sucked into the abyss.

"Kellen." Calienta turned and grabbed onto my forearm, holding on tightly.

I tried to swing my sword with my other arm, but a headless ghoul was keeping a firm grasp on my sword arm while being dragged along in the wall of water that appeared on my right side. Behind us, the walls collapsed and were immediately replaced once again by the churning sea. My hand started to slip away as I looked into Calienta's eyes.

"You have to let go of me."

Tears fell silently from her liquid blue eyes. She shook her head. "No, no, I can't."

"You *have* to." And in a moment of blinding clarity, I had the answer. "The prophecy was wrong. I'm not the king. I'm the sacrifice."

"No!"

A terrible calm washed over me; this was the right decision. "I'll always love you." I nodded, looking into her eyes, and then I let go of Crísdean and I was thrown into the abyss of darkness.

***

At first it was calming, like floating along in a dark room. My fear was detached from me, and although I could hear Calienta's cries still from within this place, she'd be safe. Then they came for me. The souls swarmed toward me, a mass of bone and flesh, with spears and swords as ancient as they. Some were whole in their appearance, but most were missing limbs: heads, arms, legs, even torsos.

The first time my flesh was pierced, I nearly cried out. Yet I refused to show weakness. They'd not see my tears; they'd not hear my cries. I wasn't a warrior physically, but I'd overcome them with my mind. I'd be brave until the very moment my body was destroyed. They continued to attack, trying to rip my soul from my body. I closed my eyes and that helped, not having to look at them.

It occurred to me that Calienta's cries, which had been slowly fading away, were getting louder, not softer. Then they were so loud that my eyes popped open. I realized that I was no longer in darkness, but in the alleyway with Crísdean and Calienta. I stood in front of something opposite them and I turned to see what it was.

The sea was growing and bonding together to form a shape. As it grew in height, the floor of the sea was exposed and a vast desert-like landscape of dry earth could be seen. The souls that made up the water had bonded together to form an enormous specter.

The creature was simply a large skeleton that wore a cloak of gray which hung open to its feet to reveal a translucent skeletal body; on its frame hung rotting flesh, which gave off a repulsive stench. The creature towered above Crísdean, several thousand feet higher than our friend, and I feared for his safety.

Crísdean whipped around to face the specter and Calienta was instantly ejected from the animal's back and propelled toward the coast, opposite the one from which our journey began. She landed roughly on the sand but didn't seem injured. The air shimmered around us, signifying the change in time. I needed to get to her if I stood any chance.

"You cannot escape us. We have taken one of your own." The creature ended its words on a moan that was as unendurable as its mangled visage. It rocked back and forth, swaying as if intoxicated.

"You may not have him." Crísdean's words were confident and I wondered what choice he had in the matter.

I tried not to look down at myself, at the wounds and blood that I was now more conscious of than when I'd been in the abyss. Even if Crísdean managed to save me, I'd surely not survive this attack.

As if reading my mind, Crísdean stared at me. As soon as our eyes met, his light, which had grown so dim, now shone brightly again. It shot into my body and out through my fingertips, my eyes, my ears, warming me everywhere. He was restoring me, making me whole again. As soon as I could run, I sprinted across the short distance that separated me from Crísdean.

"You may not have him, creature. You will battle me instead. I am the one that you want." The stag started to back up, almost knocking me down to the ground as he pushed me rather forcefully with his hind flanks.

"We shall see." The specter's voice practically dripped with evil. The creature lunged at Crísdean with surprising agility and he lithely darted out of the way in return.

"Kellen, the portal," cried Crísdean.

Turning, I realized that he'd backed me up to the beach. Without hesitation, I ran up the embankment to the door that stood there, and into Calienta's arms.

"Go. I have to try and help him. Figure out how to open it. I know you'll know what to do." She pulled away from me and ran down the small slope to stand behind Crísdean.

I looked back at the door that had nothing on either side of it. I could probably walk completely around it and not encounter a way out. It was as though someone had walked into a home improvement store, purchased a door and frame, and stuck them into the sand.

The door was made out of aged mahogany and was weathered, with a symbol carved into its core. There was writing around the door, inscribed within the frame, as I remembered from the image I'd seen earlier. However, one thing was different from the picture. There was no doorknob.

Calienta was standing at the edge of the sand with both palms extended. I was about to warn her that her powers might not exist here, might not be strong enough, but from the end of each hand fire shot out and struck the creature square on the chest. It recoiled from the heat and light and shrank in size by about a foot.

Yet it rallied, and the creature waved its hand and sent shards of ice at Crísdean and Calienta. Running back, I grabbed her arm, yanking her out of the way just in time while Crísdean melted the ice by shooting fire from his antlers.

Calienta sent a ball of light at the creature and it roared its anger, trying to charge toward us. I was supposed to try to get through the door but I couldn't take my eyes off the scene in front of me.

Then Crísdean spoke up. "Kellen, the portal. You must figure out how to open it."

I turned to face the door in front of me again. *Okay, think.* This time I paid close attention to the symbol. The symbol was familiar to me. It was in the cave; it was the symbol of the original Children of Danu.

Suddenly I understood why I was here, what I had to contribute. I wasn't the sacrifice as I'd originally thought. I alone had the key to the Ellipse. I'd been wearing it around my neck this entire time.

All thoughts flew from my head as I grabbed the pendant I wore and, without taking it off, placed it into a small, carved indentation in the door. It was a perfect fit. I waited for the door to open, but nothing happened.

What? This wasn't the way it was supposed to go. The pendant fit perfectly. *Why wasn't the door opening?*

"Kellen."

"Calienta." And my heart was in my throat, for I looked over to see her surrounded. The Hounds of Hell had returned to hunt us for their master, Arawn. Calienta could fend for herself; her strength and power were far greater than my own, yet I wanted to help her. She'd rescued me and I would return the favor.

They charged in pairs, the first pair upon us in seconds. Sword in hand, I was prepared to bring it down upon the head of each beast if necessary. Calienta leaned forward and blew a stream of air from her lips in a short puff. In seconds, each beast was frozen in its tracks, encased in ice statues.

I turned to look at her, both impressed and a little afraid. “Damn.”

“I have a few abilities.”

“I’ve seen.”

“But I only use them to protect myself.”

“Huh. Note to self: Do not anger this woman.”

We turned to look back at Crísdean. As the battle wore on, some damage had been done to his opponent and the creature was now no taller than Crísdean himself. Yet this incarnation was most definitely comprised of the most evil of souls, for it now dripped blood from its crooked skeletal mouth.

Crísdean began to back away from this creature. I didn’t believe his actions were rooted in fear but more related to strategy.

However, he wasn’t given time to plan his next move as the creature began to charge at him, its skeletal arms outstretched to seize our valiant friend. An opening in the abyss appeared above the creature; light streamed down from the crevice. And with a toss of his head, Crísdean charged the creature and they both disappeared into the light, the specter screaming in agony as he was sucked into the hole. Then there was silence.

As we looked around, there was nothing except the churning abyss. Everything else was desert, a void where even the souls of the unforgiven no longer existed.

"Did he fall?" Calienta's voice was worried.

"I don't know, but let's get the hell out of here before something else happens."

Tugging on her hand, I led her over to the door and pressed the pendant against the indentation with my palm. My memory recalled at that moment one more line of text on the picture that hung in Stephen's house. How could I ever have forgotten it? It was the only part that resonated with me, the one line that I'd focus on whenever I was forced to walk by the thing.

I am the key, I am the light.

I spoke those words now. "I am the key, I am the light." At first nothing happened…and then, with a heavy creak, the door opened a sliver. Using my hands, I pried it open. It was a small opening, but one that would be enough for two people to get through. We both hesitated.

I looked at Calienta, her eyes wide. "On the count of three?" When she nodded, I continued. "One, two, and three…"

As we stepped over the threshold, a rush of wind gusted over and around us, through us. There were a million sights, sounds, and scents in that brief moment. Then our vision blurred. This was what Crísdean had spoken of: we were regaining the four years we'd lost in an instant. We were passing through time.

Then the air stilled. As we opened our eyes, the breath rushed out of my lungs. Cabhan stood in front of us with a dagger in his hand.

CHAPTER EIGHTEEN
EYE CONTACT

The green grass of the lush valley surrounded Calienta and me, so different from the place that we'd just left. There was, in front of us, a sort of stage in a large open area, with steps rising up to a sheltered area at the top.

Glancing back, I looked for the doorway through which we'd come. Maybe we could trap Cabhan there? Startling me, the door slammed shut with a firm thud, disappearing from sight. *Guess that's out.*

On a riser behind Cabhan, sat five thrones richly covered in plush velvet of varying shades. There was a different color for each chair: royal blue, burgundy, dark purple, hunter green, and blood red. On the steps in front of these thrones, Lugh was bound and gagged with rope. It must have had magickal properties, as the rope continued to bind itself tighter around Lugh every time he struggled. His arms were rubbed raw from the effort.

Brigid was also bound, though not as inhumanely, if that was possible. She was tied to the blue throne, her arms wrapped back behind her. Our eyes met and her shock was apparent. She hadn't expected us to make it and the tears in her eyes were a testament to the weight that she'd been carrying inside of her.

Behind her stood Arawn, or at least I assumed that it must be Arawn, for one of the hounds sat at his feet growling fiercely. Looking at Arawn, my blood ran cold. He was a shadow, a non-entity, completely black and opaque. He had no distinguishable features at all, save for his red eyes. It was like someone had cut his frame out of the sky and filled in the cut out with black paint.

He was easily over six feet tall, with two long horns, jagged at the edges, extending from his head.. He said nothing but his eyes mocked me, though he had no pupils to truly give his glare any meaning. It was only instinct that told me otherwise. And there were other emotions as well. Negativity radiated off him in waves, as did the pain that seemed to come from his very core.

Cabhan's face, which had appeared in my mirror so long ago, captured my attention now. The distorted visage that appeared to me in Gran's bathroom and on the screens in the cave hadn't done him justice. Every bit the god, he stood ten feet tall, and his golden hair was blown back from his face in long waves.

His cheekbones were as chiseled as a sculpture, his skin pale but still managing to hold a healthy glow. Had these been different circumstances and his height more normal, I might have mistaken him for a soccer player, given the size of the muscles in his legs. When he spoke, everyone snapped to attention.

"This is the mortal of whom the prophecy speaks? He is hardly a man and no threat at all to us, surely. Is he truly your saving grace, sister?" He turned and looked at Calienta, howling, roaring with laughter at my expense.

Okay, this guy was a jerk.

"He's more of a man than you could ever be," Calienta cried in my defense. *Yes, you tell him.*

"Then the *man* should prepare to die because I will not let him live to challenge me. No mortal could ever take me."

Closing my eyes for a moment, I felt heat pulsating from Calienta's hand against my sweaty palm. Her sweet smell enveloped me as warm air swirled around us. How I'd miss her when it ended.

No. I would not die a coward, with my eyes closed holding my love's hand. Forcing my eyes open, I raised them to meet Cabhan's. Calienta had come to me to protect her family. I would do what I came here to do.

I regrouped. "You know, most people go to therapy and blame their parents, you nutcase."

"Kellen, don't. You'll only get him worked up." Calienta's voice held a warning note.

"If he's going to kill me, I won't go as a coward."

Cabhan's voice sounded bored. "You are tiresome when you talk, so do not."

Immediately my windpipe was sealed shut and speech evaded me. I was fighting for my very breath. Regardless of what it all meant, I had to do something. Cabhan's eyes blazed as he raised his arms, preparing to kill me, not with the dagger in his hand but with the power that ran through his veins.

The moment he released his grip on me, I gasped for air. With not a moment to lose, I raised my sword above my head with a strength and agility I didn't know I possessed. Then I was charging at Cabhan, who met my challenge running toward me.

"Kellen, no." I was frozen in mid-air. Calienta had crooked a finger at me and frozen me in place. "You can't kill him, Kellen, you're a mortal. He'll take your life. Please back down." She released me and I dropped to the ground, my knees like jelly.

Color flooded my face as humiliation coursed through my veins. I was about to tell her my real thoughts when I glanced down at the sword in my hand and noticed an inscription on the hilt: Claíomh Solais. Where had I read that before? *Oh.* This was no ordinary sword, I realized. This was the Sword of Light.

I rose to my feet, gripping Calienta's arm. "Look, you have to trust me on this. I know what to do."

Her eyes met mine, confused, afraid. I sensed her anger and fear all at once as she spoke. "How do you know what to do? How could you?"

"You have to trust me. You asked me to trust you once; do you trust me?"

Her eyes lingered on mine, intense, concerned. "I do."

"Don't stop me then." But before I could act, I was immediately brought to the ground by a pain so excruciating that I could barely stand it. A million needles were piercing my flesh and I was bleeding, dying, my soul being ripped from me in a million unimaginable ways.

Arawn's laughter rang in my ears as I writhed on the ground, my spine seemingly being plucked from my body. My back arched in pain; the color drained from my face.

"Cease, Arawn." Cabhan's voice was chilling. Arawn stopped at once and I collapsed to the floor once more. "My father is responsible for Kellen being here. I will be the one to destroy him. You are a silent partner." Cabhan walked forward and stood at the bottom of the dais, looking up at Arawn.

"A partner I may be, but silent I shall not remain." Arawn's gravelly voice sounded as though he'd gone centuries without actually speaking. Yet his articulation was cultured, flawless, despite the unpleasant tenor. "You will need me in the end, so I would not make assumptions about the level of authority that you have over me."

"And you cannot assume control without me or my family, so you would be wise to take the same precautions." Cabhan glared at him. The pair formed an uncomfortable alliance that much was clear.

"They'll never help you." My voice seemed insignificant in this arena, almost childlike. Instantly both of their heads snapped to face my direction and I mentally chastised myself for bringing their attention back to me. *Stupid.*

"There are ways that they can be made to help me, regardless of their own wishes." Cabhan dismissed me, turning back to Arawn.

"That's it then?" I was pushing the envelope, but the obvious attack was not going to work. I needed to stall.

"Kellen, be careful," Calienta said from her position behind me.

Ignoring her warning, I continued, taking a few steps toward Cabhan. "Do you hate your father so much that you would kill him and put the rest of your family in harm's way? Look at your sister. She's beautiful, both inside and out. Would you, could you hurt her, harm her at all, for some vendetta with your father over an old girlfriend?"

"If I am not given the opportunity to know love, no one should," Cabhan whined, a departure from his commanding god persona.

I rolled my eyes. "Get over it, punk." *Okay, maybe that was going too far…*

Arawn walked up to Cabhan and pushed a long spiny finger against his chest. "Enough talk. Let us kill them all and be done with this."

Before Cabhan could turn and look at me again, I was already charging. The sword had come from Crísdean for a reason, and I had to believe that this reason was to kill Cabhan. I had to try. It was my destiny.

I ran strategically, zigzagging through the empty space, ever the soldier. If I could get closer, I could have a shot. I raised my sword again, prepared to strike.

And then, when I least expected it, the oddest thing happened. I didn't die. Cabhan stopped in his tracks, staring at me, the expression on his face changing from one of unadulterated anger to incredulity and shock. My breath hitched in my throat.

Lowering my weapon, I kept my eyes on his, not daring to glance at anyone else. He stared at me, eyes wide, as his breathing started to slow. Calienta walked toward me, coming to a stop beside me again. Only her feather-light touch on my arm gave away her presence.

When he spoke again, his softer voice tone encouraged me to relax slightly. “That pendant…the one you are wearing. Where did you get it?” There was a puzzled expression on Cabhan’s face.

I looked down at the pendant that I wore around my neck. The top two buttons of my shirt had come undone and exposed it. The pendant's black insignia and silver backing stood out against my pale skin.

Meeting his eyes again, I found I couldn’t answer immediately. Of all the things I’d expected to hear, this was not it. I was almost annoyed. Was he toying with me? Delaying the inevitable?

This reaction wasn’t what Cabhan seemed to want and he was obviously angered by the delay in my response. “Answer me, mortal.” His voice was acid; his eyes raged fire. He towered over me, standing several feet taller. The beauty by my side tensed but said nothing.

“It was given to me by my mother.” I was impatient for this game to end. My sword was at my side and I was prepared to strike. This had gone on long enough. If death were coming, I'd as soon not wait for it any longer. We'd been through too much.

However, the information that I provided seemed to have the opposite effect on Cabhan. Instead of raising his hands or striking me with a weapon, he staggered and fell to his knees.

"What is this?" demanded Arawn, taking a small step down but never leaving his place next to Brigid. The hound snarled at his feet.

Cabhan ignored the outburst and instead looked into my eyes. They slowly dimmed and the anger, a constant since I had known him, faded. "You are from Clare's family?"

Although it took me a moment to recall the name, I was at last able to understand the meaning of his words. "Clare was the name of my great-great-great-grandmother on my mother's side." No sooner had I shared this information than the pieces started coming together for me, as they usually did when I was presented with a puzzle.

Cabhan turned and sat at the base of the stone steps that ran behind him, seemingly unconcerned about turning his back on me. Tentatively, I walked over to where he sat.

"Clare was your love, wasn't she?"

He looked at me as though gauging whether he wanted to share his story with me. Something in my expression must have encouraged him, because he started talking.

"When I was younger, much younger, I went to Earth to spend time among the mortals. I found your kind fascinating then, you see." He chuckled.

I chuckled back awkwardly, feeling foolish.

Cabhan continued. "It was on my second trip there that I met her. Her name was Clare and she was the daughter of a local fisherman. I fell in love with her on sight. Her soul reached out to me. I was meant for her. She said that it was the same way for her and she promised that she would marry me.

"Yet I could not marry a mortal without becoming one myself. I gave her the pendant that you are wearing to hold until I could be with her once more. She promised to wear it as a message to all that she was mine.

"I returned to my father and begged to give up my powers. Yet he would not allow me to. He refused to permit it until I considered all of my options. By the time I was allowed to return, I found her with child and already bound to another man.

"I came straight back here. I was going to tell my father exactly what he had done, but instead I became so angered that I could barely control my temper. I could not bear anyone else's happiness or hopefulness, for all of my hope was lost. My love was gone. I hid, an angry coward."

His voice broke with emotion. "And you show up here and you have my pendant and her…eyes." He looked past me at his parents, prisoners by his own doing.

Arawn laughed again. “This is quite a tale you have been telling us, Cabhan.”

Calienta and I gasped as we found ourselves immobilized on the ground in front of Cabhan.

Arawn continued. “You were the one who agreed to work together to end your family’s reign. You cannot go back on your word now. You will end this.”

Cabhan was about to speak when we all noticed that a single star had appeared in the air between us, blocking us from Arawn’s view with its brightness. It reminded me of the green ball that I’d seen at my graduation. *How long ago was that?*

Even Arawn seemed transfixed for he released us, shrinking back from the light as it grew in brightness, standing in the shadow of the throne. My heart, which had been pounding furiously before, started to slow. Then we were interrupted by an unfamiliar voice.

“Cabhan, my love. End this, please. Do not continue this madness because of me.”

As we stared at the light in front of us, one of the most beautiful women that I had ever seen appeared right on the spot. She was dressed in a gossamer gown of sea blue, with pale skin and coal-black hair. Her eyes matched mine, deep green. She glowed, seemingly lit from within.

I thought she was standing alone, but I realized that there were others with her, though their features were indistinct. I was unable to discern if they were men or women. Cabhan’s breath caught as he stood. His entire face was transformed again, from the angry young god that I had known to a man in love. It was clear that this woman was the one whom he adored, my ancestor.

"You must stop this vengeance, this hatred that threatens to harm my grandchildren. How can you act this way? You were always so kind, so generous."

His voice darkened. "Clare, you chose not to wait, not to find out what kind of man I could be."

I sneaked a glance at Cabhan. His eyes had begun to blaze again, though not as strongly as before.

"My darling, of course I waited for you, but my father wanted to see me settled and with a family. He was a very patient man, and he did not force the issue. Every year on the eve of the Summer Solstice I returned at sundown to the same spot where we first met, waiting for you.

"But after many long years my father refused to let me wait any longer for you. He insisted that I marry, and there was a man in the village that was willing to accept a spinster. When you did return, almost ten years had passed. I had given up hope at that point in time."

"Time does not pass in the same way in my world. I did not know. You, on the other hand, could have left that mortal fool for me."

"I never would have. I had already had two children."

"I remember. You had them with you when I returned that day. You were also with child again." Cabhan's expression was unreadable as I glanced back in his direction.

"Would you have denied me children, Cabhan? The children that I so desperately wanted?" Clare was pleading with him now. "If you had come back before I was married, I would have loved you. How I would have loved you."

This man, who once had looked so formidable, so powerful, now looked destroyed. "I have been wrong." He flew toward her and her to him, but they were blocked. An invisible wall kept them apart. They tried frantically to reach one another but to no avail.

"I will not waste any more time on a trite lovers' reunion. If you will not kill him, I will!" Arawn cried.

What I did next was risky, given my limited experience with a sword and general ineptitude with sports of any kind. Yet I had two things on my side: the remarkable sword and Calienta's trust. I'd figure out the rest. Bringing my fist up over my head, I ran forward, charging the demon, and launched the sword up high into the air.

I hit my target.

The sword struck Arawn squarely in the chest, the sound of a metallic-like *thunk* reverberating in the air.

Arawn looked up at me and smiled, pulling the sword from his chest. "You pitiful mortal. You think to attack me? You think that you can destroy me?"

"I can, with the Claíomh Solais." My voice was confident. This was what I was supposed to do.

Arawn's red eyes widened in shock as he looked down and took in the weapon that had struck him. The acknowledgement of the sword was all that it took. He was instantly weakened by the weapon and slumped to his feet in front of me. The dog at his feet whimpered and disappeared.

CHAPTER NINETEEN
HIGH KING

Arawn had no sooner fallen than he shattered like glass, the pieces breaking off of his hazy visage and gathering on the grass in a pile. In a matter of seconds the man, the monster, the demon—whatever he was—was destroyed.

Brigid and Lugh, who now found themselves freed from Arawn, stood and joined hands. Their voices united, they ordered, "Arawn, leave this place. Be gone."

The black shiny pieces reassembled, showing Arawn as his former self for a moment. My knees felt weak. I should have known that destroying that level of evil wouldn't be easy.

The pieces exploded apart once more before swirling into a small vortex. I closed my eyes to shield them, before a burst of wind overtook our party and the remains of Arawn were blown out of sight. No one spoke until the sky above us was once again clear.

"Wow," I breathed, still processing what had happened. I turned to Lugh and asked, "Can he come back?"

Lugh didn't smile, but he did meet my eyes. "I'm afraid that, as destroyed as Arawn appears, he is only weakened. He can, with enough souls, enough support, become a challenge again."

Before I could talk to Lugh further, our attention was turned to Cabhan and Clare. He was trying again and again to use his own magick on the invisible barrier that separated them.

"Son, she cannot be touched." Lugh's voice sounded weary. He walked to his son, gently wrapping a muscled arm around him.

"But why? Has my anger, my hatred, destroyed my chance at love?" Cabhan seemed defeated.

"It is not your actions that separate us now," Clare said. "I have left my mortal world behind for the mortal heaven. I am only here because of Kellen." She looked at me when she spoke my name, beaming proudly at me.

I returned her smile and wished that I had known her in my lifetime. Her smile matched Gran's.

"Cabhan, you were going to kill Kellen simply because he stood in the way of your revenge. You had such belief in the prophecy that you would not see the people involved in its message. I could not allow you to kill my kin, even if he is several generations removed. I thought you were a better god, a better man than that."

Cabhan fell at Clare's feet. We all witnessed his remorse at that moment, how sorry he'd been for the time he'd lost and the gruesome plans that he'd made. He rose and met Clare's gaze once more. She beamed at him, her smile lit by a thousand suns, her black hair whipping around her face as she nodded with apparent encouragement.

He then walked over to Calienta, grasping her hands in his own. “I was so very wrong, when clearly your love is true. Please find it within you to forgive me if you can.”

Calienta smiled warmly at him. “Brother, though your actions have pained me, I cannot doubt your sincerity. I forgive you.” She glanced at me expectantly.

I don't know about her, but I was a little less interested in forgiving this god who’d almost killed me. Maybe that's just me; call me crazy. On the other hand, it wouldn't be such a hot idea to provoke him further.

The once formidable Cabhan turned to me next. “Clare spoke the truth. I was so overcome by my own pain that I was prepared to destroy both you and my beautiful sister. Thank you for saving us all, Kellen. You are much more of a man than I am. Please forgive me. I will be forever in your debt.”

I had no idea how to respond to that adequately. “Yeah, it’s cool.” Not really, but what else could I say?

“That was quite a risk that you took with Arawn. You could have easily lost, you know.” Cabhan extended his hand in friendship. I took it in my own, recognizing it for the honor that it was.

A grin spread across my face as I remembered my discovery. “No, that’s just it—there was no way that I could have lost.”

“What do you mean, Kellen?” Calienta leaned closer to me.

"The sword that Crísdean gave me was the Sword of Light, the sword of the first king of Ireland. When you wield it in battle, you can never lose."

Cabhan and Calienta stared at me.

I shrugged. "I like to read. A bit." *In other words, I'm a book geek.*

"Your studies have served you well." Lugh walked over and clapped me on the back. I fell to my knees again from the impact.

Cabhan extended a hand again, this time to help me back up. "You truly saved us all today." Slowly, he turned to Brigid and Lugh. "Mother, Father, I am so very sorry. There aren't words fitting enough to undo the atrocities I have committed."

Lugh and Cabhan briefly embraced, a father forgiving his son. Brigid clasped his hand tenderly, a sign of acceptance.

"I have to ask you for one more thing. Please, Father. It is the only way I can be with her. I must be with her. I think I have had enough time to think it over now."

Lugh shook his head as he began to comprehend what Cabhan was asking. "It's condemning you to die. I can't be responsible for that."

Beside me, tears began to run down Calienta's cheeks so I pulled her toward me. "What's going on?" Everyone seemed to know exactly what was going on except me.

"He wants to go back in time and be made mortal so he can be with Clare," Calienta whispered.

"That's…sick." If there was one thing this family wasn't, it was boring. They sure kept things moving.

Cabhan continued as though he hadn't picked up on every word of our whispered conversation. "If you do not, Father, I will be dead inside anyway. Give me this chance at happiness."

Lugh was hesitant but he seemed to steel himself. "How long ago?"

"No." Brigid stood between the father and son. "We have only just gotten him back."

"And he will be no good to us now. We have each other. Calienta has Kellen. Our boy needs someone to love." Lugh looked at Brigid with all the tenderness in the world in his eyes.

Cabhan didn't waste any time. "March the nineteenth, 1889, please." He took Lugh's hand in his own.

"Son, maybe a little later. Otherwise it's possible that Kellen might not exist."

Cabhan glared at me for a moment, apparently annoyed that something as trivial as my existence was a factor.

"Kellen should still be allowed to exist." There was an edge to Calienta's voice as she stared at her brother. This brought sibling rivalry to a whole new level.

Cabhan nodded his head in consent and then smiled at Clare, as he truly realized for the first time what was about to happen. "I am coming for you, woman."

"Finally." Clare rocked on the balls of her feet, a grin on her face.

Placing his hands on either side of Cabhan's head, Lugh closed his eyes and whispered the command that would transform his son into a mortal. For a moment, nothing happened.

Suddenly small stars appeared above Cabhan's head and circled slowly. I was reminded of a cartoon character that got slammed over the head with a hammer. I almost laughed aloud until I realized that Calienta was crying. The power of the stars was leaving her brother and she'd lost yet another sibling to the mortal world.

As quickly as the process began, it ended. A flame rose up and engulfed Cabhan. In a matter of seconds, the process was over. He was gone.

"What will happen to him? My only son… Will we ever see him again?" Brigid's voice was thick with emotion.

"I think that can definitely be arranged," said a familiar voice.

A man, a stranger, appeared directly in front of us. All at once, everyone dropped to his or her knees in deference to this newcomer. I followed suit.

"Gaze upon your son once more."

Clare beamed as a younger, mortal Cabhan embraced her. He was so young looking and so happy that we all did a double take.

"Thank you, Father," Cabhan said.

Lugh's expression was bittersweet. "Goodbye, my only son. Please be happy in the heaven of mortals."

Before our eyes, he was gone again, along with Clare and her family. We were left with only our memories and the man I'd yet to meet. As if reading my thoughts, the stranger walked toward me.

He didn't extend his hand, but said my name in acknowledgement. "Kellen St. James."

"Kellen, this is Síl." Lugh gave a brief introduction, but remained penitent. "Our creator."

Síl motioned for all of us to stand as he continued to look at me curiously. "I have to say thank you. You did not fail me today. Although Arawn has not been stopped forever, you have taken away much of his power and saved Lugh and his family. For this, I will grant you High Kingship and you will reign with your High Queen here with Lugh and Brigid for eternity."

Before I could speak I started to sweat, feeling suddenly almost unbearably warm. I was trapped in the inside of an oven with no escape. My stomach roiled, my head pounded. There were black spots behind my eyes.

In an instant, I fell, but was lifted up again, levitated from the ground outside of my own control. I spun around in the air, fast, hundreds of times around and around, never stopping. Bíle rose in the back of my throat and I could taste the vomit in my mouth when I blacked out.

When I came to, I was sitting on grass, with the distinct feeling that quite some time had passed. Calienta sat beside me, her face glowing. Síl looked on indulgently.

My veins seemed to expand and I could physically sense the blood pouring through them. Though it wasn't blood but power coursing through my veins. I'd never experienced anything like it. The closest I'd come was when I'd lunged the sword at Arawn and hit my target. It was overwhelming and I didn't know what emotion to react to first.

The kid in me immediately responded to the innate knowledge that I could fly. *I could fly!* It was awesome! I was no longer afraid of heights, of anything at all. To prove my point I soared into the air from a sitting position, spun around, and landed gracefully on the lawn.

"Whoo-hoo!" I soared again and flew around the sky, this way and that between the tall trees, only to swoop down and almost touch the grass but not quite.

I was taller and stronger, too. I instantly bent down and lifted a boulder at the base of the steps and tossed it up into the air like a basketball. I caught it and continued to toss it around. The boulder was a mere child's toy.

"This is incredible." I put my palms out in front of me and shot fire from my hands. *What else could I do?*

"Kellen." Brigid's stern reprimand abruptly put an end to my fun when I realized that I had scorched the hem of her dress.

The vibrations of Lugh's sigh seemed to shake the very ground on which we stood. "Give him some powers and he gets completely out of control."

I smiled when Lugh said this for I liked him quite a bit. But it didn't take long for me to consider his words and see them under a new lens. "I'm sorry." As I calmed my breathing, the wheels started to turn. Not only did I not deserve this, but also I had never asked for this. I never asked for any of it.

I looked up at the creator in front of me, staring intently at his intelligent blue eyes. Recognition hit me.

"You're Crísdean."

He smiled but didn't confirm my statement. I didn't feel as though this was meant to shut me out. I supposed there were some questions that didn't need answers.

"You hesitate." His smile didn't waver.

"Yes." Calienta's eyes were on me. Suddenly I understood that I never wanted to do anything more than protect her.

"Usually when I bless people they are a little more responsive." This last part was shared without reproof. "When we found you, you were nothing but a child. To see you here with Lugh's family warms my heart. After all, that's what you wanted all those years ago, wasn't it?

"But the experiences that you have had have not been of your own choosing. So if you would wish for a new start, I can return you to your life right now and you can walk away. I think I can say for Lugh that he would not even insist you marry his daughter now."

Everyone chuckled, nervously it seemed, and Calienta looked everywhere but at me. Her fear, her hesitation was palpable. This was probably what Calienta would want for us. She'd want her family around her, especially since she was now an only child.

"Calienta, there's no one that I will ever want more than I want you in my life. You were made for me. Marry me?" Stepping close to her, I touched my lips gently to hers and the moment stood still as we kissed.

My reason for living had shifted, changed. I'd never be the same again. Though I wasn't sure I wanted a *High Kingship*.

"We certainly cannot doubt your love for her, that much is certain." Síl said this with a hearty laugh.

"I'm sorry. Thank you for this honor, sir…" I began.

"But he doesn't want this. He wants to remain human. He never asked for this power," Calienta finished for me.

I looked at her. "What do you mean? I'd do this for you. You're the only thing I want, the only thing that matters to me."

She smiled back and kissed me briefly on the mouth. "All you need is to be yourself. Don't you realize that's what this journey has been about for you?"

When I shook my head, she continued. "You told me that you didn't have any special powers and couldn't see yourself being able to save the world. Yet you did, and you did it with your intelligence and raw courage. If what you want is mortality, then I'll become a mortal too."

I couldn't believe that I could be so fortunate. Though she professed to love me, I'd never imagined that I would get to keep her in my life.

"Do you realize what you're giving up? What changes you'll have to make?" I asked her.

"Only the same things that you would need to give up if you changed. Marriage is about compromise." She turned to her parents, who looked back wistfully but nodded their heads in encouragement.

"Marriage." Despite my proposal, the concept still overwhelmed me.

Síl nodded in understanding. "Consider it done."

The power slowly drained away from my body as I was restored again to my mortal state. The breath flew out of my chest with a loud *whoosh* at this action.

I was thankful. Though I hadn't said so, that amount of power was too addictive, too tempting. I didn't know if I could live with that.

I took a moment to get my bearings before hugging Calienta close. "Marriage…"

"Don't tell me that you have a commitment problem after all we've been through. After all, we spent four years in Faerie." Calienta smiled, resting her head against my shoulder.

"She has a point." Lugh shrugged his shoulders. I didn't know whether I liked him or not now. I thought I might have changed my mind.

"Getting back to the matter at hand, if immortality is not what you desire, there must be something that I could do for you?" Síl asked with curiosity.

I already knew what I wanted to ask for. The question was hanging there and I didn't hesitate.

"If Clare could come back for a moment, then can everyone?"

Síl smiled and stepped aside. I looked around frantically, but didn't have much of a search. There was a blinding flash of light and my mother stood right there in front of me.

She was even more beautiful than I remembered in a stunning dress of jade green. Her dark hair fell loosely at her shoulders, ending in curly tendrils that framed her pale face. Most important, though, she was beaming, for she was now really and truly at peace.

"You performed admirably, Kellen. I'm so proud of you, of the man that you've become. I'll always love you."

Much like Cabhan had done earlier, I reached out to touch her, expecting some resistance. Yet I was able to clasp her hand in mine. "Mother." When I realized that I could touch her, I hugged her gently. I was afraid that she'd break, like a soap bubble. She smelled of vanilla and raspberries, and I took a moment to inhale her scent, hoping that I'd never forget.

Then Gran was there, her strong arms embracing the pair of us. "Kellen, you did well. Now that you've made your choice, it is time for you to live you own life. I think, if I am not mistaken, that you've found someone to live it with." Gran nodded at Calienta as she spoke this last. Calienta's encouraging smile added more conviction to Gran's words.

"We have to go now, Kellen. But you must know that we will always be here for you and are always ready to help, even though you might not know it." My mother smiled deeply at me as she and Gran silently pulled away from my grasp and faded away.

Stephen had influenced me, but he didn't define me. He was a man driven by anger but I didn't have to become him. My choices made me the man I was. The pain that I'd suffered would never again drive me. I blew my mother a kiss and looked away to face the woman who'd changed my life forever. And I'd only just started living.

Remembering something, I broke the silence. "I hope Arawn doesn't come back, because otherwise he's going to be seriously ticked off about his dogs."

Calienta giggled as we walked to rejoin her family. *My new family.*

CHAPTER TWENTY
VOWS

Lugh and Brigid brought us back to Gran's cottage—my new home with Calienta. I could see it all now. I'd write in the room that looked out over the cliffs, and we'd walk together along the sea.

Lugh clasped my hands. "We owe you a large debt of gratitude, Kellen."

Brigid reached over to hug me. "If it weren't for your bravery, for your willingness to risk your own life, we would not be here together now. Our worlds would never be the same," she added.

"I'm the one who has a debt to repay. You're giving me a wife and a family. It's more than I could have hoped for." I truly meant it.

"That leaves one question. What exactly are your intentions with my daughter?" Lugh smirked, always the character.

When I met Calienta's eyes, an enchanting smile spread slowly across her lips. This was right. I was whole now. "I don't know exactly. She didn't actually say *yes* yet."

Although our union was foreseen by many and encouraged by few, I still waited with my heart in her hands. I'd have to put my love out there and pray that she'd return it. I dropped to my knees, assuming that I'd be spending most of our marriage in this position, groveling, and waited.

Her eyes opened wide as she realized the truth. "Yes, of course I'll marry you, Kellen St. James. I will." Sliding to the grass in front of me, she took my face in her hands and pressed her lips to mine.

There was power in her kiss. This was a woman who could bring men to their deaths if she chose, but she didn't; she was as merciful as she was ruthless.

The laughter reminded me that we had an audience. Scrambling up from the ground, I assisted Calienta up before facing Brigid and Lugh.

"Do you have a ring for her?" There was slight accusation in Brigid's tone.

I blushed. I was just so cool I couldn't stand it. "Yes. I have a ring, but it's with my grandfather for safekeeping. I'll ask him to bring it here for the wedding."

Brigid and Lugh smiled, seeming to find this answer acceptable, but it was Calienta who spoke up next.

"How soon can he get here?"

***

Alistair didn't seem at all shaken when I called to tell him I'd be getting married and to ask for the rings. He was more upset about where I'd been for the last five months. The Faerie time-travel experience hadn't worked as seamlessly as I'd hoped on the mortal side.

"I just needed some time, Alistair." I'd let him think I'd been bumming around Europe for a few months. "You're really not surprised that I'm getting, well, you know, married?"

"Not at all, my boy. Your grandmother never ceases to amaze me, even from the grave."

"Alistair, I don't understand."

"I received a letter with the paperwork in her will."

"Another letter?" *Who writes letters anymore, anyway? E-mail would have been faster.*

"I know. I'm getting tired of the damnable things myself. Let me get it out."

I waited as Calienta and Brigid argued on the back lawn about what kind of dress she should wear. Though she hadn't yet become mortal, she insisted on buying her dress from a shop in Kerry. Brigid wanted to create it from magick, I guessed.

There was the sound of papers shuffling on the other end of the line as Alistair searched for the letter. "It says, 'Alistair, enclosed are my rings. Kellen is going to call you one day and tell you he needs them because he's getting married. Don't ask any questions. Just be supportive. You may have to obtain permission for him because of his age, but be creative.'"

"Huh." I was completely taken aback. "She's good."

"Yes. I miss her so much."

"Me too. How quickly can you get here, Alistair?" I continued to watch the epic battle continue on the back lawn. Lugh was nowhere in sight, and I needed all the reinforcements that I could get.

There was again more shuffling as he checked his schedule. “I can be there on Friday.”

***

Just three days later, I found myself standing on my lawn. My good buddy Gabe was at my side. When I’d called him and asked how soon he could get to Ireland, he was incredulous to say the least.

Although his feelings seemed hurt, he was easily forgiving when we got to the reason for my call. “Dude, I’m still royally pissed about you going on a European vacation without me, but look at this babe you found to marry! Maybe I should go to France…”

Of course he was there the next day, loyal Gabe as always. I’d been having quite a time explaining some of the odd behaviors that Brigid and Lugh demonstrated, but Gabe wouldn’t be in town long.

“I guess I have that kind of effect on the women here.” I put my tongue in my cheek. Gabe shook his head and fussed with his suit and tie as we waited at the end of the lawn with the local vicar.

“Maybe I should, like, get a job here or something?” Gabe said aloud, and I smiled as I imagined him chasing countless Irish women. He’d probably extend his stay now.

Alistair walked out of the house and came to stand beside me. “Here are the rings.” He patted me on the back. “I want you to take these and be happy now, you hear me?”

I nodded and accepted a brief hug from him as I turned toward the house. We were all on the lookout for the bride that I hadn’t seen all day. Although I had objected to this delay, many things that I hadn’t believed in before, faeries and fairytales, did exist. It made sense that I should start giving some credence to old wives’ tales. Why tempt fate any further?

I wore a navy jacket and pants with a crisp white shirt that was open at the neck. There was little point in trying for a more tailored look; any look would have seemed contrived when I considered the beauty that I was marrying.

That’s when I saw her. I could tell from my peripheral vision that she walked with her mother. Yet I never once looked at Brigid.

Dressed in a simple sheath of ivory satin that came from a shop in Kerry, Calienta was the embodiment of everything lovely. Her hair was pulled up into a simple knot at the nape of her neck. At her throat my pendant sat at the base of her neck, glistening in the light of the slowly setting sun. She wore no other adornments, save for Gran’s engagement ring that I’d given her only yesterday.

She was a queen, walking calmly and proudly to meet me at the end of our makeshift aisle. And when I met her eyes, her smile could have lit up the sky. I was struck with the realization that she loved me. She really and truly loved me.

Here she was, leaving her family, risking everything for me. I promised her I'd never doubt her love, for she gave me the world.

As we began to say our vows in the lingering dusk overlooking the cove where we'd met, I took both of her hands in mine. And all of the missing pieces of my heart, the ones I'd been searching for my entire life, returned home.

EPILOGUE
A NEW ORDER

Dillion was absolutely certain that Arawn was either destroyed or at least weakened. He did not feel the bindings that tied him to Dei any more. He tentatively mounted a small pony and began to travel into the forest, searching for others.

It did not take him long to find that many of his folk had gathered together, having sensed the same sort of thing. Arawn and the Hounds of Hell were nowhere to be seen, their great hulking forms no longer hovering in the distance.

"Can it be true?" squeaked a grotesque looking faerie called Cana.

Dillion didn't want to look at her. Some of the original Children of Danu had been punished for certain weaknesses with physical impairments. Cana, who was always so vain, now had one large eye in the center of her face. Others suffered similar transformations.

"We must consult the water to find out." Dillion raised his small hands, slowly waving them over a tiny pond. In seconds, the pond's surface turned to glass and a scene appeared before them. Dillion had brought the image to life, but he didn't need to do any more.

Immediately the story of Arawn's alignment with Cabhan played out before them, which included Lugh and his initial destruction. Some among them cheered at this, still furious at Lugh's failure to save them. Dillion looked on, trying to hide his excitement as Kellen and Calienta successfully crossed the Upside-Down Ocean. They watched as Arawn was vanquished, many jumping up and down with elation. Finally, the mortal transformation of Cabhan took place before the scene ended.

The Trooping Faeries who'd tried to take down Kellen St. James shouted in their eagerness. "We are freed from this place. We can leave!"

Dillion started to protest. "The mortals. We cannot just go busting out of this place, and we cannot return to the heavens until my brother calls us back."

"Who cares about the mortals anyway?" Far Darrig said with characteristic coldness. "The more mortals we come across, the more we can terrify."

The situation was out of control and Dillion could do nothing to squelch the excitement of the crowd. "But he *could* come back," he threatened.

"Hah. Let him," replied Far Darrig as if issuing a challenge. "By then we will be gone." And with that, the group began dispersing through mounds left and right to the mortal world above.

Dillion was left behind with a feeling of dread in the pit of his stomach. The second half of the prophecy was about to come true, and he didn't know how to warn his brother.

***

Several thousand miles away, in upstate New York, Sarah Kelly was exhausted. The master was so particular about his meals, so precise. Everything was of the finest quality and the service had to appear as though it was from a gourmet restaurant. It was outrageous, especially with the master coming in at all hours and wanting a five-course meal for supper. *Better he eat out than do that to me.*

Yet for fifteen years she'd been the St. James family cook and Master Stephen paid her well, so she kept his secrets. Where money left off, threats took over—enough so that Sarah would never leave.

Yawning, she snuggled down into her bed, thinking that she never wanted to wake up. Sleep had nearly claimed her when a crash shook the whole house. Instantly she was sitting up in her bed, heart pounding. Quietly, she snuck out of her room and knocked on the door to Beatrice's room to the right.

"Did you hear that, Bea?" Sarah stood in the hall, speaking to the closed door. Bea hadn't had a chance yet to answer it.

A moment later the door opened and Bea pulled her inside. "God, yes, but I'm not about to go see what it is, now am I?"

"What if someone's been hurt?"

"And what if they have? What can we do about it? Now, back to bed before Master Stephen hears you and *you're* the one who gets hurt."

Sarah blanched but didn't argue. In her bare feet, she silently padded back down the hall to her room and her bed, but couldn't sleep. She had this intense feeling that something evil was in the house. Clutching her aged rosary beads to her chest, she said her prayers and held her eyes tightly closed.

Two floors above, after putting up a fight, Stephen St. James's soul had been sent to the abyss. His body stood motionless as it accommodated the soul of a new master. Anyone running into him now would see him exactly as he'd always been…except for the blood-red eyes. He blinked once and then they turned dark brown. There, that was better.

Now he had only to take revenge on the one who had weakened him, his "son", Kellen St. James.

FROM THE AUTHOR
THE MUSIC

Music has always been an inspiration to me, particularly when it comes to setting the mood for my characters. The following is a short collection of character melodies that I created while writing *The Star Child.*

Come Walk With Me

Far Darrig's Theme

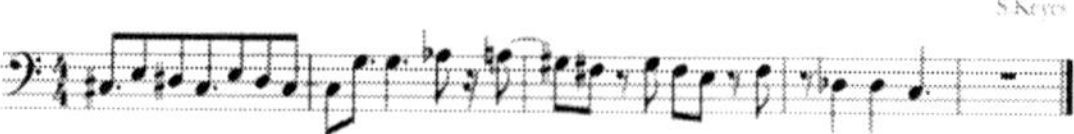

The Star Child

S. Keyes

Trooping Faeries

S. Keyes

Acknowledgements

To my family, especially my Mom, for believing I could do this.

To the real-life Gran, my grandma Betty, who shared with me stories about Ireland and the "good people". You made me believe that magic really does exist.

To my little boys, I love you more than life itself. Every day that I see you, I know that I did at least two things right in my life.

And to my husband, Aaron, my best friend, my savior, thank you for telling me that I had to write this book and making sure I listened.

ABOUT THE AUTHOR

Stephanie Keyes was born in Mt. Lebanon, Pennsylvania and has worked for the past twelve years as a corporate educator and curriculum designer in the Telecommunications industry. She holds a Master's degree in Education with a specialization in Instructional Technology from Duquesne University and a B.S. in Management Information Systems from Robert Morris University. She is a classically trained clarinetist, but also plays the saxophone and sings.

When she's not writing, she is a wife to a wonderfully supportive husband and mother to two little boys whom she cites as her inspiration for all things writing. The Star Child is Mrs. Keyes' debut novel.

Website: http://www.stephaniekeyes.com

Enjoyed This Book?

Try Other

Fantasy and Paranormal

Romance

Novels

From Inkspell Publishing.

Buy Any Book Featured In The Following Pages at

15% Discount From Our Website.

http://www.inkspellpublishing.com

Use The Discount Code

GIFT15 At Checkout!

THERE IS NO ONE SHE CAN TRUST. NO ONE THAT IS, UNTIL SHE ENCOUNTERS A MOST UNLIKELY ALLY

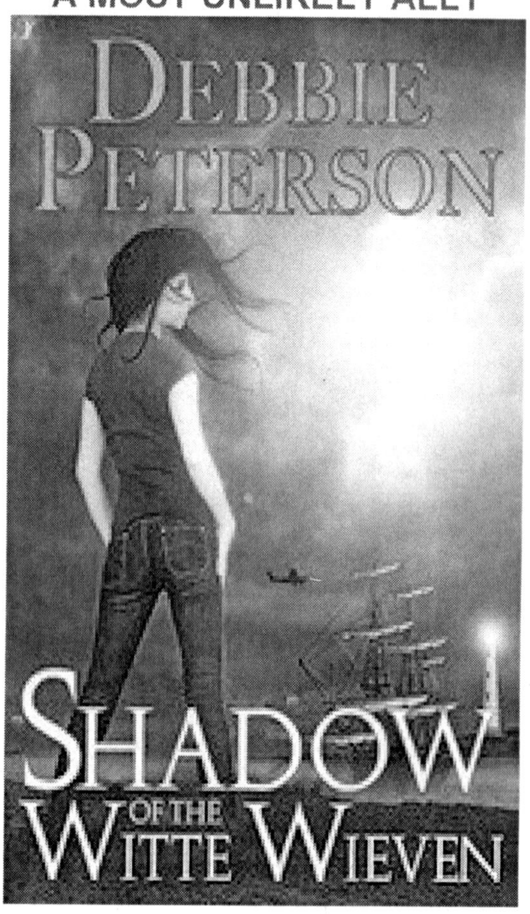

NEITHER CAN DENY THE CALL OF THE SEA, BUT HOW LONG CAN THEY DENY THEIR FEELINGS?

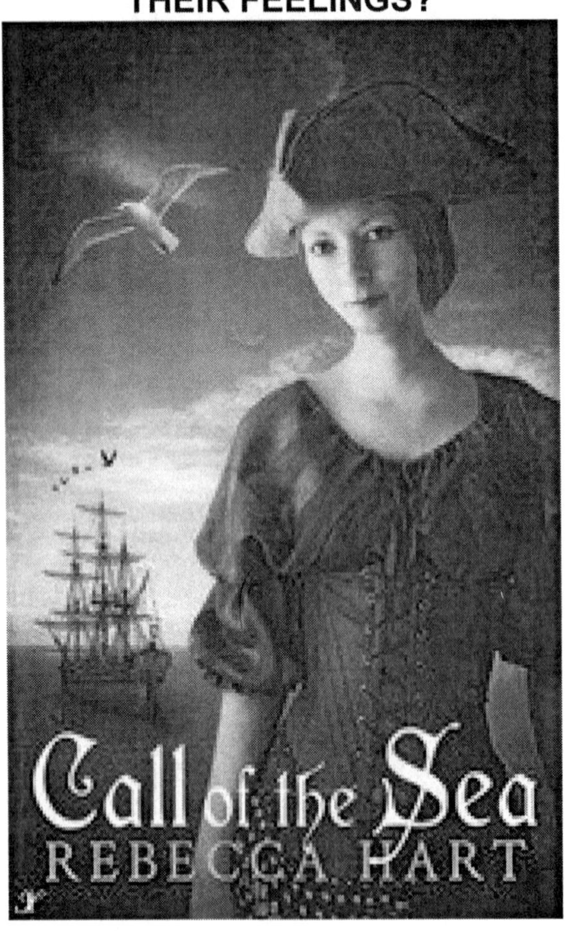

**A DECADE SURVIVING ON HER OWN.
THREE DAYS WITH THE ENEMY.
CAN LOVE CONQUER ALL?**

CPSIA information can be obtained at www.ICGtesting.com
Printed in the USA
BVOW020514090713

325135BV00001B/2/P